GET YOUR FREE BOOK

Discover how Acid Vanilla transformed from a typical London teenager into the world's deadliest female assassin in the Acid Vanilla Prequel Novel: *Making a Killer* available FREE at:

www.matthewhattersley.com/mak

THE HUNT
ACID VANILLA BOOK 3

MATTHEW HATTERSLEY

BOOM BOOM PRESS

CHAPTER 1

When gaseous ammonia is introduced to the delicate inner membrane of the nasal passage, it creates a reflex reaction. One of deep inhalation. As the lungs fight to clear the airways of this marauding foreign scent, breathing becomes faster, sending oxygen rushing to the brain and rousing consciousness. For this reason, ammonium, in one form or another, has been used for over two hundred years to resuscitate those in need. Boxers, fainting victims. But there are also other side effects. When the gas permeates the nose, the person will instinctively, reflexively, try to move away from the source of intense nasal pain – like you would if you put your hand on a hot iron – meaning the head will often lurch violently backwards.

So when Acid Vanilla smashed the back of her skull into something hard and metallic, she was unsure whether it was this that had woken her or the smelling salts. Either way, a second later she was fighting herself awake and gasping for air.

What in the name of bloody hell?

As her cognition grew and her awareness spread, a forceful pressure invaded her ears. She shook her head, a thunderous strumming sound filling the air, like industrial machinery on full throttle. It did nothing for the searing pain boring at her temples. She tried to sit up but her body was still in shock, the noxious, almost oppressive effects of the smelling salts mixing with the sedatives (Benzodiazepines? Barbiturates?) still circling the drain in her system.

She blinked into the gloom, sensing other bodies nearby, movement coming towards her. She widened her eyes, trying to focus as the conspicuous muzzle-tip of an UZI 9mm swam into view.

Well, shit.

Here we go again.

Acid traced her gaze along the barrel to take in the man standing on the other side. He glared down at her, snarling in the way a comic-book villain might do.

"Don't try anything stupid."

He spoke in an American accent but was possibly Taiwanese, or Cambodian. A safe bet said he was a mercenary. Behind him, Acid could now make out a low roof that curved over the other side of the room. Although, it wasn't a room. It was the holding bay of an aircraft. That explained the noise. Explained the pressure in her head as well. Some of it, at least.

She cast her gaze around the space. It was an ex-military plane by the looks of it, the sort often used for dropping cargo or vehicles behind enemy lines. Long benches ran down the length of the plane on either side.

The man holding the UZI nodded at something over Acid's shoulder and she turned to see another mercenary standing at the far end of the hold. A tall, muscular woman who had a look of the Middle East about her. Ex-Mossad, maybe. She held an M16 assault rifle at hip-height pointed Acid's way. Behind her an open hatch revealed a rectangle of cloudless azure blue.

The woman raised her chin. "On your feet, bitch. Slowly."

Acid flinched as an image flashed across her prefrontal cortex. The kid.

She was tied to a chair. Her face bruised and bloody. Acid shut her eyes to better focus on the memory. On Spook. Despite the spit-soaked gag around her mouth she'd been trying to tell her something, mumbling desperately through the material, gesticulating as much as her constraints allowed. Acid took in a sharp intake of breath, remembering the sting as a sharp needle pierced the skin on her neck. The benign numbness had happened almost instantly, spreading through her body like a punishing tsunami as her legs gave way beneath her.

"I said, on your feet!" the mercenary growled, snapping Acid back to the present.

She did as she was told, her mind racing, looking for a reason, for a way out. If Beowulf Caesar was behind this, it was an awful lot of effort to go through to get rid of her. But then, if she was to be forcefully ejected out the plane like she suspected, no one would ever find her body. She'd literally be a drop in the ocean.

But why rouse her to throw her out of a plane?

It made little sense.

She glanced down the length of the holding bay and made a quick assessment. The mercenaries were standing far enough apart that even if she could overpower one of them, the other would take her down before she had a chance to move. She rolled her head around her shoulders and took a deep breath. An attempt to centre herself. Right now she couldn't see a way out of this. But that didn't mean all was lost. Even in the old days – back when Acid Vanilla was the highest paid assassin on Caesar's books, and arguably one of the deadliest killers in the world – it was unlikely she stuck to a rigid plan. Unlike most of her colleagues (meticulous in the way they went about their hits), Acid preferred a more instinctive approach, trusting that when the time was right she'd know what to do. She'd never call her methodology 'winging it' like her detractors might have done, but it was certainly unconventional.

Unconventional. Unplanned. Instinctive.

But wasn't that Acid Vanilla all over? Unfortunately, at this present moment, all those traits were dampened somewhat by the fact she was a few thousand feet in the air, unarmed, and unsure how the hell she'd got there.

"Put this on," the female mercenary said, tossing a large pack. It hit Acid on the chest and fell to the floor. A parachute. She stared at it for a moment and chewed on the inside of her lip.

"Quickly," the woman yelled. "Another minute and we'll be out of range."

With a thousand thoughts fighting for dominance in her fogged mind, Acid reached down for the parachute and put it on. The woman checked the straps without making eye contact, yanking on them and tightening as needed. She nodded at her partner. "She's ready."

Grabbed by the arm and pulled towards the open hatch, Acid's hair whipped about her face. Her eyes streamed with salty tears.

"You jumped out of a plane before?" the woman asked.

Acid nodded, squinting out into the brightness. From her reckoning, they were around five thousand feet up. Give or take. Down below she could see a large island, rocky in places and covered in dense vegetation. A band of pure white sand traced the perimeter, disappearing into crystal-clear sea on all sides. As her eyes grew accustomed to the sunlight, she noticed other things. Orange blooms of various sizes, drifting in the air. More parachutes. All making their way to the island. She counted seven in total.

"Time to go, bitch," the woman spat, jabbing Acid in the kidneys with the end of the rifle.

"Listen, doll," Acid said, finding her voice at last. "I'm aware you've got me over a barrel here, but if you call me a bitch one more time, I'll kill you. Okay?"

The woman raised her chin. A slow smile spread across her face. "I'd like to see you try. *Bitch.*"

Acid blew out her cheeks. "What's down there?" she asked. "Who's in the other 'chutes?"

"You'll find out soon enough." She leaned over and flicked a plastic handle hanging from the strap of Acid's parachute. "When you leave the airplane, pull this. From this altitude you need to open up straight away."

Acid swallowed. "No sky dancing, got it."

"That's if you want to make it down there alive, of course." The woman sneered. "But I'm not sure that's your best option."

To a burst of the woman's laughter behind her, Acid took a half-step towards the edge of the plane, holding onto the sides of the hatch with both hands. She turned and yelled over the wind pressure pummelling her face, "Well, it's been swell flying with you. I guess I'll see you around."

With that, Acid grabbed the M16 and swung a sharp elbow that caught the woman hard in the chest. Surprised and winded, she released her grip on the rifle as Acid leapt backwards out of the hatch and squeezed off a burst of fiery rounds that peppered the sides of the plane and sent the mercenary jerking backwards into the hold. Job done.

Acid pulled on the ripcord but the wind-pull was stronger than she'd expected. As the parachute blossomed in the sky above her, the upwards drag shook the rifle from her grasp.

Shit.

The M16 spiralled through the air until it disappeared, leaving a tiny foam eruption in the ocean's vastness. She gripped the steering line tight. Something told her a high-powered assault rifle would have been valuable for whatever happened next.

The other parachutes had all touched down by now. All in different parts of the island. Some she could see. Some were hidden by the rainforest canopy. Over to her right on the upper edge of the island, she also spotted what looked like a large hotel complex. A huge sprawling building made of glass and steel, complete with swimming pool, helipads and a large radio antenna.

With the parachute open, Acid reckoned she had around two minutes before she reached the island. Not long to plan her next move. She scanned the horizon all around but there was nothing but ocean in any direction. This was the southern hemisphere, she was sure of that. The searing heat gave it away. The deep green of the island's rainforest just as much. If she had to guess, she'd say Indian Ocean, but it could be the Caribbean.

Sixty seconds until landing. She could now see the island in more detail, and a clearing directly below her. The torn, orange material of a parachute hung from a tree, but there was no one in sight. She squinted against the glare of the sun. It was low in the sky, but the high temperature told her it was setting rather than rising. Meant she was facing west, and the building complex was on the northern tip of the island.

As her boots skimmed the treetops Acid braced herself for landing, pulling the steering lines taut and raising her legs as high as her tight jeans allowed. A second later and she touched down, falling into a steady run to compensate for the impact. Difficult, with a hundred square feet of ripstop nylon trailing behind you. She came to a stop next to a large eucalyptus tree and leaned against it to catch her breath.

Below the tree canopy, the humidity was already oppressive, and not for the first time in her life Acid realised she was unsuitably dressed for her surroundings. She wiped the sweat from her eyes, and removed the parachute pack, followed by her leather jacket, which already stuck to her clammy skin. She tied it around her waist, thankful she'd chosen to accompany it with a thin t-shirt this morning. Or yesterday morning. Or whichever morning it had been when she'd last got dressed. She rubbed her neck. Definitely benzodiazepine she'd been given. Quick and effective. She scanned her recall, trying to further piece together the events leading up to now, when she heard a noise behind her. Then a familiar voice cried, "You're alive."

Acid gave it a beat before turning around. Enough time to stifle the relief that would be evident on her face. "Hey, kid. Good to see you."

Spook Horowitz hopped from foot to foot for a moment before launching herself forward and flinging her arms around Acid's neck. "I was worried I'd never see you again," she whimpered. "You were so out of it on the plane. I thought you weren't going to make it."

Acid shook her off. Took a step back. "What's going on, Spook? Where are we?"

The young American opened her mouth to speak, but before she had a chance a crackle of static emanated out from the undergrowth, followed by a high-pitched shriek. The sound of a speaker system feeding back. Acid scoped the area, homing in on the source of the noise and finding a battered old horn speaker hanging from a tree a few feet away. As they listened, the feedback gave way to a loud hissing sound and then a robotic voice.

"The island is now operational," it sputtered. "All guests are checked in and the quarry is now in place. Repeat, quarry is now in place. Everyone to first positions. This year's hunt is now in session."

Acid and Spook exchanged confused glances as the voice gave way to the tinny pre-recorded sound of a bugle. It played a tuneless refrain for a few bars, as if announcing something, then fell silent. In the distance Acid heard a familiar sound.

"Hunt?" Spook screwed her nose. "What the hell?"

Acid scanned the area, trying to find her bearings. Through the tall trees she could just make out the roof of the hotel complex. More impressive from this angle than it appeared from the air. It was standing atop a high mountain range, looking out over the island.

"This way," she yelled, already setting off at pace. "We need to head away from whatever that building is. Get under the cover of the jungle."

"What was all that about?" Spook asked, skipping along behind her. "The announcement."

"I'm not sure," Acid replied. "But it didn't sound good."

She stopped at the edge of the clearing and raised her ear. Yes. That was the sound of gunfire all right.

"How do you know where to go?" Spook asked. "What's going on?"

Acid twisted her mouth to one side. "I know as much as you do, kid." She grabbed her by the wrist, dragging her along as another gun fired off in the distance. "But I do know one thing. If someone's shooting and you're unarmed, the best thing to do is run in the opposite direction as fast as possible."

"But I don't get it," Spook stammered. "What did they mean, hunt? What are they hunting?"

Acid glared back at her. "Isn't it obvious?" she said. "It's us, Spook. They're hunting us."

3 DAYS EARLIER...

CHAPTER 2

Up to the point of being drugged and thrown out of a plane, Acid Vanilla had been having a relatively good week. That's if you considered tracking down and torturing two of the people responsible for your mother's murder synonymous with 'a good week'.

Acid did.

So flick back to three days earlier and you'd find her weary but excited on the sixth floor of a disused tenement block in Vauxhall, South London. She was weary because she'd spent the last hour dragging the unconscious bodies of Ethel and Doris Sinister from the back of a stolen Transit van, through the boarded-up yard, past the signs announcing the building's imminent demolition, and up the six flights of stairs. She was excited because all that effort was going to be worth it.

Acid smiled to herself as the harridans' eyelids flickered. The grim reality of their predicament would soon be apparent. She watched as their heads lolled, their arms bracing at the cable ties fastening them to the chair. Acid had to hand it to the Sinister Sisters, they were always well turned out. With their sour-puss demeanour and pale, watery eyes, you wouldn't call them good-looking, but despite being knocked out and shoved in the back of a van, they'd maintained that air of malevolent cool. Even now, the matching bobbed haircuts were immaculate. Not one hair out of place. Although Acid had noticed whilst dragging Doris up the stairwell that her roots needed doing.

"Wonderful. You're awake," she purred, hitting them with the sweetest smile as they opened their eyes. "Now before we begin, I apologise, you might have a bit of a headache after the Propofol. But don't worry, it won't last long."

The Sisters stared at her without speaking. As was their want. They did however manage to twist their wizened mouths into hateful sneers.

"Now I'm aware neither of you are too fond of talking at the best of times." Acid sniffed, sidling up to Doris' chair. "But if anyone knows where I can find Caesar, I reckon it's you two. So, here's the deal. You tell me what I want to know, and I'll make it quick. Otherwise, the next few hours are going to be pretty bloody horrific."

She glanced from Doris to Ethel and back again. They were tough old birds. Despite a combined age of well over a-hundred-and-thirty they were still the best clean-up team in the industry. Add to that their silent stoicism and extremist loyalty and anyone could see why Caesar valued them.

Acid leaned back on the heels of her Dr Martens. "I should also warn you, ladies – keeping shtum won't help the big man as much as it'll hurt you. I'm closing in, you see. With Spook's help it's only a matter of time." She leaned into Doris. Close enough she could smell her rose-scented face cream. "And I'm not sure if you're aware, but I've got The Dullahan on my team now. He's been helping me fill in a few blanks. Helped me find you two, as it happens."

She straightened up, gauging the Sisters' reactions. Ethel in particular had a look on her face like she'd just tasted something rather unpleasant. Still neither of them spoke.

"So, as I say," Acid went on, walking over to a small metal table on which she'd laid out a selection of surgical knives, pinwheels, gauging devices. "You can tell me where Caesar is now, or I can find out myself in a week or two. It means zip to me. But to you girls it's the difference between a quick send-off, or hours – and I do mean hours – of pain and torment and agony. I'm talking real horrorshow stuff here, ladies. I'm in the mood for it."

Doris stuck her nose in the air. "You're bullshitting," she said. "You know nothing."

"Bloody hell," Acid drawled. "She speaks! I honestly don't think I've heard you say that many words at once in all the time I've known you."

Doris turned her mouth down. "Words aren't important. Actions count."

"That they do. Which is why I've had Spook do a little digging for me." She produced a piece of note paper from her back pocket and held it up to the light, giving the paper a flourish as she read. "'Ethel and Doris Sinister. Otherwise known as The Sinister Sisters.' It's funny, I used to call you 'Silent but Deadly' when I first met you. Not sure if you knew that." She peered over the piece of paper and shot them both a big shit-eater. "Anyway, I digress. As you know, your real names are Diane and Enid Barker. Twins, born twenty-fourth of January, nineteen-forty-four in Ealing, West London."

Acid raised one eyebrow, delighted at the surprised looks on the faces of the two harpies.

"I've seen pictures too. A real couple of honeys and no mistake. Good work, girls. It says here, Enid Barker even went out with Mick Jagger for a few months in sixty-three. You dark horse, Enid. Sorry… Ethel."

The Sisters exchanged glances, the same shock and confusion in their eyes, but something else too. It was there in the twitching mouth and furrowed brow of Doris. Bitterness. Deep-rooted envy.

"Must have been a blow for you, Dor?" Acid sighed. "Couldn't bag yourself Keith? Or Brian? Or even Bill? Pretty shitty for you." She went back to her notes. "Then in seventy-one you both joined up with MI5. Had a good run, too. Until Doris got overly involved with a Russian agent. Deary me, girls. You were a real couple of goers, weren't you? I mean, I can't talk, can I? But just saying. Always the quiet ones."

It was Ethel's turn wearing the jealousy hat, looking daggers at her sister, who surprised Acid by allowing a thin-lipped smile to spread across her sour chops.

"So instead of waiting around to be discharged and dragged through the system, you went underground. Changed your names. Became special contractors. Cleaners. Met Caesar at the same time he was setting up Annihilation Pest Control. And here we are." Acid put down the notes and looked at the women. "You can tell me if any of that is wrong, of course. But from the looks on your faces, I'd say we got it bang on."

Neither Ethel nor Doris met Acid's gaze but eventually they acquiesced, giving just the slightest of nods. A blink and you'd miss it confirmation. It pained them to admit it. But there it was.

"You see, girls, it might take me a little longer to find Caesar, but I have the tools now. Which returns us to the million-dollar question. Do you want to save yourselves a lot of suffering?" She walked back over to the women, carrying a surgical knife prominently in front of her, letting it sway from side to side. "Obviously I still have to kill you both for your role in my mother's murder, and because, deep down, I've always despised you and can't think of anything I'd like more. But I will be fair. You give up Caesar now and I promise I'll do it quick, painless. But if not…" She held up the knife and pressed her thumb onto the blade tip, grimacing dramatically at its sharpness, then following up with a manic grin. "I'll take your eyes first. Then we'll work our way down. Slowly. Methodically. By the time we get to your toes, golly, can you imagine what we'll all look like? Good job I'm wearing black."

She laughed. The Sisters didn't. But they were taking her seriously now. Their breath sharp and shallow.

Acid gripped the cold steel of the knife handle. "I'm out of the killing business these days. You know that. Hell, I'm even trying to go straight. Whatever that means. But I'll be honest, I'd rather you didn't tell me anything. I want you to suffer. I really do. After what you did to my mum. So you keep your little cat's-arse mouths shut. Because I'm more than happy to make this a long, painful, drawn-out affair."

She glanced at her watch. It was just after 6 p.m. She'd give them one minute to decide. Then the carving started. Doris pulled at the plastic cable ties that strapped her arms to the chair. A pointless action. She sniffed, her eyes roaming the floor.

"We don't know where Caesar is," she whispered, something phlegmy stuck in her throat. "Since operations went global, only Raaz Terabyte has access to operatives' whereabouts. Even Caesar. Especially Caesar."

Acid flinched at the name. Raaz Terabyte. The 'In-field Analyst and Communications Officer' at Annihilation Pest Control. Though, Acid had always thought 'tech-nerd' was more on the nose. The flinch was because she'd heard that name too often these last few weeks. Spook had been on at Acid non-stop. Trying to convince her that Raaz should be taken off her kill list.

It had become increasingly irksome to Acid to hear the young American's protestations. Saying how Raaz wasn't really to blame for her mother's murder. That she herself hadn't actually ever killed anyone. She was an IT boffin, she said. Like her. Only doing her job. As though that excused it. Just following orders? You could ask Joachim von Ribbentrop or Hermann Göring how well that argument went down.

Acid glared at Doris. "Where can I find Raaz?"

A sniff. "No comment."

"Are you fucking kidding me?" Acid yelled. "You're going all procedural on me?" She leaned in close, holding the steel blade against the bone of Doris' eye socket. "I'm going to slice you open if you don't tell me."

"You haven't got the guts. Everyone knows you've gone soft. Turned civilian."

"Oh yeah?" Acid replied. "Try me. After what you did, I can't wait to start."

The old woman scowled at her. "We did nothing you didn't deserve."

"You killed my mum. An innocent, sick woman. She didn't even know her own name, never mind who I was. What was the point?" The exertion of the speech had her pressing the knife blade down hard. A small bead of dark crimson ballooned out from the thin skin next to Doris' eye.

"We had to send you a message. After what you did. Surely you didn't think you could take out three of Caesar's best operatives and expect no fallout."

"Was it your idea?" Acid whispered.

She'd suspected as much. From the moment she'd met them sixteen years earlier, she'd always had Doris and Ethel pegged as particularly ruthless people. Coming from someone with well over three hundred kills under her belt, that was saying something.

Doris stared forward. Didn't answer.

"It was my idea," Ethel said with a sneer.

Acid straightened. "I see. And there was me thinking you were the least heartless of the two of you." She turned, tracing the knife along Ethel's loose jawline. "So while you're in such talkative spirits and spilling the proverbial beans, why don't you tell me where I can find Raaz?"

The old woman opened her mouth to speak when a dull buzzing noise emanated from the pocket of Acid's leather jacket.

Ethel eyeballed her. "You going to answer that?"

"Ignore it," Acid said. "You were saying?"

The phone continued to vibrate noisily in her pocket. It was a new burner phone, meaning the caller was Spook or The Dullahan. Meaning she really should answer it.

Shit.

She stood, pointing the knife at the women. "Hold that thought, ladies, okay? Back in a tick."

She walked between the two chairs over to the far side of the room and pulled the phone from her pocket. Caller ID blocked. But that was normal. She tapped answer.

"Hello?"

"Acid, I've found her." It was Spook. Though her voice was an octave higher than usual. She was also breathless.

Acid glanced at the backs of the Sinister Sisters' heads. "Found who?" she asked. "I am kind of busy, kid—"

"Raaz, of course," Spook said. "I infiltrated an email she sent to Magpie Stiletto last week. An image file, with a message encoded in the metadata. Same as before. But this time she forgot to mask her IP address in the source file. I've been tracing it all week. And now I've found her."

Acid considered the news. Spook's skills were certainly impressive, but something felt wrong. "That's good work," she started. "Thank you. Once I'm done with the Ugly Sisters here, I'll be home and we can discuss how to move on her."

"No, Acid, you don't understand," Spook went on. "I'm here now. About five minutes away. There's an underground bunker set up in the middle of a forest a few miles outside of Epsom."

Acid chewed on her bottom lip, seething with a silent rage that threatened to knock her out of balance. She'd been managing her moods well recently, eating properly, exercising. But it didn't take much for the chattering bats of her hypomania to bubble up in her system. Hearing things like this didn't help.

"We discussed this, Spook," she replied through gritted teeth, aware that the Sisters were listening. "I told you not to do anything without talking to me first. And you agreed."

"I know. But I thought if I can get to Raaz first, maybe I can make her see."

"See what?"

"That helping us can benefit her. If she gave us Caesar and Magpie, couldn't you spare her life?"

"Spook, don't do this," Acid told her. "It's dangerous. She's not who you think she is."

"She's a techie," Spook said, that worrying tone in her voice. Like she knew better. Like Acid wanting Raaz dead was somehow an affront. "I get that she's part of the organisation, but she didn't kill your mum. She wasn't there that night."

"She set it up. She's as guilty as any of them. Plus, let me remind you, she was the one who sent all those people to kill you. Myself included."

"Yes. But you didn't."

"So?"

"So, people change. You changed. Why can't she? Let me talk with her. I'm here now. Please, Acid. It'll be fine. I've got this. Trust me."

"Spook," Acid rasped. "I'm serious. Do not do this."

But the line was dead. The kid (clearly getting a little big for her boots) had bloody well hung up on her. Acid stared at the phone for a moment, then let out a compressed scream that remained in her chest. Her first thought was to leave the petulant fool to her fate. Let her deal with whatever consequences were coming her way. But even as the notion swam across Acid's awareness, a deeper part of her was already preparing to leave. Spook had a good heart, and she was becoming a useful ally in Acid's search for those who'd betrayed her, but she was still naïve. If Raaz's location was discovered so easily (and yes 'easily' was a relative term, but to a fellow hacker like Spook it *was* easy), then something told her that was a problem.

She looked down at the surgical knife still gripped in her fist.

"Shit. Shitting bastard hell."

She couldn't enjoy this now. Not with Spook in danger. In front of her, the Sinister Sisters seemed to grow a little in stature. Acid imagined their faces. The prim 'told-you-so's' of their exchanged glances.

No.

Wasn't happening.

She flung the surgical knife over her shoulder. Then, as she strode towards the women, she slipped a Glock 17 from out of her waistband. Without missing a stride she shot them both in the back of the head, killing them instantly. Nowhere near as much fun as she'd planned. As the Sinister Sisters slumped forward into their sizeable bosoms, Acid was already out the door and calling a new number.

The Dullahan answered in one ring. He always did. "It's me," Acid told him. "I think Spook's in trouble. Can you trace a call for me? My usual line, just now."

"Aye, shouldn't be a problem." The old man sighed. "Give me twenty minutes."

"Thanks."

She hung up and ran along the short landing to the stairwell. A few miles outside of Epsom, Spook had said. A forest. Acid looked at her watch. It was seven minutes to seven and it looked like she was going to Epsom. Not what she had planned this evening. But wasn't that always the way.

CHAPTER 3

In Spook's head the plan was going to work like a dream. She'd confront Raaz, reason with her (one computer genius to another), and explain to her in no uncertain terms how she understood her predicament. There weren't many high-end jobs out there for female techies, even in this day and age. So she really did empathise with her taking the job at Annihilation Pest Control. She got it. It was an exciting job. A way to utilise new skills and develop existing ones. And didn't all hackers have a foot in both camps of justice and corruption, anyway? Hacking was a grey area, always had been, but that was the way it was. Spook knew that. She'd tell Raaz as much. Once they'd bonded, her plan was to offer her a way out. Give up Caesar and the rest of the organisation and Acid would spare her life.

So when Spook made her way into the seemingly unguarded and unlocked bunker and felt a heavy blow to the back of the head, she couldn't help but feel a little disappointed. Although, the feeling did only last a split second, before the world went black and she hit the floor like a rag doll.

"You really are a blight on the world, aren't you?"

Spook opened her eyes and tried to blink the room into focus. No dice. She tried again before whimpering, "I can't see."

"Oh for heaven's sake. Here!"

Spook jumped as her thick-lensed glasses were thrust onto her face. She leaned back. An attempt to better take in the sudden rush of visual stimuli, but not easy when you were strapped to an uncomfortable wooden chair. The room she was in was windowless and dark. In fact, the word 'room' was a misnomer here, implying some degree of domesticity. Warmth, even. Cold concrete box was a more apt description. Along the wall to Spook's right were three large shelving units that were stacked high with hard drives, modems and servers. Red and green lights blinked incessantly, flashing in time to their own silent song. Along the wall opposite stood two large desks, laid out in an 'L' shape. Spook cast an inspecting gaze over the computer set-up on top. Three monitors, two of them linked and displaying what looked like a secure messaging program. From this distance she couldn't make out any more than that. The third monitor looked to be running a brute-force attack on some foreign government's website, the progress metre paused half-way.

A few feet away, standing with her arms folded in front of an open doorway, was Raaz Terabyte. It was the first time Spook had seen her in the flesh and she was surprised how short she was. Five-three at the most. This, along with the plaited pig-tails, hoop earrings, baseball cap and pink Adidas tracksuit, gave her the appearance of a little kid. Made Spook think she'd been right to try reasoning with her. Despite the bling and urban-streetwear, Raaz was a woman of science and math. Not a killer. She didn't deserve what Acid had planned.

But then Raaz spoke, and all that went out the window.

"You really are a stupid bloody pest, aren't you?" she said in her Cockney-Asian accent. "Spook Horowitz: ace hacker, fucking annoying bitch. Though I guess you must have something about you, to convince Acid to help you the way she did."

Spook struggled at her constraints. Thick electrical tape had been wrapped around her shoulders and the tops of her arms, fastening her tightly to the chair. Her hands were tied behind her back.

"She saw some sense, that's all," Spook told her. "Realised she was better than all of you. That she had more to offer the world than killing people."

"Is that right?" Raaz scoffed. "So how's that working out for her? Because as far as I can see, all she's done since she left Annihilation is kill two of my colleagues. Not really stopped the killing, has she?"

"She will," Spook said. "That's the reason I'm here. I've got a proposal for you."

"A proposal?" Raaz walked over and sat on the large leather chair next to her desk. She swivelled it around to face Spook. "Do go on."

"If you give up Caesar and the remaining members, I'll make sure Acid spares your life. You could do anything. Go to America. Someone with your skillset would kill it in 'Frisco."

Raaz smiled. Nodded to herself. "You're right. I would. But where would the fun be in that? And I suspect Caesar might have a little problem with me giving him up."

"He'd be dead," Spook replied.

Raaz laughed. It was a weird sound, a few octaves higher than her normal speaking voice. Like she was trying it out for the first time. She halted and, still sitting, walked her chair over to Spook.

"You're wrong by the way," she whispered.

"Acid's going to find Caesar. With or without your help."

Raaz shook her head. "Not what I meant. You're wrong because that isn't the reason you're here. The reason you're here, you dumb fucking bitch, is that I lured you here. You really think I'd be stupid enough to leave my IP address unmasked?"

Spook swallowed. "Oh."

"Oh. Exactly. So don't start with your pathetic nonsense."

"What are you going to do to me?" Spook asked, scanning her eyes around the room.

"You'll find out soon enough,"

"You're going to kill me?"

"Not me. Not Caesar either. We've got much bigger and more lucrative plans for you and your goth girlfriend."

"Lucrative?"

"Let's just say there's some incredibly wealthy people who want to meet you both."

Spook opened her mouth to speak, but before she had a chance an alarm sounded.

"About time," Raaz said, getting to her feet and pressing a button on the computer desk. The alarm stopped and Raaz pulled a long strip of black material from out of her pocket. "We have a visitor."

Spook raised her head. "What's going on? Who—"

Raaz stepped behind her and pulled the material between her lips, halting any further protestations. She wrapped the gag around her head a few times and tied it around the back. Then, as a faint scuffling noise drifted in from outside, she moved over to the corner of the room where an open trapdoor was concealed behind a bank of flashing servers. She held her finger up to her lips before disappearing around the side and down into the space below, closing the hatch.

Left alone, Spook struggled again at her constraints, but it was useless. She tilted her head back, tried to scream. Same story. All she could do was sit there and wait.

A minute later a cherry-red Dr Martens sixteen-hole boot appeared around the side of the doorway and Acid Vanilla peered into the room, leading with a large handgun. Assuming a defensive position she moved into the room, holding one hand up to Spook in acknowledgement as she scoped out the space.

Spook glared back at her, shaking her head and opening her eyes wide. As if this would somehow deliver the message.

"Aggg," she tried, over the thick cotton. "Eeeztrrrrrr."

"You hurt?" Acid asked, eyes darting left and right as she moved around the edge of the room. "Is anyone here?"

Spook opened her eyes as wide as they'd go, nodding over at

the server unit and the trapdoor, straining desperately at the material in her mouth.

"Rzzz."

"Yes, I know. Where is she? I was expecting trouble."

Where is she?

The answer to that was she was creaking open the trapdoor and raising a trank gun over the top of the server unit.

"Asssdddd!" Spook tried. "Rzzzz!"

"Okay, fine." Acid leaned down to remove the gag.

Spook gasped. "Raaz. There—"

But it was too late.

"What the—"

Acid spun around, one hand on the dart in her neck, the other going for the gun in her waistband. But Raaz had already moved away from the unit and side-stepped around the back of her. Acid stumbled forward, mishandling the gun and letting it fall to the floor. She made to pick it up, but Raaz kicked it away and the momentum sent Acid over on one knee, her whole body visibly wilting as the drug took her over. She glanced up at Spook, opened her mouth, then fell unconscious onto the hard floor.

"Well, there she is," Raaz said. "The big hero. What a fucking joke."

That laugh again. Even shriller than before. More menacing. She walked over to the desk and picked up a second syringe, held it up to the light.

"Now it's your turn," she whispered, squirting a little fluid out of the end. "Sweet dreams, Spook Horrorbitch, and good luck on the island. You're going to need it."

CHAPTER 4

Spook had jolted awake on the plane, knowing straight away she'd excelled herself in the messing-things-up stakes. After being shoved out of the hatch ahead of Acid, she'd spent the parachute ride taking stock of her predicament. Trying to keep her analytical head in play rather than let anxiety take over.

Of course, it didn't work.

All she could think about as she approached the large green landmass below her were the words that Raaz had uttered before everything went black.

Good luck on the island.

Despite what some of her classmates at the MIT had supposed, Spook wasn't on the spectrum. Shy, yes. Socially awkward, absolutely. But she understood emotions, understood empathy and sarcasm and cynicism. (Although the more time she spent with Acid, she wondered if it might have been a blessing if she didn't.) Still, she'd mused as her feet brushed the treetops and she'd pulled on the guide-ropes to straighten herself, even an autistic person would have clocked the sarcastic malevolence in Raaz's voice.

Good luck on the island.

Meaning, you're going to need it.

Meaning, this was bad.

Very bad indeed.

Now, on the mysterious island (and reunited, thankfully, with a roused and rejuvenated Acid), Spook was able to make a little more sense of their plight. Raaz Terabyte was behind this. And if that was the case, then Beowulf Caesar was behind it too. The only problem was, that made little sense to Spook's rational mind. He'd had both Acid and Spook exactly where he wanted them.

Why were they still alive?

As if to jerk Spook out of her confusion, a loud gunshot echoed through the humid air. Someone was on their trail. She stuck close to Acid as they ran through the luscious undergrowth. Large leafy plants scratched at her skin, whilst mosquitoes and other creatures she'd rather not think about took tiny bites out of her. It was so hot here under the tree cover. Like being in a furnace. There was no air. Just uncomfortable, sticky heat. The jungle was darker than she'd imagined too, even in daylight. Shards of light cut through the trees at intervals, creating an eerie atmosphere unlike anything Spook had ever encountered.

In front of her, Acid craned her neck around and yelled, "Come on. Keep up."

"Where are we heading?" Spook asked. "You got a plan here?"

At least they were moving. Spook didn't have the best hearing in the world, but the gunfire was getting louder. Whoever it was, they were closing in.

"When do I ever have a plan?" Acid replied. "The plan is to keep moving. We'll think of something."

Which would have been all well and good – Spook had been privy to Acid's on-her-feet-thinking many times since they'd met and she hadn't let her down yet – but neither of them were counting on the dense jungle suddenly dropping away to leave them teetering on the precipice of a large rock face.

"Well, shit," Acid mouthed, peering over the rim at the fast-flowing river below.

Spook grabbed Acid's arm. "What now?"

Acid cupped her hand around her ear and closed her eyes. In the distance Spook could hear more gunfire. Male voices. Something like, *We've got the bitches.* Acid had heard it too. She moved closer to the edge as Spook's stomach did a backflip.

"Ah, no, Acid. I can't. It's got to be a hundred feet or more. And that water looks deep. We could drown."

"Yeah, well, we wait here we'll get our heads blown off," Acid retorted, eyeing up the drop. She fixed Spook with a steely gaze. "You ever seen Butch Cassidy and the Sundance Kid?"

Spook frowned, wracking her brain. "Is that the one where they—"

"Yeah, they do this," Acid yelled, grabbing Spook around the shoulder and running them both off the side of the mountain.

"Ahhh, shiiiitttt!"

Spook's internal organs shifted into her chest, threatening to burst out of her throat. The drop was intense and scary and exhilarating all at once and she wondered if she might piss her pants. Then she actually did piss her pants. Not a problem though, as a second later she disappeared under the water. The impact knocked all the air out of her but, driven by instinct over strategy, she'd had the foresight to grab onto her glasses. Now she held them tight in her fist as the water slowed her trajectory. A second later she felt the rocky riverbed below her feet and pushed off, searching for the surface.

She flailed her arms, kicked with her legs, but she was getting nowhere. She tried to open her eyes, but the water was murky and the subsurface view confusing. She closed them and kept going, stretching her neck upwards, as if the few millimetres this allowed would do any good. Her chest felt tight. Her lungs ached. The crushing water was beating her. She kicked some more. Desperate now. There was no air left in her body.

She was drowning.

Actually drowning.

Then, finally, she felt heat on her face. Bright sunshine permeating through the skin of her eyelids. She opened her eyes and gulped down a deep lungful of fresh air, treading water as best she could. The river current was rapid and was moving her quickly downstream. She scrambled to put on her glasses, frantically searched for Acid.

"Spook get over here quick."

"Wha—" She squinted into the sunlight, seeing Acid a few metres upstream, holding onto a large rock that jutted out of the water.

Spook doggy-paddled over to her, letting the current do most of the work. As she got nearer, Acid reached for her hand and dragged her around the side of the rock. Just as a bullet pinged off the other side.

"Woah. Who is that?" Spook rasped.

"I can't see with the sun behind them. But there's at least two."

"What do we do?"

Spook flinched as another bullet ricocheted off the jagged rock. Beside her, Acid strained her neck and squinted. "They've got hunting rifles, look like Mauser 18s."

Spook nodded, unsure why she was doing so. "What does that mean?"

"If memory serves, they hold five rounds a piece," Acid went on. "I've counted eight shots so far, so they've got two more before they have to reload. We wait till they've used those and we move." She gestured downstream at where the river disappeared around a low-hanging tree. "Push off from the rock and keep under water as much as you can. Once we get around the bend, we should get a little breathing space."

Spook sniffed. "But what if one guy shoots then reloads, leaving the other still loaded?"

"Yeah, well." Acid sighed. "I didn't say it was a good plan. But we can't cling to this rock forever. We don't know what's in these waters."

That got Spook's attention. She stared at Acid, searching her face for a sign she was joking but got nothing back. Another shot pinged off the rock, sending loose gravel crumbling over their heads.

"You're right," Acid said. "We can't wait for him to reload."

Before Spook could reply, Acid hauled herself up over the top of the rock and shoved her index finger in the air. "Come on, you bastards."

She dropped back just in time as the final bullet struck the rock a few inches from her head. "That's the one," she yelled. "Move."

Spook didn't need telling twice. Finding purchase against the side of the rock she pushed away with all her strength, following Acid and dipping her head beneath the fast running water. The current transported them around the bend and under the cover of the dense vegetation.

They were safe.

For the time being, at least.

CHAPTER 5

Once safely out of sight, Acid swam over to the riverbank and hauled herself out. Exhausted, she lay back in the shade of an enormous tree that arched over her head. She had no idea what species it was. Nothing she'd ever seen before. Its large plate-like leaves were a dark bottle-green and the thick sinewy bark spiralled around itself like the veins on a weightlifter's forearm. She closed her eyes, letting her other senses take over, enjoying the rich floral notes that drifted into her nasal passage, still stinging a little from the ammonium. Each smell was alien but exciting, taking her back to childhood and London Zoo's tropical house. She remembered visiting with her mum. Back when things were happy and well, which in reality was a small window and would have made her around six years old, before her mother had her fall and life sank into a quagmire of shit. It was a gentle time and one that Acid had always hung onto, but now the memory had pain attached and she brushed it away.

She propped herself up and looked over to see Spook cleaning her glasses on her shirt.

"You okay?" Acid asked.

"Just about. You?"

"You know me, Spook. Hard to love. Harder to kill." The remark got zero response from the kid.

Tough crowd.

Spook shoved her glasses onto her face and got to her feet. "Should we keep moving?"

Acid paused, savouring the relative tranquillity and sliding her tongue around her lips. Fresh water. That was something, at least. She sat up and held her hand out to Spook, who obliged, straining hard to pull Acid to her feet.

"You don't seem too concerned that people are shooting at us," she said.

Acid rolled her shoulders back and looked about her. "Obviously, I'd rather those things weren't happening. But there's no point getting stressed. Is there?"

"Easy for you to say."

"Listen, sweetie," Acid said, attempting something close to a compassionate smile. "I've spent the last sixteen years handling my emotions. Staying cold. Clinical. But it doesn't mean I don't take things seriously. Doesn't mean I'm not worried about our current situation."

Spook nodded. "I'm not sure if hearing that is reassuring or not."

"No. Me neither." She laughed humourlessly. "The sooner we find out who the hell is shooting at us and where the hell we are, the better. We might stand a chance of getting off this island alive."

She threw her gaze up the river as another loud gunshot cracked the atmosphere in two. A flock of tiny birds burst through the treetops, squawking their distaste.

"This way," she said, already brushing aside a leafy fern and heading into the darkness of the trees.

"Will we be safe?" Spook asked, almost on her shoulder as they pushed deeper into the humid jungle.

Acid didn't turn around. "Relatively safe."

She knew it wasn't the answer Spook wanted, but it was the

best she had. Truth was, her heart was pounding heavily in her chest and she could sense the bats awakening in the pit of her soul. Times like this, the bats (the anthropomorphised way Acid related to the manic side of her bipolar energy) could be a huge help. But not always. Over the years, she'd created an array of coping methods to best deal with her condition, honing the frantic, chaotic energy to her advantage. Indeed, in her old life, taking huge risks, requiring little or no sleep, and having access to wild, off-the-wall creative thinking was incredibly helpful.

Until it wasn't.

The two women reached a clearing and stopped for a moment to catch their breath. The deeper they went in the jungle, the more oppressive the heat and humidity. The air here was wet and heavy and hard to grab hold of, as though at high altitude.

Acid wiped the back of her hand across her forehead. "We need somewhere to hide out," she mused to herself. "Find weapons of some description."

"Weapons?" Spook said. "You want to take these people on?"

Acid turned and screwed up her nose. "What did you think we'd do?"

"I don't know. Find some sort of boat. Escape. Did you see the big building as you parachuted in? What do you think it is?"

"Not somewhere I expect we'd be welcome," Acid replied. "But as far as I could see, that's the only man-made thing on the island. Wait. You hear that?"

Acid closed her eyes. Another benefit when the bats were in town was her senses became super-heightened. Sometimes unbearably so. Like needles in her head. She listened. Someone, or something, moving fast through the undergrowth, brushing against bark and tendrils. She could hear panting. The sound of desperation. But more than that, she sensed fear. Could feel it in her guts. Bad energy coming through.

"Hide," she told Spook, gesturing at a large rubber plant whose leaves were big all the way to the ground. Big enough to hide them.

They hurried over, ducking behind the plant as a woman appeared, glancing anxiously about her. She was an older woman, of indiscernible age. Which meant she was probably wealthy. Her caramel skin was stretched taut on her cheeks and forehead. The result of surgery rather than Botox. But it was excellent work. You wouldn't have looked twice if it wasn't for the pronounced sternocleidomastoid muscles and the crêpe paper skin on her neck. Her dark, short hair was cut into a pixie style, longer at the back and sides. Her black tights were laddered and ripped in many places and the grey power suit she wore was covered in dirt.

"Help," she whispered into the leaves. "I saw you. Please. If you can hear me. I need help. They're trying to kill me."

Acid glanced at Spook and shook her head. *No. Not happening.* In turn, Spook did that weird thing with her mouth that made her look like a frog. Albeit a frog with the power to twist Acid's arm.

Bloody hell.

She got to her feet and moved into the open. "Who are you? Quickly."

The woman spun round and stared at Acid, her face frozen in startled shock (though it could have been the surgery.) She flapped her mouth a few times before speaking.

"M-My name is Grace Philips. I'm a high court judge. From Bakersfield. California."

Acid moved a little closer. "Why are you here?" she asked her. "Do you know who's trying to kill you?"

Grace gasped. "Don't you know? This is their game. They're sick. All of them."

"Who are they?" Acid grabbed her by the shoulders and held her at arm's length, locking eyes. "Who are you talking about? What game?"

She sobbed, falling limp in Acid's arms. "My husband kept on telling me to be careful," she wailed. "Said I was skating on thin ice with those people. But I never thought… I never thought…"

Through her tears she gazed into Acid's face and raised a hand up to her cheek. "We're all going to die. And it's all my fault."

Acid gritted her teeth. Tried again. "What do you mean? Talk to me, Grace. Explain. Properly."

Grace let her hand drop, her shoulders too. Acid released her grip and took a step back. Waiting.

But the answers never came.

A loud bang splintered through the undergrowth, followed by a low whooshing sound, followed by Grace lurching to one side and blood and brain matter splattering up Acid's face.

"Shit. Get down."

She ran for cover, dragging Spook with her into the jungle and putting distance and a labyrinth of dense trees between them and whoever had fired the fatal bullet. Over her shoulder she could hear voices, laughter. But no one was giving chase.

Why would they?

This was their game.

It made sense now. These people, whoever they were, they didn't see this as combat. It was sport for them, something to savour and enjoy. And Acid and Spook – and whoever else was unlucky enough to be in one of those parachutes – were nothing but prizes.

CHAPTER 6

The hunters may have been less than hasty in their pursuit, but that didn't stop Acid and Spook from running as fast as they could go, for as long as possible. Which, incidentally, wasn't that far. What with the stifling heat and the thick vegetation they had to deal with.

Soaked with sweat, and with her leg muscles burning and pulse points throbbing, Acid slowed her pace. Up in front, through a gap in the leaves, she could see a rock formation. Caves, perhaps. She stopped by a large banana tree and waited for Spook to catch up.

"We need to keep going," Spook wheezed as she got closer. "They could be coming for us."

Acid leaned against the rough bark of the tree and narrowed her eyes into the sprawling mass of vines and fern leaves.

"I don't think they are," she said. "Not with any real purpose."

Spook put her hands on her hips, still battling through the pain of exertion. "What does that mean?"

Acid twisted her mouth to one side, pondering how much she should say. "I mean, the way those guys were laughing and joking back there," she said. "They aren't worried about us fighting back. We're not a threat to them."

"Yeah, I think you're right. But does that mean they'd come after us?"

Acid pulled at her lip. Thinking. "No. But I think they're toying with us. Dragging it out. We're part of some bizarre game." She frowned. "But maybe we can use that to our advantage. Somehow."

Spook shuffled her feet, toeing a small rock. "This is all my fault."

"In what way?"

Spook raised her head, opening her eyes wide to fight the tears. Acid looked away. When the kid got like this, it was best to keep quiet. Let her work through whatever worries were nibbling at her without interruption. She sat at the foot of the banana tree and leaned against it. The floor was moist and soft. The tree bark springy. Comfortable almost. In front of her Spook paced back and forth with a face like a constipated hamster. Every so often she stopped, as if about to speak, before thinking better of it and carrying on pacing.

Jesus. Spit it out, will you?

Acid took a deep breath, working on slowing her heart rate. No point both of them being stressed. She wished she had a pair of sunglasses to hide behind. The pacing continued for another few minutes before Spook moved over to join her at the foot of the tree.

"I'm guessing you don't remember much about what happened before you woke up on the plane," she said, all in one breath.

"Yes. I do." Acid picked up a triangular piece of bark and sliced it through the dirt. "I'd come to rescue you."

"Ah, I see. I figured you didn't remember. Otherwise..." She trailed off.

"Otherwise what? I'd have kicked your arse?"

Spook forced a smile. "I suppose."

Acid pointed the bark at her. "I am pissed off, Spook. Especially after I told you to leave it alone. But that can come later.

Right now we need to stick together. Work out how we survive this."

Spook sighed. "Yeah. Cool. It's just, Raaz mentioned something about an island. Said I'd need good luck. So I can't help but think if I hadn't gone looking for her then we wouldn't be here running for our lives on this goddamn island in the middle of an itchy, smelly jungle that is *so fucking hot* I can hardly take it— Oww!" She recoiled as Acid slapped her hard across the face, almost knocking her glasses from her nose. "Hey, I wasn't being hysterical or nothing. I was just venting."

"I know," Acid said, getting to her feet. "But I've been itching to do that since I found out you were alive." She reached down and helped Spook up. "Let's call it even, shall we?"

She flashed Spook her best smirk. Sassy, but with the devil behind it. The kid scowled back, but eventually signalled her acquiescence with a slight giggle and nod of the head. Worked every time.

"You said we might use something to our advantage?" Spook asked. "What do you mean?"

"Not totally sure yet. But if they continue to underestimate us, treat this like a game they can't lose, that's a good thing. When that happens people lose focus, they make mistakes."

Spook nodded, but she didn't look convinced. "So what happens now?"

Acid huffed down her nose. This was going to be a hard sell. "I'd say what happens now is we try and get hold of some guns," she replied.

"Sounds good. How do we do that?"

She scratched at her neck. "How do you feel about luring those guys over here?"

"Not great. You mean use me as bait?"

"Sort of. I was thinking some kind of ambush."

Spook's shoulders sagged. "What stops them from just killing me and taking off, like they did with Grace?"

"I had considered that. But I was thinking…"

She stopped. Off in the distance they heard the sound of a woman screaming. Acid closed her eyes, allowing her deeper instincts to take over. She knew from experience the key to survival was to stay out of your head. Muscle memory and intuition trumped intellectualising any day of the week.

The screaming continued. Like a banshee wail filtering through the trees. But these were screams of fear, not pain. Whoever it was, they were still alive. The timbre and volume told Acid they were getting closer. Two hundred metres away at the most. She turned to Spook. Put a hand on her shoulder.

"This might be our chance. Are you with me?"

Spook nodded, her face serious. "I'm with you."

More screaming. Coming in rapid bursts. Frantic. Desperate. Acid set off in the direction of the sound, fighting through a bed of gigantic ferns as a cloud of buzzing insects kamikazed themselves into her face. The screams had now taken a turn, morphing from desperate wails to a softer more sorrowful whine. The sound of someone realising they had no power left.

Acid quickened her pace. A few yards in front, the ferns opened out to reveal a large rock formation with a ledge that jutted out over a small clearing.

"Over there," she whispered, ducking behind the last of the large ferns and pulling Spook to her. "By the far side of those rocks. Two guys and a girl. Do you see?"

Spook narrowed her eyes. "Not really. What are they doing?"

"Nothing good, kid."

From what Acid could tell, the men (two of them, possibly those who were shooting at them earlier) had bound the woman's hands to an exposed root that stuck out of the rock formation above her. She looked to be in her late twenties and was wearing tight blue jeans and a dark hoodie, ripped under the left arm. Despite the heavy mascara tracks running down her cheeks and her dark hair stuck to her face, she was clearly attractive, with a good figure. The men obviously thought so. The way they were prowling around her, sizing her up, stroking her face, it made

Acid sick. Made her blood run cold. It didn't help they were both over six foot, well-built too. Dressed in full army camouflage. One of them, the blond-haired one, even had war paint on his face. Yet no amount of dress-up could disguise the fact they were city boys. Acid couldn't make out exactly what they were saying, but she caught the accents. American. New York, possibly. A couple of classic Gordon Gekko devotees. Acid held her nerve as the dark-haired one got up close to the woman and grabbed her face, squeezing her cheeks together so she'd look at him. He leaned in and kissed her forcefully on the lips, his friend falling about laughing as the woman cried out. She got a slap for that.

"Pathetic pricks," Acid mouthed, digging her fingernails into her palms until her knuckles cracked.

"We've got to help her," Spook whispered.

Acid sighed. "They're armed. We don't stand a chance."

The kid curled her lip. "Are you serious? You're going to let them rape her?"

"We can't save everyone," Acid rasped back. "It's rotten, I know. But we have to think of ourselves."

"Are you for real?" Spook was adamant. "We have to help her. Please."

Acid fell silent. This was a suicide mission. But then again, weren't most of the things she got herself into? And here she was, still breathing. Just about. For now at least. She narrowed her eyes, scanning the area.

"Up there," she whispered, gesturing at the overhanging rock. "See that boulder a little way back on the ledge, about as big as a football? You reckon you can get up there and move it?"

Spook looked. "I can try."

"You'll be all right," Acid said, looking her up and down. "Take it on a wide arc. Stay out of sight. But if they hold their position, I reckon the blond one is in the perfect spot for you to go Lord of the Flies on his arse."

The kid sucked in her top lip. Didn't get the reference.

"Drop the rock on his head." Acid sighed. "Do you think you can manage that?"

Spook closed one eye and gave an unconvincing nod. "What about you?"

"I'll move around the perimeter. Get a bit closer. Once you're up high, I'll move in on the other guy. If we strike them both at the same time we might pull it off. You ready?"

Spook's voice cracked. "Now?"

Acid looked over as the woman screamed again. The blond guy had undone her jeans and was working them down her thighs.

"Yes, Spook. Now."

She gave her a gentle push and waited as she scurried off through the flora, approaching the ledge in a wide arc as instructed. Although it had to be said, Spook's take on what 'wide arc' meant was a little extreme. But she was scared, being cautious. Eventually she reached the bottom of the steep incline where the ground rose up to form a flat roof over the jagged rocks. Once she got there, Acid set off, moving swiftly and stealthily through the trees, staying low until she was in place behind a low rock a few feet from where the dark-haired man was standing. He had his back to her, but she could now hear the conversation.

Again, nothing good.

"Come on, Lance," he sneered, slapping his buddy on the back. "Let's get this party started. Get our first points in the bag."

"Calm it down, Riggs," the blond one – Lance – snapped back. "I want to enjoy this. I've been going through a dry spell lately."

To her credit, the woman still had some spirit left. "Fuck you," she spat, as the men closed in. "Just get it over with, needle dick."

She was another New Yorker, her accent easier to place. Refined, but with a distinct Brooklyn twang. She gnashed her teeth at this Riggs as he approached her undoing the thick leather belt on his trousers. Up on the overhanging ledge, Acid spied the top of Spook's head. She'd made it up there at least, but if she made a noise, or that rock fell in the wrong spot, they were all screwed.

Acid got to her feet as Spook rolled the rock to the edge of the overhang. Their eyes met. Acid raised her hand. Gave the kid a curt salute. Then, as Spook pushed the rock over the side, Acid leapt forward. She was on Riggs in three steps. Another leap, and she was on his back, one arm around his throat and the other around his head, legs tight around his waist. He yelled out, surprised, but less so than his buddy Lance, who a second later had a large rock dropped onto his skull, killing him instantly.

The woman screamed.

Riggs dropped his rifle and twisted around, striking out with his elbows, to shake off his unknown assailant. "Get the hell off of me. Lance?"

He punched over his head, but Acid dodged the blows and tightened her hold around his neck.

"Acid?"

It was Spook. She'd climbed down from the rocks and was holding Lance's rifle. She aimed it at Riggs' chest.

"What shall I do?"

"Dumb bitch." Riggs said, fighting to breathe. "Go on. Shoot me. See what happens."

"Do it," Acid yelled. She let go of Riggs and sprung from his back, pushing away as she did so to put space between them. "Shoot him."

"I'm trying," Spook cried. "It's jammed or something."

Acid scrambled over and grabbed for the rifle dropped by Riggs. Lying back on the soft jungle floor, she aimed at his head and pulled the trigger. Nothing happened. The trigger loose and unresponsive. She looked at Spook. Looked at Riggs.

"Help me," the woman screamed.

Riggs rubbed at his neck. "You killed Lance. You're going to pay for that." He straightened himself and advanced on Spook, grabbing the rifle from her with one hand and delivering a vicious backhand with the other. The force knocked Spook's glasses off, and she stumbled to the floor.

Resting the rifle over his shoulder, Riggs turned to Acid, looking her up and down with a lewd sneer.

"You're the Cerberix bitches, right? Shit, man. You're big scores. Damn."

"What the hell are you talking about?" Acid asked.

Riggs sighed dramatically. "You're Acid Vanilla, yes? Your catalogue photo does not do you justice, baby. Wow. Almost seems a shame to kill you. But that's the game. I'd rather get my score up than my dick wet." He handled the rifle, aiming it at Acid's head. She didn't move. Riggs laughed. "Oh, you think it's bust? Nah. Works just fine. They all do. Just not for the prey."

Acid frowned. "The prey?"

"That's you. The one about to get that pretty head blown off." He adjusted his grip on the barrel as Acid homed in on his trigger finger. Pre-emption was her only chance. But a split second either way and she was dead. The bats screamed in her psyche. Every nerve tingled with energy.

Go left, her guts told her.

Go left.

Time slowed down like it often did in these situations. Enough that Acid could almost see things before they happened. Riggs tensed his finger on the trigger. Her fate was sealed. The gun fired, piercing the air with a loud crack.

Spook screamed.

Riggs stumbled forward with a loud grunt.

Acid raised her head to see the woman, still hanging from the root had swung her legs up to kick Riggs in the back, sending his shot into the sky.

That was all Acid needed.

Twirling the broken rifle around to create a makeshift club, she ran at Riggs, smashing the heavy wooden butt into his jaw and knocking him unconscious. She stood over him, gave him another smack around the head for good measure.

"Is he dead?" Spook asked, appearing alongside her.

"Not sure," Acid said, heading for the jungle. "But let's not wait around to find out."

"Wait," the woman yelled. "You're not leaving me tied up here?"

"Acid?"

She turned around to be met with a disappointed scowl courtesy of Spook. "Fine." She walked over and worked on the thick knots around the woman's wrists. "But you can't come with us. I'm sorry."

"Excuse me?" the woman spluttered.

"Yeah, what?" Spook spluttered. "We should stick together."

Acid shot her a look. "The more of us there are, the easier it is to find us. Plus, we can't afford to get slowed down."

"Hey, Joan Jett," the woman said. "I don't know if you recall, but I just saved your freakin' ass back there. That prick was going to blow your brains out."

Acid finished with the knots. "I had it handled."

"Is that so?" the woman replied, rubbing at the raised red whelts on her wrists. She reached down and pulled up her jeans. "And who are you? Super Woman?"

A shrug. "Something like that."

"Jesus H. Christ," the woman muttered, shaking her head and doing her belt up.

"Hi, I'm Spook," Spook cut in, holding her hand out. "Spook Horowitz. This is my friend, Acid Vanilla. She's all right, I promise. She just takes a little getting used to."

The woman stared at Spook like she was speaking an alien language. "Spook Horowitz? Acid Vanilla? What is this, some kind of joke?"

"No joke, sweetie," Acid replied. She picked up one of the rifles and examined it. "And only one of those names is made up. I'll let you decide which."

"And you are?" Spook asked.

The woman considered the question, no doubt weighing up

how much she should say. "Sofia," she replied, all spit and consonants. "Sofia Swann."

Acid stuck out her bottom lip. "Good name. Okay, Sofia Swann – you're free. I suggest you head off that way and keep your head down."

Before Acid had even finished speaking she sensed the response. Spook was now staring at her, open-mouthed, as though she'd just told this annoying Sofia chick to *fuck off and die*.

And she hadn't. She was only thinking it.

"Please. She has to come with us," Spook said, staring at Acid in that way she did. As though trying to implant her own thoughts into her head. "Safety in numbers. Isn't that what they say?"

Acid went to reply, but pulled it back. No point arguing with Spook when she was like this. She'd just whine and complain and make Acid want to slap her again. Besides, maybe she was right. Maybe another set of eyes and ears would be helpful.

Acid nodded at Sofia. "You want to come with us?"

The question elicited a fleeting shrug. "It's that or take my chances with lover boy over there." She gestured to Riggs who was beginning to stir.

Acid walked over to where he was lying and swung the rifle butt at his head, knocking him out cold.

"All right, fine," she said, straightening up. "Stay alert, stay quiet and do as I say. First things first, we need to find out how to get these rifles to work. Then we need to know who's behind this, and why we're here. The sooner we know that, the sooner we can work out how to get off this damn island."

CHAPTER 7

But Sofia Swann already knew the answer to most of Acid Vanilla's questions. She knew exactly why she was here and who was behind it. She even knew where the island was. One of two privately owned landmasses smack-bang in the middle of the Indonesian Ocean. Each one around ten thousand acres or sixteen square miles. Big, but not huge. The owner of both islands was one Thomas Engel, a multi-billionaire hedge-fund owner, originally from Boston, now based in California, Paris, the Maldives. You name it, he had a place there. Sofia knew all this because for the last six months she'd been working on a hard-hitting exposé of the semi-retired playboy billionaire. Or more importantly, the kind of activities he got up to in private. Rumours had long since thrived between those in the know about his secret islands and what went on there. The story goes that Engel had won them in a card game with a Saudi entrepreneur in the late eighties, and since then had spent millions of dollars transforming them into high-end recreational facilities, to be utilised by his wide-reaching social circle of the rich and powerful. Those happy to pay millions of dollars for a few nights on the islands. Such was the experience on offer.

Sofia had been getting close, too. Two months earlier she'd

been put in touch with a source who seemed legit. An ex-employee of Engel's who – with a little coaxing and promises of anonymity and a decent pay check if her claims could be proven – agreed to go on the record. The woman, Catherine, had confirmed to Sofia that the rumours were true and told her how she'd worked as an assistant to Engel, back when he was setting them up.

The dream was to create an experience for his guests that they could get nowhere else. Something truly unique. The fact that these experiences were widely considered unlawful, ungodly and unhuman, mattered not to Engel who considered himself on a higher plane, unfettered by the constraints of polite society. The way he saw it, Catherine had told Sofia, morals and laws were for people stuck in the old world. His vision was for something brand new and pioneering. Twin islands. Havens. Exotic playgrounds where those unencumbered by ethics and morality could live out their basest desires.

And that's exactly what he did.

Over the next ten years Engel had pumped millions into creating his mythical islands. One based around pleasure. The other pain. No prizes for guessing which island Sofia had found herself on after being drugged and bundled into a van forty-eight hours earlier.

She'd almost got him, too. The piece was written. A two-thousand-and-sixty-six-word exposé on Thomas Engel's elicit empire. Covering everything: trafficking of underage girls, links to the last three sitting presidents and the British royal family, not to mention the Albanian mob and the Taliban. Even now, after everything that had transpired, Sofia couldn't help feeling a little ashamed she'd not had the courage to go for the big coup de grâce. She'd believed the stories. Started to, at least, the more she'd heard about Engel. But in the end she'd left any mention of Pain Island out of the piece, concentrating instead on the more salacious and illegitimate goings-on over on its sister island. It all just seemed too implausible. Too hard to get one's head around, that people would really pay money to do that sort of thing in the name of sport and recreation. Made her sick. But now it made her more sick that she'd left it out.

Back in the jungle, Sofia unzipped her torn hoodie and flung it into the bushes with a shudder. She'd been handling herself well enough, right up to the point those bastards had jumped her. She shuddered at the thought. Their hands on her. If these two weird chicks hadn't turned up when they did, she'd be dead right now. Or at the very least, wishing she was. She pulled at her Abercrombie and Fitch t-shirt, peeling it from her sticky torso. The sun was on its descent, the air growing cooler as day merged into dusk, but it was still damn hot. It was the humidity that got you. That and the bugs. Creepy crawlies. She hated the outdoors. She was a city girl, Brooklyn born and raised, with an attitude and a mouth that often got her into trouble. But never anything like this.

She spun around and walked backwards, taking in the two women trailing behind her. The small nerdy one with the glasses was whispering animatedly at her slightly taller and much ruder friend who, despite the attitude, was a good-looking woman. Or would be, Sofia mused, if she ever cracked a smile. But then as Sofia watched her, she rolled her eyes in a way that was all too familiar. What was it Mike called her? *The queen of the eye-roll.* Maybe that was it. She'd met her match. Still, you didn't need to be an investigative journalist to figure out this Acid character was not happy about her tagging along.

Well you know what? Screw you, honey. Makes two of us. But right now, we're all we've got.

Sofia's hope was they'd reach the shoreline before encountering any more of Engel's cronies. Catherine had told her the islands were unreachable by large boat (something about submerged sand dunes in the surrounding oceans; Engel and his guests always arrived by helicopter), but she had also mentioned in passing that staff moved between the islands on rowing boats.

"You guys all right?" she asked her new companions.

"Of course. We're having a wonderful time," Acid replied. "Best holiday ever."

"Funny girl," Sofia muttered to herself, turning back to lead the way. "Just what I need right now. Some good old British cynicism."

Over her shoulder she heard Spook going for it again with the urgent whispering. Perhaps she was telling her friend to play nice, because a minute later Acid called out. "Hey, do you have any idea where you're going?"

Sofia raised her hands, palms up. "Not really. But I figure the deeper we go, the more leaf cover, the less chance we have of being found so easy." She stopped, serious-face on. "I'd suggest we find somewhere safe to hold-up until it gets dark. Then we move towards the shoreline. We can trace around the island. Hopefully find a boat."

Acid stuck out her bottom lip. Was she impressed? "Not a bad plan," she mused. "You're sure there are boats?"

"Pretty sure. Yes."

"Unguarded boats?"

Sofia resisted an eye-roll. Settled for a heavy sigh. "We'll find out. Won't we?"

"Who are you, Sofia Swann?" Acid frowned. "What do you know?"

Sofia couldn't help the involuntary smirk that tickled the edge of her lips. "Who says I know anything?"

"Me. I say so," Acid said.

Before Sofia could respond, Acid had her hand gripped around her throat, pushing her backwards into the prickly bark of a thick sago palm.

"The fuck!" Sofia said, grabbing at Acid's fingers. But it was no use. She was strong. Stronger than she looked. "Get off of me, ya psycho bitch."

"Enough with the bullshit, honey," Acid said, shooting her a look that made Sofia's blood run cold. "Start talking. Now."

She struggled a second longer. "Fine. I'll tell ya everything I know. Just let me go."

The pressure on her neck intensified for a second before releasing altogether, leaving her gasping for air.

"Talk," Acid told her. "Now."

She rubbed her neck in an attempt to compose herself. Buy a little time. "Fine. I'll tell you everything I know," she said, voice hoarse, throat raw. "But not here. Like I said, let's get settled somewhere first. Somewhere those sick fucks won't find us so easy."

CHAPTER 8

The night was drawing in, the cloudless, ultramarine-blue above the eucalyptus canopy turning to crimson and then orange, and finally inky purple and black. With the night came the cooler air. Within half an hour of the sun going down the dank heat had dropped dramatically, turning the hot sticky sweat that soaked their clothes to a cold, uncomfortable clamminess.

The three women trudged on in silence. A frosty atmosphere hanging in the air between them wasn't just the drop in temperature. By the time they'd reached a small clearing surrounded by long trailing vines, it was so dark Sofia couldn't see more than a few feet in front of her. She kicked at the ground, moving her once-white Converse in a wide arc, making sure there were no snakes or other nasties present before sitting down.

"Should we make a fire?" Spook whispered through the darkness.

"No fire," Acid said. "It's too dangerous. It'll give away our location."

"No shit," Sofia muttered.

"What's that, sweetie?" Acid came at her. "You got something to say to me?"

"Forget about it," Sofia said. "I mean, I appreciate your wariness. But I don't think anyone's after us right now." She folded to the ground, crossing her legs under her.

"How do you mean?"

"Well, you got to understand, *sweetie*," Sofia continued. "This weekend is a big party for these guys. A holiday. Right now they'll all be back at the resort, safe and warm, drinking themselves stupid. Regaling each other with exciting tales of their first day on the island."

"You think?"

"I know. I'm an investigative journalist. The reason I'm here right now with you losers, rather than safe and warm in my loft apartment in Clinton Hill, is that I found out about this place. And what goes on here."

"And what does go on here?"

"It's a hunt. A big game hunt. With us as the prey. People have paid millions to be here. To kill us. And my guess is, we ain't been picked by chance either."

That was it. She'd got them. Acid and Spook settled down a few feet away, leaning in eagerly.

"Go on then," Acid snipped. "What's the story?"

Sofia took a deep breath and told them everything she knew. About Thomas Engel. About the two islands, and that one of the islands – the one called Pain Island (Pleasure Island being the other) – was a gigantic hunting ground. A sprawling tropical jungle where billionaire playboys could hunt the biggest game of all. Human beings.

"I had the article written," she told them. "I just needed to dot the i's and cross the t's. You write an article like that, you better make sure you've got all your facts checked. After that, the plan was to float it to the majors. New York Times, maybe. The Post."

"No way," Spook cooed, sounding genuinely impressed. Next to her, Acid let out a soft tut. Not so much.

"I've been a struggling freelancer most of my career," Sofia continued. "I had the big time in my sights. But then two days ago I received a manila envelope. Opened it up to find a photo of my source. A young girl called Catherine. Used to work for Thomas Engel. In the photo she's lying in her kitchen in a pool of her own blood. They'd cut her from ear to ear. I found the chick's tongue in the bottom of the envelope."

"Oh shit." Spook groaned. "What did you do?"

Sofia placed her hands on the ground behind her and looked up. Above them the moon had taken its place in the sky, shining down through the leaf cover.

"I shit my pants. Obviously. I mean, I knew I was putting myself in the sights of some seriously dodgy people. But I'd been so careful. Catherine and I had only ever talked via a secure messaging site. The article didn't mention her. Just an unnamed source. No clues as to who she was."

"There's always a way to find out," Spook said.

Sofia lowered her head to take in the young woman. So full of panic and rage earlier, she hadn't really taken much notice of her, except the trope-ish accoutrements. The oversized glasses. The boys' jeans and little girl plaits. Seeing her up close now, illuminated in the moonlight, she seemed more intense and intelligent than Sofia had given her credit for. Nervy, yes. A little odd. But worth listening to, perhaps.

"You know what you're talking about?" she asked.

"Yep. I've been a coder and a hacker since I was seven years old. White hat stuff mainly. But hire the right person, pay the right price, nothing is secure anymore. So what happened then?"

"I didn't know what to do," Sofia continued. "Eventually I called the police, but I knew they didn't believe me. They said they'd send someone to interview me, but they never got a chance. To be honest that was the worst thing I could have done. Should have backed off. So stupid." She looked away, emotion gripping her throat as if from nowhere. She closed her eyes, fought the tears. This wasn't like her. She was tough. Street-tough. A deep breath and she continued. "I'm still a little hazy with what happened next. I remember hearing the door. Thinking it was Mike, my fiancé, arriving home from work. I called out to him, but he didn't reply, so I went through to the kitchen. There were two men there. One grabbed me and stuck a needle in my neck and that was it. I woke up with a parachute on my back and a gun in my face."

"Similar stories here," Spook said. "Do you think there's a pattern? A reason they took us specifically?"

"I have my theories," Sofia said, before locking eyes with Acid Vanilla, who'd been gazing at her the whole time. Normally when you met someone's eyes in this way, societal norms had them look away. But not this one. Sofia swallowed. Held her ground. There was something about this Acid Vanilla that unsettled her. Sure, she was a grade-A bitch who clearly thought a lot of herself, but it was beyond that. Sofia was good at reading people (an empath, Marcy, her yoga-teacher-slash-life-coach had told her). But for whatever reason, Acid had her baffled.

She sat upright and hugged her knees. "So what about you?" she asked her, keeping the tone light. "What's your story?"

Acid Vanilla held her gaze a while longer, a smirk forming across her full lips. "You don't want to know about me."

Sofia ran her tongue over her teeth. "Let me guess then."

Acid's shoulders dropped a little, and the smirk twisted into the hint of a genuine smile. She peered through her bangs. Flirtatious suddenly. "Go on then, Miss Hot-Shot-Investigative-Journalist. Let's see what you got."

Sofia scanned her up and down, taking in her shapely but firm body. Clearly she worked out, but she had the air of someone with a penchant for decadence. Her long thick hair was unwashed. It said 'rock chick' in a way that was a little obvious, but it worked for her. Coupled with the leather jacket tied around her waist, and black jeans, and the obvious guess would be someone in the music industry. But there was more to her than that.

"I couldn't help notice your eyes earlier," Sofia said, dampening the coquettish smile inadvertently playing across her lips. "Very striking. Very unusual."

"Yes, so they tell me." Acid sighed, but looking away as she did.

"It's called heterochromia, isn't it?" she went on. "Something like that. I bet people always tell you they're like David Bowie's, right?"

Here Acid's diffidence turned into a smirk. She opened her mouth to speak, but Sofia got in first.

"But obviously you know that's not true. Bowie had one pupil bigger than the other, which only made them look different colours. Whereas you really do have one blue eye and one brown eye. I'm guessing it kind of pisses you off when people get that wrong. Yet you also get off on correcting them. You like to be right."

"Very impressive," Acid said. It was sarcastic, but her smirk had faded.

Sofia tilted her head, buoyed by the reaction. "Okay, wild guess, I'd say you're in PR."

This provoked a loud scoff from the two women.

"You can fuck right off," Acid said, but hitting her with a playful look. "PR? Bloody hell."

A shiver ran down Sofia's back that wasn't entirely unpleasant. She hugged her knees tighter.

"Are you cold?" Spook asked. "Acid, why don't you lend Sofia your jacket if you aren't wearing it?"

The question provoked a stern look from Acid. She eyeballed Spook, trying to convey her displeasure via those intense, different-coloured eyes. Sofia saw it. Spook not so much. Or was pretending not to.

"Just for now," she went on. "If you aren't wearing it…"

"Fine," Acid said, untying it from her waist and flinging it at Sofia. "But I want it back."

Sofia held the old thing up in the moonlight. Up close she smelt a heady stench ingrained in the leather, a cocktail of sweat, spilt alcohol and expensive perfume. "Gee, thanks," she said, putting it on. A perfect fit.

Spook grinned and elbowed Acid. "She looks just like you. Same hair, same build. Same jacket."

Acid chewed on her lip. "I mean it, I want it back. There's a lot of sentimental value there."

Sofia straightened the cuffs. "I see. Gift from an old flame?"

"You could say that. You could also say it was a trophy. Of sorts."

"A trophy? Geez, you sound like a serial killer."

The two women exchanged a weird look.

Sofia frowned. *What the hell was this?*

"Did you hear about all the business with Cerberix last year?" Spook asked, her face serious.

"Who didn't? Deserved everything they got, you ask me. I saw the keynote. Saw what those two evil bastards had been up to."

"Well, that was me," beamed Spook. "I was the one who made the recording that exposed them."

"Woah. Heavy," was all Sofia could say. Wasn't often words failed her, but she hadn't been expecting this. Though it made sense now. She waved her hands, gesturing for Spook to continue.

"Long story short," Spook went on, "the CEO, Kent Clarkson, found out I had that recording and hired an assassin to take me out. A company called Annihilation Pest Control. You heard of it?"

She shook her head.

"No one has," Acid said. "Unless you're in the business of having someone killed. Caesar, the boss, he runs a tight ship."

"Sorry," Sofia asked. "How do you fit in to this?"

Acid threw up one eyebrow. "Best you don't kn–"

"She was the assassin sent to kill me," Spook cut in.

Sofia gasped. "Woah. What the fuck?"

"Yeah, Spook. What the fuck?" Acid spat, viciously. "You're telling this to a journalist? Really?"

Spook looked down. "What does it matter now?"

"It matters. Sixteen years I've been a shadow. Anonymous. I'd like to keep it that way."

Now words really did fail Sofia. She glanced from Acid to Spook and back again.

Was this for real?

"We're all screwed here, Acid," Spook went on. "The only way I see us getting off this horrible island is if we trust each other. That starts with telling the truth. About everything."

Acid sighed pointedly into the trees. "*The truth.* Fu-ck-ing hell."

Sofia held up her hands. "You're actually serious? She's a hit man – woman – whatever?" Spook nodded. Acid kept on sighing. "I don't believe ya."

"It's best for you that you don't."

Sofia kept on glancing between the two women. Acid's face was heavy with rage. She glanced at Spook like she wanted to smash her face into the nearest tree.

"Okay, so say this is true, you didn't kill her in the end?"

"Nothing gets past you, does it?" Acid said, still not looking at her.

"But why not? If that was your job?"

Acid met her eyes and pouted. "Let's just say I was already questioning my prescribed career path. Spook here helped me see I had other choices."

"But you kill people. For money."

"I did. Not any more."

"Don't worry," Spook told her. "Acid has put all that behind her. She saved my life. Many times. Got a price put on her own head while she was at it."

Sofia didn't move. "So, what? You just turned good all of a sudden?"

Acid shrugged. "I'd say the term 'good' is a rather subjective term, wouldn't you?"

"Ah, shit, Acid," Spook yelped, animated suddenly. "I never asked. How did it go with the Sinister Sisters?"

"The Sinister Sisters?" Sofia asked, but then shut up quick when she noticed Acid's expression turn dark.

"It's done." Acid rubbed at her palm with the thumb of her other hand. "I didn't have chance to get any intel out of them, but they're off the list."

There must have been something in Sofia's expression Spook clocked, because she went on to explain. "Acid has been searching for her old colleagues the last few months."

"Oh yeah? And what does 'off the list' mean?"

She knew full well what it meant, just couldn't believe it. Or didn't want to. A goddamn assassin. In the flesh. Talking like killing people was nothing.

"It's a long story," Acid said, still looking at her hands. "After I met Spook and defected from the organisation, they killed my mum. Their way of sending me a message. You don't get to choose when you leave."

Stone-cold killer or not, there was something else there, something more to Acid Vanilla. Sofia sensed it even if she couldn't quite catch it beneath the tough talk and the hard jaw. "I'm sorry," she muttered.

"But it makes sense now." Acid's head came up, eyes piercing even in the dim light. "Ever since I woke up on that plane I've been confused as to why Caesar wouldn't just kill us both when he had chance. We've been a pain in his side since Spook and I met. But from what you've told us, Sofia – and the way those two pricks were talking – I get it. He's sold us to Engel." Acid got to her feet and pulled a leaf from a nearby rubber plant. She split the stem down the middle and picked away at the leafy web. "You know, I got to hand it to him. He's clever. This way he gets rid of us and gets paid for it. The sly bastard."

Sofia kept her eyes on the enigmatic assassin as she paced about in the clearing. Suddenly she seemed unhinged, wired, like she'd snorted a big line of Colombia's finest. She carried on, speaking fast and without breath. Telling Sofia her life story. How she fell into killing people for a living. Poor chick had a rough time, it seemed. But hadn't everyone? Was that a good enough excuse to turn to a life of death and destruction? Taking fathers from sons, husbands from wives? Sofia listened but kept her emotions in check. There was something about Acid made her real uneasy.

Eventually she finished pacing and sat back down. "We should probably get some rest," she said, turning to Spook and then Sofia, nodding. "At first light we'll move towards the shore. See what we can find."

Spook yawned. "Shouldn't we keep watch? Take turns?"

"No point. I agree with Sofia. This really is a hunt, isn't it? A game. So they'll be tucked up in bed right now. Probably won't start again until late tomorrow. There might even be another announcement. Think about it. To them we're sitting ducks. They're in no hurry. But we can use that to our advantage."

"Yeah? How?" Sofia asked.

Acid lay back. "I haven't figured that part out yet. But don't worry, *toots*. I'll think of something. I always do."

Sofia settled down herself, snuggling as best she could into the collar of Acid's leather jacket. Which had once belonged to one of her victims, she was now certain. She closed her eyes, sensing sleep on the horizon. Whether she could trust Acid Vanilla and Spook Horowitz, she wasn't yet sure. But if she was going to survive this island and get back to Mike in one piece, a clear head and a revitalised body was the first step. After that, it was anyone's guess.

CHAPTER 9

Acid opened one eye and groaned. In her initial waking moments, still basking in the haze between benign slumber and total awareness, she'd wondered if it had all been a dream. A silly dream (probably alcohol-induced), where she was being hunted by a group of shadowy billionaires. The top prize in a grisly game of death where there were no winners and so many losers.

But it was no dream.

She propped herself up on one elbow and rubbed at her eyes. A few feet away, sat on a low rock, Spook was examining one of the hunting rifles they'd taken from those pricks yesterday. They'd had that girl tied up. The journalist. Sofia. Sofia Swann.

Shit.

Acid sat bolt upright as her awareness swam into focus. She glanced around, her breath catching in her chest. "Spook," she said. "Where is she? Where's Sofia?"

Spook placed the rifle down. "Please don't get angry."

"Where is she?" Acid repeated. "Where's my jacket?"

"I don't know," Spook whined. "I'm so sorry. I don't know what happened. I heard her moving around about an hour ago. I figured she might be going to take a leak or stretch her legs. But she's gone."

Acid got to her feet. The sun was already making its presence known through the trees. "Did she say anything?"

"I was only half-awake."

Acid held her finger up. "What did I say? I knew something like this would happen."

Spook's head dropped. "I'm sorry. I know how much you loved that jacket."

Acid turned away, stopping herself from saying what she was about to. She closed her eyes. Counted back from ten. It didn't help.

She gave it a beat, then turned back to the kid.

"Screw her," she sneered. "She'll get herself killed. Stupid bitch. At least we know why we're here. And who's out there."

"Does that help us?" Spook asked.

"It tells me most of these people are amateurs," Acid replied. "Yes, they've got weapons, but they aren't real hunters. They don't have a killer instinct." She ground her teeth together as a million tiny bat wings fluttered in her chest. "I'd say with a little ingenuity and a lot of luck we might survive this grim little holiday."

Spook didn't look convinced. "Survive? How?"

"First thing, we get this working," Acid told her, picking up the rifle. "Will be a start."

"Yeah, about that. I've been taking a look while you were asleep. It's not good news."

Acid held the rifle straight and pulled the bolt handle towards her. There was a round in the breech. She removed it and held it up in the light. No misfire. She replaced it and closed up the breech. Next, she flipped the rifle upside down and checked the magazine. It was full. Made no sense. She aimed the rifle at a tree fifty yards away and pulled the trigger. Same problem as before. The firing mechanism was loose and unresponsive. Like it wasn't there.

"What the bloody hell is it with these things?"

"Like I was saying," Spook said softly, padding over to her and gently lifting the rifle away. "It's not good news. See here?" She turned the rifle over and pointed to a small black square on the underneath of the grip, below the barrel.

"What is that?" Acid asked.

"Fingerprint technology. I had wondered, especially after what Riggs said. I've been reading about it for years. Smart guns, they call them. They use embedded technology to ensure only authorised users can fire them."

"The crafty buggers. But surely then all we need to do is find the guy's body and unlock it with his finger."

Spook pulled a face. "Normally yes. In every article I've read, it's like that. You lock and unlock the gun with your fingerprint, the way you'd open an iPhone. Other smart guns I've seen rely on radio waves from a wristband to unlock it. But these ones are different. There's a spring mechanism underneath the sensor that only makes contact when the right fingerprint is engaged. So the registered user has to be the one firing it at all times."

Acid puffed her cheeks out. "Well, bollocks. That's us screwed then. No workaround?"

"None that I've come up with so far."

"Okay. So we've got no firepower. But we might have a start on them today. It sounds like me and you are pretty big targets in this game. But we can use that. I don't know how it works amongst psychopathic billionaires, but I'm guessing there're some rules here."

"Oh shit. We're going to die." Spook took off her glasses and wiped the sweat from her nose before replacing them.

"Don't worry," Acid said, placing a hand on her shoulder. "We'll get through this."

"You think?"

"We've come this far. Let's keep moving. I could do with finding water and something to eat."

As Acid was speaking, an indistinct sound rumbled through

the jungle. Quiet at first, but as she listened it grew louder, morphing into the definite sound of a helicopter. Possibly two.

"This way," Acid yelled, already setting off at a run.

The helicopters were moving fast but Acid was able to keep sight of them as she zig-zagged around thick roots and fibrous vines. On she ran, past densely hanging foliage and an impressive display of tall pitcher plants. The smell coming off those things. Even in her haste Acid couldn't help but wince at the intensity of it. Like rotten meat mixed with unwashed genitals.

"Look there," she said, as they reached the edge of the jungle, pointing to the two choppers disappearing over the trees, heading for the complex. Yesterday, on her parachute down, she'd counted two helipads. But after what Sofia had told them, wouldn't the guests (the players, the hunters, whatever the evil pricks called themselves) already be on the island?

It wasn't a question she could deal with presently as next thing she heard a shout, then noise of a claxon horn, then the crack of gunfire as a bullet whizzed past her head at four thousand feet per second.

"Get down," she yelled, grabbing Spook and diving for cover behind a large boulder as a second bullet ricocheted off the other side.

"We're screwed," Spook whimpered, with tears in her eyes. "Acid, do something."

Acid bit her lip. She could really do without a meltdown right now. From what she'd seen in the split second before leaping behind the rock, there were two shooters, approaching from the north and a few hundred metres away. But their aim was off and, like before, they didn't seem to be in any kind of hurry.

She closed her eyes, tensing every muscle in her body before consciously relaxing each one in turn as she cleared her mind of thought. It was a practice she'd developed a long time ago. A way of calming her oft-chaotic mind and shifting into a persona that was composed, sharp and super-focused. Ready to do whatever she needed to survive. Brutal? Bloody? Risky as hell? Bring it on.

She was ready. With this killer's mindset, and the bats screaming across her nervous system, there was nothing Acid Vanilla couldn't, or wouldn't, do. She was Lady Macbeth, Genghis Khan and Bloody Queen Mary all rolled into one. Part of lineage going back through the ages. Spook had been correct before about Acid trying to go straight (straighter, at least), but the heart of a killer still beat behind her ribs. And right now, she was glad of that.

"Did you say you've seen Butch Cassidy and The Sundance Kid?" she asked, cricking her neck to one side.

"Not sure. Why?"

"No reason. Only, this situation," she gestured at the two of them crouching behind the boulder. "Kind of reminds me of the end. Butch and Sundance are holed up in the bank with the Bolivian police surrounding them."

"I don't think I've seen it," Spook replied. "So what happens?"

Acid opened her mouth and then shut it again, avoiding Spook's blank stare.

"Never mind," she muttered to herself. Then, straightening her back. "Okay, listen, we need to make a call on this. So when I give the word, we're going to run as fast as we can into the cover of the trees. Back the way we came there's a row of tall plants on your left as the trees open out. Sort of tubular things. Pitcher plants or something. I want you to head over there and hide behind them."

"What are you going to do?"

"Leave that to me. Just keep your head down and stay quiet. No matter what happens. You hear me?"

"But there's two of them," Spook squealed. "With weapons. They'll kill you."

Acid tutted theatrically. "Hey now, Sundance. When has something so trivial as being outgunned and outnumbered ever held me back?"

CHAPTER 10

Spook considered Acid's plan, wishing, hoping, trying for a better idea. But she had nothing. Reluctantly she got in position, ready to run when Acid gave the word.

Acid edged to the side of the rock and peered around. "Okay, they're getting closer. Wait. What is that?"

"What?"

"One of them is carrying a crossbow," she said. "The idiot's wearing full hunting gear as well. In this heat. But this is good for us, Spook. Really good."

For once, Spook understood. Crossbows were more rudimentary than rifles. Meaning they wouldn't have the same Smart-Lock technology as on the rifles. If they could get their hands on it, it would be a big help. Not that this knowledge made her feel any more confident. They still had to get hold of it somehow, and a crossbow bolt in the wrong place was as lethal as any bullet.

Whilst she was considering this, Acid was reaching for a large piece of wood that lay a few feet away. She pulled it close and examined it. It was actually two pieces of wood joined together, about five-foot long, slightly curved, and with the flaky remnants of turquoise-blue paint along the length. Possibly it had been part of a boat. It was hard to tell.

"A weapon?" Spook whispered.

"No, a shield." Acid sniffed, holding the wreckage at arm's length.

Despite its age, it seemed sturdy. The wood was an inch thick, with heavy metal rivets holding the two joists together.

"Will it, though?" Spook asked. "Shield us from a bullet?"

Acid shrugged. "We'll see, I suppose." She looked up, lips morphing into a wicked grin. "Don't fret, little one. From this distance, I'm almost certain it'll take a bullet."

"Almost?"

Acid hit her with a now familiar look. The one that said, *Trust me*, whilst simultaneously giving the indication you really, *really* shouldn't.

"Look sharp," she said. "Here they come."

Spook got alongside Acid, tense behind the makeshift shield. A glance at the clearing told her it was a good few strides away across sand and loose gravel. Not conducive for running fast.

"You can do this," she whispered to herself. "Stay cool."

Next to her, Acid raised her head. "Come get us, you pathetic pricks!" she yelled. Then, elbowing Spook in the ribs, "Move."

They set off, scrambling clumsily in the uneven dirt but pushing off together. Spook kept her head down and her arms and body in-line with Acid and the wooden shield. She could hear the men hollering something as they found firmer footing on the long grass at the edge of the rainforest. A few seconds more and they'd have cover from the trees. But a few seconds was relative. An unwelcome image flashed across her mind's eye. The men taking aim. Then an insidious bullet splintering the wooden board. Burrowing its way through Acid's skull and then into her own. Or what if these hunters were cleverer than they'd realised, shooting at their exposed feet instead? A more difficult shot, for sure. But a well-placed bullet would take them both down. They'd be crippled. Unable to run. Ripe for execution.

Spook screwed up her face. An attempt to squash the intrusive thoughts. Two more steps and they'd be in the comparative safety of the jungle. She saw the narrow clearing in front of her. Saw the grove of pitcher plants. They'd almost made it. A loud bang fractured the air. The jungle rustled with commotion as Spook's heart dropped like lead into her stomach. Her first thought: Acid had been shot. Was injured. Was dead. But the bullet had only split the wood.

Acid flung the broken shield to the ground and grabbed Spook by the arm. "Move it, kid."

A step and a leap and they were back in the stifling sauna of the rainforest. But with no time to waste. The hunters had upped their game and were giving chase, the gung-ho jubilance of their initial hollering turning to angry shouts, as their prey disappeared into the jungle.

"Okay, Spook, you know what you have to do," Acid told her as they reached the row of pitcher plants. "Not a peep."

"But—"

"Trust me. I'll be fine." She cast her a flirtatious wink and began to side-step away.

Spook watched until she was out of sight before hurrying behind the largest of the carnivorous trumpets. Up close, the stink coming from inside the pitcher tube was unbearable. She had eaten nothing since yesterday, but if she had, she'd surely be throwing it up. The plants did however provide ample cover, their pink mouths open and waiting, glistening with moisture from the early morning dew. Their appearance was strangely sexual, she realised, before shuddering visibly and shaking that thought from her mind.

A freakin' plant? Geez.
Not the time.

It was safe to say, however, that she had been a little jittery of late. Living in that cramped rental in such close proximity to Acid, it got to her. She knew nothing was going to happen between them, of course. She told herself that every day. But there was still a small part of her that wondered.

What was it they said, it's the hope what kills you?

If Spook hadn't already spent most of her adult life on the shitty end of unrequited love, it might have set her back. As it was, it was just another dull ache in the pit of her stomach. Something she could live with. Although, last night, the way Acid had been flirting with that journalist, Sofia. That stung.

But it really wasn't the time. A few feet away Spook heard the rustle of leaves and the deep murmurings of male voices. Keeping low, and moving slowly so as not to disturb anything, she peered around the side of the pitchers. The men were facing the other way, scoping the area with their weapons poised at waist height. One of them was indeed carrying a crossbow. He had grey, thinning hair, slicked back with pomade and was wearing a khaki shirt with a padded green hunting vest over the top. Must be hot as hell. As Spook watched, he turned around, his red, bloated face jerking nervously at every sound, his piggy eyes peering into the gloom of the rainforest.

"You see anything?" he asked.

His companion – a man of similar age and build but dressed more appropriately (if not more stylishly) for the climate in camo shorts and a dirty undershirt – shook his head. "They've got to be around here somewhere. We were right behind them. If they were running we'd see them."

The way the hunters were moving around the clearing with their backs to each other, it wouldn't leave Acid much scope for a surprise attack.

"Come out, ladies," the one holding the crossbow shouted. "You're only delaying the inevitable. Show yourselves and we promise it'll be quick."

"That's right," his pal continued. "Myself and Patrick here are married men. We're only here for the rankings. The points. But some of the other guys, well, I'm not so sure. They find a couple of lookers like you girls, they might want to draw this whole thing out. If you know what I mean. Have some real fun." The men snickered to themselves, the miserable laughter turning into a violent coughing fit for Patrick.

"Why are you doing this?" Acid's voice rang out. "Who are you?"

Spook swallowed a gasp. Held her nerve. She couldn't place the direction of the voice. The two questions seemingly came from different places. The men looked at each other, then back to scanning the surrounding greenery.

"All you need to know is what the brochure says," Patrick replied. "On this island, we're gods. Willing and able to smite you for our own pleasure and enjoyment."

"But we know who you are," his friend added. "The Cerberix girls, right? Two for one. Top scorers, as well. We bag you today, I'd say we've got this year's trophy in the bag."

"Lay down your weapons." The voice came from behind a rubber tree ten feet from where the men were standing. "This is your only chance. Then you die."

Not for the first time, Spook was intensely glad that she had Acid Vanilla on her side. This despite her sinister statement making the two men laugh heartily into the trees. But they underestimated Acid Vanilla at their peril. Through a gap in the plants Spook saw the men making elaborate hand gestures to each other, signalling a strategy. Hollywood's influence, no doubt. Spook would bet her entire Manga collection neither one of these stout, pompous fools had a military background.

The man who wasn't Patrick was now walking backwards, moving slowly and methodically, aiming behind each tree as he passed by. At the same time, Patrick had his crossbow on his shoulder and was moving in the opposite direction. They were closing in on Acid.

Spook knew she had to do something. Casting aside the fearful thoughts already whizzing through her mind she grabbed hold of the nearest pitcher and shook it forcefully, leading the tall plants in a crazy, disjointed dance. She continued for a few seconds and then stopped, but the hunters had noticed the commotion. Patrick gestured to his friend, shoving two stubby fingers towards his eyes, then over at the plants, the universal sign he was going to investigate. He turned his back on his friend. And that was all Acid needed.

As Spook watched, too scared to even blink, the furtive ex-assassin slipped out from behind a large rubber tree and grabbed a small paring knife from the belt of the over-dressed and under-prepared Patrick. With one hand clamped around his mouth, she drove the knife deep into his side, twisting as she did before yanking it free and shoving the blade into the side of his neck. All the way up to the hilt. Another twist and she'd ripped out his throat, the whole performance over in less than three seconds. She lowered Patrick silently to the ground as Spook scurried back into position.

The second man was almost over the top of her. If he looked down and to his right, he'd have a clear shot. She held her breath. Waited. Down here behind the plants, she couldn't see what Acid was doing, but hell, she hoped to heaven she had it handled.

"What the—"

She jumped clear as the plants parted and the man stumbled onto his knees with Acid riding him, an arm gripped tight around his neck. Purple-faced, he clawed desperately at her as the blood supply to his brain was shut off. But it was ineffectual. He was already fading, eyes bulging with rage and confusion.

"Still feeling god-like?" Acid asked, through the exertion of her grip. "I like a good smite myself, truth be told."

She released her arm from around his neck before grabbing him by the hair, forcing his head through the thick leaf folds of one of the larger pitcher plants and submerging his head into the well of tepid rainwater and whatever pheromone receptors produced that revolting smell.

He flailed around in a final death throe, desperately trying to get her off of him. But Acid tightened her grip, shifting her weight onto his upper back and shoving his whole head into the plant's greedy stench pit. There was a loud gurgling sound. A guttural groan. Then nothing.

Acid stayed on him a while longer, before slowly relaxing her grip and getting to her feet. The look and smile she emerged with sent goose bumps cascading down Spook's arms.

"See. I told you I'd handle them."

Spook brushed herself down and nodded at the man, face first in the pitcher plant. "What a way to go."

"Tell me about it. I remember Davros drowning a mark in one of the chemical toilets at Glastonbury. On the final day too, if I remember correctly. Horrible. But that can't have been far off."

Acid prowled over to the fallen friend. Careful of the stream of blood still gushing from his throat, she removed his belt and fastened it over her own. She wiped the paring knife on his shirt and slipped it into a leather sheath hanging from the belt.

"Does it suit me?" she asked.

"Beautiful," Spook replied, feeling her cheeks burn. "What now?"

Acid picked up the crossbow and eyed it lustfully. "Well, that's easy," she purred, her eyes shining with intensity. "Now we hunt."

CHAPTER 11

The blistering sun beat down on the two women as they trudged onwards through the sticky rainforest alive with millions of tiny bugs and stinging insects. Eventually they found themselves at a large clearing, revealing an idyllic scene that wouldn't have been out of place on an expensive shampoo advert. A small waterfall flowed down a series of layered rocks that looked almost man-made, to collect in a small but incredibly inviting splash pool. The perfect environment for a cornucopia of exotic plants to thrive. Flurries of exotic orchids the colour of raw meat stood out amongst sprawling masses of dazzling purple tendrils. Blood-red flowers the shape of lobster claws hung down beside vermillion gourds and neon yellow flowers. Every extreme of the colour spectrum was here. And the smells. A sweet and heady mix of deep and mysterious scents filled Acid's soul with a renewed life force. She couldn't have pointed them out, but she was certain there were coffee plants and cacao trees nearby.

"Woah," Spook cooed beside her, and for once Acid couldn't help but share the sentiment.

"Yes. Pretty special."

"It's amazing. Like something from the movies. Shame we can't stay here a while."

Acid looked at her. Threw up an eyebrow. "Who says we can't?"

"Umm, not sure if you remember, but there's a bunch of billionaire trophy hunters trying to kill us."

She placed the crossbow down. "Five minutes won't hurt."

"Acid, please. I don't think we should."

But Acid was already heading for the inviting waters of the splash pool, and scooping up handfuls of the refreshing H_2O that burnt her parched throat but instantly revived her.

"You need to drink, Spook," she called over. "We're both dehydrated."

Spook shuffled closer. "We don't have time for this. Hunters could find us any second."

Acid sat back, listening to the gentle sound of the waterfall as it trickled over the rocks and into the pool below. "Don't call them that – hunters. Makes what they're doing sound normal. And yes I know coming from me that's rather hypocritical but there you go."

"What should I call them?"

Acid considered the question. "Dead pricks walking." She nodded at the crossbow. "It's going to be fine. Don't worry. So come here, will you? You've got to be bloody thirsty."

Spook hunched her shoulders and knelt beside Acid before shoving her entire head into the clear water.

Acid laughed as she came up for air. "Quite the technique you've got there."

Spook looked over, wet hair covering the top half of her face. She grinned childishly and they both laughed some more. A moment of relative calm amongst the dark chaos.

Acid leaned back, enjoying the pleasing chill of the water vapour as it bounced off the rocks onto her skin. The last few days had left her frazzled. The last few months, if she was really honest.

Her muscles ached and her nerve endings throbbed with brittle energy. Tiny bat fangs nibbling at her psychology. Acid Vanilla still talked a good talk – tried to at least, especially in front of the kid – but lately she'd noticed her resolve slipping. Not that she'd gone soft. She was still raging at the world, and a mighty force to be reckoned with. But once she'd been the best. The most feared assassin in the business. Now, every day she spent in the civilian world she felt her mind and body growing weaker. So despite the desperateness of the situation, it was important to take a time-out. To reset and refocus. Remember who she was. Who she could be. And sure, a dingy bar with a bottle of whisky for company, and something loud and snotty on the juke box, would have been her first choice for a therapeutic escape. But when in Rome...

She glanced at Spook who was sitting on the edge of the pool, face towards the sun.

"See?" Acid said. "Much needed."

Spook smiled through a shiver. "I guess. I don't think we should stay here too long, though."

"Yes, yes." Acid squinted into the scorching sun peeking over the tops of the trees. "Excellent work, by the way, distracting Dumb and Dumber back there."

"No problem."

Her tone was nonchalant, but it was clear she was pleased with herself. Acid's resolve may have softened over the last six months (and she blamed Spook in part for that), but in return she'd toughened the kid up. Timid nerd to slightly less timid nerd. Still, it was something. Plus, when Spook wasn't getting them caught up in a lethal game of cat and mouse, she was good to have around.

"What do you think happened to Sofia?" Acid asked. "We scare her off?"

"You did, maybe. Her whole demeanour changed when she found out who you were. What you were."

"I noticed that, as well. Poor girl seemed rather perturbed."

Spook snorted. "Oh, you noticed, did you? I bet."

"What's that supposed to mean?"

"Nothing. Just, I saw how you were looking at her. What was it, some kind of self-love fantasy?"

"Excuse me?" Acid sat upright.

"Well, you obviously were attracted to her. Thought maybe because you look alike."

"Oh my god," Acid shrilled. "Are you jealous, Spook?"

"No. I think it's odd, that's all."

Acid smiled to herself. "Well, don't worry. I'm not planning on running off with her. Besides, she's probably dead by now. Stuffed and mounted on some banker's wall."

"Acid! You know I hate it when you talk like that."

Acid got to her feet and picked up the crossbow. "Gallows humour, sweetie. You know how it is. Gets one through the dark times."

Spook turned away. "She'll be okay. She seemed pretty tough."

"That's what I meant to say," Acid replied, aiming the crossbow at a brightly coloured parrot that was sitting in a nearby tree. "Smart too. Although not enough to realise we're her best chance of getting off this island alive, but still."

"Do you think she's right?" Spook asked. "About there being a reason we're all here on this island?"

"A reason other than bored, psychopathic billionaires wanting to blow our brains out?"

"But why us specifically? The woman we met, the judge, before she died she said something about it being her fault. And Sofia was clearly brought here to shut her up. Is it all linked somehow?"

Acid leaned back, the sun's rays like hot hands on her face. "I have been wondering the same. But why me and you? If Caesar is behind it, which he seems to be, why send us here? Why not just get it over and done with? Cleanly. I know he's getting paid well, but the more I think about it, I don't think that's enough."

"But this way we suffer before we die."

Acid shook her head. "He could have made us suffer more

than this if he kept us captive. No. I don't get it. I've killed five of his best operatives in the last year, not to mention the damage done to his reputation after the whole Cerberix disaster."

"Maybe that's it. He needs money," Spook offered. "This Engel guy must have paid him a fortune to bring us here."

Acid scrunched up her face. "There's something else. If everyone on this island is here for a reason, then I want to know why."

"This whole set-up is so scary-weird," Spook mused. "Hunting human beings. Murder as sport. It's the sort of thing you imagine rich white men doing, but never really believe it would happen."

Acid swung the crossbow over her shoulder. "Well, you know what they say, doll. If you can imagine it, no matter how sick and twisted it is, somebody somewhere is already doing it." She helped Spook to her feet, ready to give examples, when she noticed something out of the corner of her eye. She stopped dead.

"What is it?" asked Spook.

Acid held up her hand for quiet, her already heightened senses in overdrive. She scanned the trees, certain she'd seen movement just now, but it was more than that. A strange feeling in her abdomen told her someone was watching them.

"Don't move," she whispered.

Putting herself between Spook and the trees, she heaved the crossbow to her shoulder.

"Who's there?"

Nothing.

"Come out, you fucking coward."

Still nothing.

She gulped down a deep breath, consciously allowing her awareness to spread, shifting into peripheral vision. Her nerve endings itched with manic energy. Her muscles were taut, ready to move when required.

"What are you doing?" Spook whispered, as Acid padded

over to the edge of the clearing. With one eye down the crossbow sight, she traced a wide arc, her finger firm on the trigger.

"I know you're there," she hissed at a large banana tree, its plentiful green fruit hanging down at eye level. "What are you waiting for?"

She remained static, ears pricked for movement. But except for the white noise drone of a thousand chirping insects, the jungle was calm. Slow, cautious, she advanced into the trees, moving all the way around the perimeter of the banana tree until she was back where she'd started. No one in sight. She relaxed her aim, about to tell Spook she'd been mistaken, when she heard a twig snap.

Got ya!

In a flash Acid was in kill mode, her vision zooming from macro to micro. She spun around, swerving out of the way of a tall figure as they emerged from the gloom and stumbled forward. Homing in on the target, she aimed the crossbow.

"Wait," Spook yelled.

"Wait," the target yelled – now identifiable as a man in his early twenties. "Please. I'm on your side."

She held her ground. Her finger quivered on the trigger. The bats screamed in her head.

Kill him.

Destroy.

"Acid, please," Spook tried again. "Look at him. He's not one of them."

She kept the crossbow raised as she snorted back a long deliberate breath, stepping away from the edge mentally if not physically. She assessed the situation, taking in the man's pleading eyes. Pure white globes shining out from his dark skin wet with perspiration. No danger here, her guts told her. But she'd been wrong before.

"Who are you?" she asked.

"M-My name's Will. Will Foster," the man stammered. "I'm an activist. Don't shoot. I swear I'm on your side."

"I don't have a side," Acid told her. "What sort of activist?"

"Political corruption. Big Pharma. All sorts of righteous shit. You name it," he splurged. "I'm one of the Nameless Greys. The hacker group. We're the good guys. I swear it."

Acid shot Spook a look.

"I've heard of the Nameless Greys," she said, nodding emphatically. "They're awesome."

Acid lowered the crossbow a touch as her sharp tunnel vision began to fade. Looking at this weedy character, with his high-top fade haircut and ironic bow tie, it was hard to think of him as anything but a harmless computer geek.

"What were you doing watching us?" Acid asked him, not ready to let him off the hook so easy.

"I was wary. I've been running for my life the past twenty-four hours. I wanted to make double-sure it was you."

"You know us?"

Will held his hands up. "Can I get up? I'll explain everything."

She lowered the crossbow finally. Gestured for him to stand.

"Thanks," Will said, getting to his feet.

Upright, he was well over six-foot tall but with no real muscle mass to speak of, as though a regular-shaped person had been stretched. Along with the bow tie, he wore a button-down short-sleeve shirt that had once been white. Dark blue chino shorts and a pair of old Nikes completed the look.

He brushed himself down and looked sheepishly at her. "You're the guys who took down Cerberix, right?" he said. "Acid Vanilla and Spook Horowitz."

"That's right," Spook exclaimed, before catching Acid's eye and backing off.

"How did you know that?" Acid asked.

Will held his arms out. "Like I said, I'm a hacker. I live for that sort of shit. Saw the keynote live. The video you made. Man, that was fire. We all knew those cats were dubious motherfuckers."

"Okay, granted," Acid replied, as beside her Spook bristled

with silent pride. "But that doesn't explain how you knew we were on the island."

"No, it doesn't," Will went on. "But I can explain. I found something yesterday that blew my mind. If you come with me, I'll show you."

She tensed. A glance at Spook didn't help. Her just nodding and smiling like an eager puppy. As if to say, *let's go*.

"How can we trust you?" Acid asked. "You could be part of this sick game."

"Seriously?" Will asked, waving a limp hand down his body. "You think I look a part of this macho hunter bullshit?"

"No. Course not," Spook butted in. "We can trust him, Acid. I'm sure of it."

Acid let out a loud sigh, as much to signal her scepticism as anything. "Fine," she told Will, holding the crossbow at waist height. "You lead, but the second I see anything I don't like…"

"Got it," Will told her, raising his arms. "But I swear, I'm on your side. Now follow me. This is something you're going to want to see."

CHAPTER 12

Sofia Swann shrieked as a bullet zipped past her ear and splintered the trunk of a young fig tree a few feet in front of her. Only now did she hear the crack of gunfire echo through the trees. So, it was true what people said, you never hear the bullet that kills you. Pushing the thought away, Sofia swerved into another turn, scrambling through the dense vegetation as fast as her aching limbs would carry her. A cursory glance over her shoulder told her she couldn't let up. The old bastard was sprightly, despite his wizened appearance, and with Sofia now weak with hunger, he was gaining on her. Another bullet whipped past as she ducked under a trailing vine. He was getting closer, but still firing wide. If Sofia had been a glass-half-full kind of gal she might have felt herself lucky her pursuer's aim was so poor. As it was, she could only curse herself and Engel and every other one of these evil pricks for her being here.

Around the next bend and the trees opened out to reveal the crumbling walls of some old building. An ancient temple, perhaps. The footprint of the building was about twenty square metres, with the largest remaining wall disappearing beneath a low-hanging eucalyptus tree. There was plenty of rubble lying around, so Sofia grabbed up a decent-sized rock, felt the weight of it in her hand. Moving swiftly but silently, she swung around the side of the ruined wall and knelt beside it. It was a risk, hiding rather than running, but she felt sick with fatigue and it was only a matter of time before she was caught. She crouched further, pressing her body against the ruined wall and secluding herself from the path. With any luck the old man would pass straight by, but she kept the rock in her hand all the same. Kept her eyes fixed on the path. Every pulse point in her body throbbed.

She waited, gasping silently for air but not daring to move. Not for the first time in the last few hours she cursed herself for being so dumb, running off on her own like that.

Who the hell did she think she was?

She might have fancied herself as a tough cookie but she was fast realising it was all relative. City girls weren't cut out for the jungle. Especially when it was full of damn psychopaths. Besides, there was safety in numbers. Three heads were better than one and all that shit.

Yet at the time it had been a no-brainer for the wily New Yorker. There was just something not right about those two chicks, with their weird-ass names and even weirder personalities. Plus one of them was an assassin, for Christ's sake. She'd killed people. Plenty of people.

How could she have trusted someone like that?

But as Sofia's time on the island had ticked away, her predicament had become more and more desperate. She was alone, hungry, despondent, terrified. To the point where she was now starting to reason that a trained killer might be the exact sort of person to help her through this. Well tough shit, right? She'd made her own bed. Thinking that way was the road to nowhere good. Sofia had to accept it, she was on her own and no one was coming to save her.

Staying low beside the cold surface of the ruins, her thoughts turned to Mike, her heart firing out over oceans and continents.

What was he doing right now?

Worrying himself sick, most likely. Poor guy. She could hear his voice, telling her to drop the article, as more damning and grotesque allegations came to light. They'd fought over it. Many times over the last few months. Mike saying she was playing with fire, that it was a job for the FBI, not a journalist. But Sofia being the hot-headed person she was, had framed his protestations as a lack of belief in her. Only now she saw the truth. He was scared. Worried for the safety of someone he loved. Someone he was due to marry in a month's time.

Her focus snapped to a disturbance in the leaves a few feet away. The old guy. He was here. Nervously, she peered through a small gap in the stonework. He was standing with his back to her, on the far side of the ruins. This close, he looked even more ancient. Pale skin and bone, with a shock of white hair sticking out from beneath a canvas bucket hat. Still, people like this you underestimated at your peril, and that large hunting rifle clutched tightly in his liver-spotted paws was nothing to be complacent about.

As he turned around, Sofia's breath caught in her throat. She was sure she recognised him. But from where? She narrowed her eyes, racking her brain. Her best guess, he was an old-school business tycoon. A Warren Buffett type. Deep troughs ran down each side of his face but not what anyone would call 'laughter lines'. This tight-lipped old fucker hadn't laughed in many years. Same as every other wealth-lord Sofia had ever met. So damned scared of losing even a dime it made them sick. Sick and twisted.

She gripped the rock tight, broken fingernails and chipped nail polish digging into the hard stone. The old man was walking backwards, nearing the edge of the wall. One step closer. She imagined herself leaping forward and caving his skull in, surprised to find she felt nothing but rage. She could do this. One step closer.

The old man stopped. Straightened his back.

Come on, you piece of shit. What are you waiting for?

Every muscle, every orifice in her body was clenched tight. She raised herself up off her haunches, rising above the level of the wall where she had a clear shot at him. Right on the back of the head. Drop the frail old prick like a sack of shit. Slowly, silently, she lifted the rock above her head. This was it.

She could do this.

She was going to do this.

But before she had a chance, the old man gained a sudden surge of energy. With a guttural growl he spun around and swung the rifle butt.

"Take that, you stupid bitch!"

The hard wood connected with Sofia's cheekbone and sent her staggering into a large bush. Keeping a hold of the rock, she swung wildly at her assailant but only glimpsed the material of his cream hunting jacket. The unspent momentum sent her tumbling over the side of the wall and she smashed her ass-bone on the hard, cobbled floor of the ruins.

Man, that hurt.

She made to get up but got instead the end of a hunting rifle shoved in her face. She raised her hands, gazing up at the old man. His eyes were pale blue, cold as ice. The sort of eyes with no soul behind them. Sofia grinned at him, joylessly. She'd remembered.

"Edward Menks," she said. "I always suspected you were a rotten sonofabitch."

The backstory on Menks (the one you'd hear told on the likes of CNN or Fox, at least) had him portrayed as a self-made man from humble beginnings. After a short career as a Wall Street financial analyst he'd founded his own oil company in '82, amassing a fortune well into the fifty billion mark before he turned forty. Glorious capitalism in full effect. The epitome of the American Dream. But Sofia knew that was only half the story. Because a huge chunk of Menks' wealth had come from semi-illegal weapon dealings. In fact, if the stories were to be believed, most of the militia groups of central Africa, along with Al-Qaeda and ISIS, had benefitted from Menks' nefarious arms dealings. But of course, he was well connected. With one foot in Congress and a big arm around the military industrial complex of America, he was untouchable. But weren't they all?

Until they weren't.

"And who might you be?" he shrilled, in a high-pitched nasal tone.

"I'm no one," Sofia answered. "I'm just a piece of meat. A trophy. Isn't that right?"

Menks smiled, revealing two rows of jagged, discoloured teeth. Clearly his immense wealth hadn't stretched as far as dental work in the last thirty years. "What can I say? I like to hunt."

"You evil fuck."

The old man laughed at her and raised his gun. "Come along, girly, it's just sport. You wouldn't be here if you didn't deserve to be. This is a cull. We're doing the world a favour."

"What you're doing is sick and wrong," she yelled. "I don't deserve this. I'm innocent. A journalist."

"Innocent?" Menks muttered, moving the rifle-sight to his eye and aiming at her head. "I'm not so sure about that."

Instinct had Sofia raise her hand to her face. A pointless gesture, she knew, but she had nothing else. She was done. Finished. She was going to die here at the hands of this bitter old man, hundreds of miles away from Mike and her friends and her beloved New York. She scrunched up her eyes. Waited.

Get it over with, you miserable prick.

She heard a click. A surprised gasp. Then an ear-blistering crack reverberated through her skull. For a second she thought she was dead. Then she opened her eyes to see Menks slump to his knees and fall, face first, into her lap. The left side of his head and most of his jaw had been blown away, leaving a mess of bone and blood and brain matter.

She screamed.

Or at least, she opened her mouth and went through the usual motions of what screaming entailed. Only she couldn't tell whether she was making any sound due to the intense ringing in her ears. Next she felt a calloused hand close over her mouth and a large, broad-shouldered man loomed in front of her. On seeing the hunting vest and rifle, she leapt back, ready to scream some more, before the man held a thick finger to his lips. His eyes were almost bulging out of their sockets, pleading with her to shut up. But even in her heightened state of confused panic, she could tell they were kind eyes.

The sort of eyes with a soul behind them.

"Can you hear me?" he mouthed at her, his full lips over-enunciating the words. "Are you hurt?"

She gasped for air. The panic subsiding some as her hearing returned. "Who? What?" she spluttered. "You saved me."

"Let's not get complacent," the man said, helping her up. "We need to move. Now."

He hurried her away from the relative open of the clearing and ruins into the dense vegetation beyond.

"Who are you? Where are we going?" she blustered, tripping over an exposed root as the man dragged her into the undergrowth.

"My name is Andreas Welles," the man replied, coldly. "I'm FBI."

"No shit!" she exclaimed, trying to avoid getting swept away by the sense of hope washing over her. "What are you doing here?"

"I'll explain more when we're clear of danger," he said. "There's four hunters heading this way and they mean business. Tough guys. Not like Mr Burns back there. So stay close to me and don't stop until I say so."

"No problem, sir," she said. "Lead the way."

CHAPTER 13

Andreas Welles had hit the ground running after touching down on the island. Quite literally. He'd unclipped his parachute and was already making a bee-line for the relative cover of the rainforest as the man he'd parachuted down behind was still trying to work out which way was north.

Like, who gives a shit, man?

This isn't some fishing expedition.

Welles had tried to get the guy to follow with him. But he was panicking and being weird, so he left him to it. You can't save everyone. Welles had spent twenty years as a detective in Lincoln Heights before joining the Bureau, so he knew if danger reared its head you didn't wait around to talk nice or brainstorm how to best proceed. You got the hell out of there. Fast. Actions first, questions later.

Still, time spent as a uniform in one of the most dangerous areas of LA had prepared him well. Despite his age, Andreas Welles was still a fit and guileful sonofabitch, make no mistake. Six-two in his stockinged-feet and almost as wide, he'd handled himself well so far on this hellish island. Day two and he'd already taken out three of the bastards, four including Mr Burns back there. How many more of them there were, he wasn't sure. But he was damned certain he wasn't going out without a fight.

"Wait, please. Can we hold up a second?"

Welles slowed his pace, coming to a halt next to a large fig tree. He waited, fighting the urge to give this girl some less-than-friendly advice. With both barrels. Like, *no, we can't damn well hold up a second. People are trying to kill us.*

He turned around, the hard trapezius muscles in his neck knotted tight. "What is it?"

"I just need to rest a second." The girl panted. "I think I'm going to throw up."

She was red-faced, and her thick hair stuck to her face with sweat. She leaned over, dry retching as tears streamed from her eyes.

Welles scanned the area, listening for movement. Over to the south of the island (Welles could have told that dithering fool where north was if he'd only listened) he could hear the flow of water. A river, perhaps. But that was all.

"Okay, miss," he said, throwing the rifle over his shoulder. "Let's get to the water and we'll rest for a while. Ten minutes. You can handle that?"

The woman's mouth hung open. She nodded wearily. "Thanks."

The two of them headed south, following the noise of the running water, whilst all the time Welles kept one eye and one ear on the surrounding area.

"Andreas, huh?" the woman asked, once she'd gotten her breath back. "Where you from?"

Welles side-eyed her as she trotted along beside him, trying to keep up with his large strides. "Born and raised in City Terrace, Los Angeles," he told her. "Moved to Lincoln Heights when I joined the force."

"Heavy. But you can obviously handle yourself. Big guy for a Latino."

He gave her a look. Didn't reply.

"Hey, I didn't mean nothing," she spluttered. "All I mean is most of the Latinos I've ever known have been kind of short. Not that it's a bad thing, just a thing, ya know, and—"

"My father was white," he mumbled. "Okay?"

"Right, gotcha. Makes sense," the woman continued. "Well, good to meet you, sir, and *thank god* you showed up when you did. My name's Sofia Swann. I'm a journalist from New York. Brooklyn. I'm immigrant stock too. Italian."

"No fucking shit," he muttered to himself. Up ahead, through a gap in the trees, he could now make out a river. It was fast-flowing and seemed deep in places. He stopped and turned to Sofia. "We can rest here under these trees."

"Awesome. Thanks."

The two of them settled down, Welles positioning himself with his back against a large boulder that stuck out of the ground below a bunch of low-hanging vines. He closed his eyes, gave thanks for the imposed rest. Truth was, he hadn't stop moving since he'd arrived on the island, but he'd fared well. Had the answers he wanted. Had firepower, too. The evil bastards weren't getting away with this.

"Hey, I just realised," Sofia called out. "The rifle. I thought they didn't work unless you were one of the bad guys. Finger-print technology, or something?"

Welles smiled to himself. That's what he'd thought too. But he'd spent long enough in law enforcement to know there was always a workaround. He held up his hand, waving his fingers at her.

The shrill New Yorker stared at them, unsure what she was looking at. Then slowly her confused expression turned to realisation. Turned to disgust. "Oh my god, are you kidding me? That's gross. Gross, but fucking genius."

He let out a laugh that emanated from the depth of his throat and didn't travel much further. "Thanks. Pretty pleased with my handiwork. Excuse the pun."

It hadn't taken him long to realise the hunting rifles worked with the smart gun technology he'd been reading about on GunBuyer and other forums for the past number of years. It would herald a new era in gun ownership, they all said. Only no one had mastered it up to now. Or so he thought. After ambushing his first target (some wet-behind-the-ear hedge-fund prick who lasted all of one second once Welles had cut the blood supply to his brain), the idea had come to him. He hadn't always lived in downtown LA. In fact, after his parents' divorce he'd spent a few summers with his uncle up in Santa Clarita. He had many fond memories of the two of them shooting and skinning rabbits. Using the skills his uncle had taught him (along with the aforementioned hedge-fund prick's pristine hunting knife), he'd removed the skin from the guy's hand in one piece and stretched it over his own. Fit like a glove. All fingerprints intact.

"So now I can use his rifle," he growled at Sofia. "Good thinking, huh?"

"Fuckin-A." She grinned. "Now I really am glad you came along when you did. Makes me think I might have a chance of getting off this island in one piece."

"You know why you're here? You know what this place is?"

Sofia raised her eyebrows. "Oh yeah. I know everything."

Over the next few minutes, she relayed to him everything she knew. Everything that had happened up to the moment she said she expected Menks to turn her head into a firework.

"Quite a tale," Welles mused once she was through. He leaned forward, contemplating what he'd just heard. "Don't think I've ever met a real-life assassin."

"Really?"

"Cartel hitmen, sure. *Sicarios*. Plenty of those *vicioso* bastards. But not the sort you're talking about. That's crazy. And her name's Acid Vanilla? That for real?"

"She said so. She was odd. British, so…"

"Why didn't you stay with her? Sounds like she might have been a useful ally. On this island at least."

She twisted her mouth to one side. "Yeah. Maybe. Like I say, there was just something about her made me uneasy."

"If she's on this island, someone rich, powerful and evil wants her dead." Welles shrugged. "I don't know, miss. Maybe she's on the right side of whatever this is."

Sofia ran her fingers through her matted hair, pulling it back from her face and letting it drop over her shoulders. "Well, you found me. Thank you. I was starting to give up hope." She closed her eyes, a bitter smile spreading over her face. "I kept telling myself I was done for. Maybe I've seen too many movies. Situations like this, it's always someone like me who gets it first."

"Someone like you?"

She shrugged, coyly. "I'm due to get married in a month's time, and ain't that always the way? The one with the sweetheart back home or whatever, something good on the horizon, they usually end up dead before the end of act one."

Welles coughed through another deep laugh. "You think you got problems. I'm an ageing cop of ethnic origin. Due to retire in six weeks too." Her mouth dropped open. A *no fucking way* kind of look on her face. "I'm not kidding you. Looks pretty shitty for me, doesn't it?"

The two of them stared at each other for a moment before simultaneously breaking out in fits of laughter. They laughed long and hard, until their jaws ached and tears streamed down their faces. It was a release, but as quickly as it started, the laughter stopped. A strange atmosphere hung heavy in the air between them.

"Should we make a move?" Sofia asked, wiping a hand across her cheek.

Welles was about to respond in the affirmative when an alien sound broke the relative calm. He froze, the noise now distinguishable as a PA system crackling into life. He jumped to his feet as the static crunch turned into high-pitched feedback and then a voice boomed through the trees.

"Security team three needed in quadrant four. Repeat – security team three needed in quadrant four. We have a Code One security breach. Subject AW is armed and dangerous. Proceed with extreme prejudice." Sofia moved to Welles and grabbed his arm as the voice's tone changed. You could almost hear the malevolent grin over the speaker as they continued on. "To the prey in quadrant four. That's you Mr Welles and you Ms Swann, don't think you'll outrun our security team. Look in the trees. In the sand. In the bushes. We have eyes and ears everywhere."

More static as the voice let out a shrill laugh.

"There's nowhere for you to go. It's over. Goodbye Mr Welles, Ms Swann. It's been enjoyable watching you fail."

The speaker clicked off. The jungle silent once again.

"What does that mean?" Sofia asked, squeezing his arm tighter.

He snorted angrily down both nostrils. "Means this whole thing is worse than we thought. Sick bastards. This isn't just a hunt for them. It's a goddamn spectator sport."

CHAPTER 14

Beowulf Caesar reclined on the black leather couch and took another sip of Champagne, smiling to himself as he drank.

"I've got to hand it to you, dear boy," he growled. "This really is some set-up you've created here."

He cast his gaze around Thomas Engel's impressive office, taking in the tiger-skin rugs, the matching desk and drinks cabinet in dark mahogany with gold and leather embellishments. The appearance was more in keeping with an old-fashioned gentleman's club than any office. But Caesar liked that. He'd come a long way since his days as an East End thug, and he relished any time spent with bona fide billionaires. People like Engel. So above and beyond even the upper echelons of polite society. Shadowy and untouchable. Plus, they all seemed to have a certain air about them he found enchanting. A deep confidence that came from knowing you could do whatever the hell you wanted with zero reprisals. Screw financial security and all that poppycock, that's what real money brought you – freedom to do whatever you wanted. One day Caesar too would be part of this world. He was sure of it. Told himself often. The deal with Engel had helped. The most money Caesar had ever earned from a hit, and all he had to do was deliver him his ex-protégé and her pathetic girlfriend. Easy money.

He glanced at Raaz Terabyte, who was sitting beside him and nursing a glass of fizz with a face like thunder. He angled his head to one side, giving her a look he hoped she'd understand.

Cheer the fuck up. Don't embarrass me.

"I've got to hand it to you, Thomas," he went on. "When Raaz here first told me about your islands, I had my doubts. But now I see it in action. Well, it's delicious. Absolutely delicious."

Thomas Engel spun his chair around, putting his back to the enormous bank of monitor screens – twelve in total – each showing a different part of the island. "I'm glad you like it," he purred, steepling his fingers under his heavy-set chin. "Of course, with the presence of our special guests, and the enormity of the purse, it makes this year's hunt even more exciting. It's you we have to thank for orchestrating this."

Caesar slapped his large hand on Raaz's knee. "It's this one you have to thank," he said. "Raaz was the one who captured those stupid girls."

Engel smiled dismissively at Raaz before turning back to Caesar. "Stupid girls. I like that. Regardless, getting them here was a real triumph. I don't want to blow my own trumpet but this year's guest list – both in terms of the hunters and prey – is one of the best we've ever had on the island. And tomorrow we have the closing ceremony. It's going to be wondrous."

"Closing ceremony?" Caesar enquired. "Intriguing."

Engel flicked up his eyebrows as a lascivious grin spread across his face. "Oh yes. The closing ceremony for each hunt is a spectacle to behold. You wait and see." Back to Raaz now. "And how are you finding your accommodation on the island? Settling in okay?"

"It's fine," Raaz muttered, for which Caesar gave her a sharp jab in her ribs with his elbow to remind her of her manners. "Thank you."

"I put you in the Marina Suite especially," Engel told her. "I find the ladies who visit my island have a real affinity for that room."

"Is that so?" Raaz sneered. "Well, I am sorry to disappoint you, but I've disabled all the recording devices."

Engel's eyes widened.

Caesar sat upright, quickly turning to his tech-guru. "Recording devices? Surely a misunderstanding on your part, Raaz."

She didn't look at him. "The camera in the bathroom was hard to disable. But I managed it."

"Now, now," Caesar said. "Let's not get ahead of ourselves. We're guests here, Raaz. I'm sure Mr Engel has valid reasons for having such equipment in place. Security measures and all that jazz." He smiled at his host. An air of calm on the surface whilst his brain turned over ten to the dozen. Raaz Terabyte was a loyal worker and her tech-skills invaluable, but if she messed this up for them he'd crucify her. Literally. Nail her to the damn door. He hadn't worked his fingers to the bone for her to ruin it because of ridiculous feminist pride. Annihilation Pest Control was arguably the finest and most exclusive assassin network in the world, and here he was rubbing shoulders with the likes of Thomas Engel, for Christ's sake. He'd hit the big time, and he wasn't going back. Not for anyone.

He gritted his teeth. Casting a big shit-eater around the room.
We cool? We're cool.

Thankfully, Raaz's outburst had only amused Engel. He closed his eyes over a supercilious smile before clearing his throat.

"Sure, I have valid reasons. If you count a healthy dose of voyeurism as valid. Which of course I do." He glared at Raaz. "But I apologise if I overstepped the mark. Just a bit of fun. I'm actually impressed you found the devices. Not to mention disabling them."

Raaz didn't respond. Caesar watched her out of the corner of his eye, willing her to stay quiet. They were so bloody close.

"Fine," Raaz said. "No harm done. I suppose."

Caesar's shoulders dropped. "Wonderful," he bellowed, clasping his hands together. "Just a bit of fun. No harm done."

He got to his feet and moved over to the side of the room where a table was set up with an extensive array of liquor and wine. He reached for the already-open bottle of Cristal and glugged out a large glassful. He saw Engel watching and held up the bottle.

"Not for me, thank you, Mr Caesar," he said. "I don't drink whilst the hunts are in session. Prefer to keep a clear head."

"Yes. Quite wise," Caesar replied, feeling a familiar sensation stir in his trousers. Thomas Engel had a way of looking at you. Made you feel like the most important person in the room. It was there in the slight tilt of his handsome, half-German, half-American face. There in the way he nodded along to what you were saying, showing real concern, real interest. Not to mention those sparkling blue eyes that held your gaze just the right amount, and that just-sincere-enough smile. Coming from someone else, you'd be forgiven for thinking it was nothing but a carefully constructed pose. After all, this kind of behaviour was covered chapter one in any book on presence, on charm, on how to be charismatic like Clinton and Clooney. But with Engel it was different. For real.

Caesar turned his attention to the bank of monitors as a familiar face flashed up on the screen, top left.

"Bastard bloody Christ. There she is."

He moved closer to the screen, squinting at the grainy footage of his old protégé and (yes, say it as is) friend, Acid Vanilla. She was making her way across a small stretch of water accompanied by a man and woman. The man he didn't recognise, but the small woman with the thick-framed glasses was unmistakeably Spook Horowitz. The sight of her, along with Acid, sent a hot ripple of rage shooting up his spine. They wouldn't get away this time.

"Don't worry," Engel said, sensing Caesar's ire. "They won't last much longer. Why don't we move into my main viewing room? We can watch their imminent demise in a more luxurious setting."

"Sounds ideal," he replied, annoyed with himself for being so pliable, but unable to argue with Engel's stark white smile. "But tell me," he added, genuinely curious, "where is the guest of honour? I assumed he would have arrived by now. Is he not joining us?"

Engel brushed a piece of invisible lint from the sleeve of his shirt. "Oh, did I not say? He arrived yesterday."

"Oh?" Caesar frowned. "Then I assumed he'd be watching the proceedings with us."

"He's doing more than that," Engel replied, getting to his feet and gesturing for Caesar to lead the way. "Let's just say he wanted a more hands-on experience this year. He's actually out there on the island. Hunting. Wants to take down those two – what was it – 'stupid girls' himself."

"I see," Caesar cooed. "Well, good luck to him."

"Luck?" Engel said, the charm slipping for an instant. "He doesn't need luck, Mr Caesar. We don't leave anything to chance here on the island. It might be today, might be tomorrow – might even be as part of the closing ceremony, wouldn't that be a treat – but mark my words, Acid Vanilla will die. As will Spook Horowitz and the rest of the pathetic vermin crawling about my island." Engel pressed a button on the wall and the door slid open. "You see, this is my hunt, Mr Caesar. My island, my rules. And as you know, the house always wins."

CHAPTER 15

Whoever had likened tropical islands to paradise clearly didn't wear glasses, Spook thought, as she pushed the thick frames back up her sweaty nose for the fifth time in as many minutes. The afternoon sun was relentless. The UV rays like hot daggers stabbing her already sunburnt skin.

Still they kept on, having already walked for many miles, Spook and Acid traipsing along wearily behind Will Foster's gangly frame. Over rocky terrain and swampy ground they went, through dense rainforests oppressive in their humidity. And all this to a soundtrack of a million exotic creatures vying for attention. The song of the jungle. It actually reminded Spook of a relaxation CD a fellow MIT student had recommended whilst studying for her finals. *Rainforest Melodies*. Something like that. The gentle sounds of chirping insects, windchimes and babbling streams was supposed to aide rest and boost mental clarity. Unfortunately, the extra soundscapes on offer today (claxons, human screams, the terrifying crack of distant gunfire, getting closer all the time) negated any calming ambience that may have been found. Tropical paradise? Not so much.

"Will. Wait," Acid called out as they reached the edge of the jungle and he disappeared between two leafy banana trees. "Where are you taking us?"

The lanky hacker turned, a wide grin on his face, all teeth and dimples. "You'll see. We're nearly there. Trust me."

Out of the corner of her eye, Spook saw Acid raise the crossbow a touch.

"Hey," she whispered, shooting her a look. "He's one of us."

"Is he?" Acid asked, still eyeballing Will. "We don't know this guy from Adam. So let's step careful."

"Come on, Acid, you've got to trust people a little bit. Will's one of us. You can see that."

"Excuse me," Acid said, but with the hint of a smirk tickling the corner of her mouth. "One of you, maybe."

"Yeah, yeah." Spook shrugged. "We're both nerds. I get it. So trust him. He wants to show us something important, so let's keep going."

Will held his arms out, watching the exchange with a bemused look on his face. "It's through here. Couple of hundred feet along this path, and we'll be there."

"We'll be where?" Acid tried again.

"You'll see." He set off, gambolling through the trees with his gangly arms swinging at his sides. Spook stifled a snicker as Acid silently seethed next to her.

"Come on," she said, setting off after Will. "Let's see." She spun around, walking backwards so she could watch Acid, who's face morphed from twisted fury to something closer to acceptance. Playing it cool.

"Fine," she said, marching past Spook into the gloom of the trees. "But if this is a trap, don't expect me to save you."

"Aww, come off it," Spook yelled, skipping along behind her, feeling brave for once. "Not like you to be so timid."

"I am not timid," Acid told her. "I've just got a lot going on in my head right now. But sure, do your usual disassociation act, pretend everything's cool."

Spook's face sagged. "I wasn't. I just thought…"

"No, Spook. You didn't think. Because you never do. Which is why we're in this bloody mess." She stopped walking, one hand on her hip. Those intense eyes like laser beams, burning into Spook's soul. "I'm sorry if I'm taking this seriously for once, kid. But I'm not feeling too special. And I'll be honest with you, right now I don't fancy our chances."

Spook gazed in front of her as Will beckoned them close. "Sorry," was all she managed. "I'll keep my head in check from now on."

"That's all I ask." Acid let out a deep sigh before setting off to catch up with Will.

Spook remained where she was, trying her best to ground herself. She'd been on the receiving end of Acid's agitated moods before, of course. Yet most of the time it was that same manic, bipolar energy that made her who she was. She'd explained to Spook on more than one occasion how, honed correctly, her condition felt almost like a super-power. But then, Spook also understood being Acid Vanilla every single second of every single day was a whole lot to deal with. If they ever got off this horrific island she'd be a better friend, she told herself. Told the heavens too. So please, God, help them get off this terrible island.

She caught up with Acid and Will around the next bend standing and looking at a small wooden building with a flat wooden roof about the size of a family garage. The entire unit was painted green to fit in with the surroundings and, indeed, passing by even fifty feet away you might miss it through the tree cover.

"Here we are," Will announced proudly.

"What is that?" Acid asked.

"Our way out of here," he said. "Look, see."

The three of them made their way over to the strange building and Will guided them around to the far side where a metal door lay slightly ajar. A large swing lock with a padlock still attached hung from the wall.

"Took me all morning to break in." Will opened the door and

held it for Acid and Spook to enter. "It's a control room. For the entire island."

They stepped inside and Will shut the door, plunging the room into darkness but for the light from three large monitor screens attached to the wall.

"Woah," Spook whispered. "Good find, dude."

"I know, right?" Will moved into the middle of the cabin, giving the tour. "We got the monitors here, as you can see, complete with control unit. From what I can see they've got cameras all over the island. Plus over in that corner, we got food supplies, bottled water, that sort of shit."

"Weapons?" Acid asked. "Guns?"

Will drew his lips back over his teeth. "Afraid not. There's a flare gun, but that's all. But I'm thinking we might not need them."

Acid shuffled over and grabbed up a bottle of water. She drank it down in one go before passing a bottle to Spook while Will explained.

"The system's connected to a single server in the resort complex. I reckon I can get in and get a message out to the world. Tell them what's going on."

"Why haven't you already done that?" Acid asked.

"I was working on it. But I had one eye on the camera feeds. Some hunters were approaching so I had to make a run for it. I already had a location on the two of you and I figured if I found you, together we could come back and get this done. You keep watch while I do the necessary."

"Oh my god! Yes!" Spook yelled. Then, quieter, after Acid and Will had shushed her. "Can I help? What are we looking at?"

She leaned on the control desk, squinting at the monitors. The two in the middle showed camera feeds from the island, changing location every ten seconds. She watched the grainy footage with an air of detachment, people running around, men with guns. If she stopped and thought about what was going on she'd choke, so she tried not to. Instead she kept her analyst head on, focusing on what she could do. So, it was the third monitor that interested her, the one which Will had already commandeered. He opened up a terminal window and began typing out lines of code.

"Ah, I see what you're doing. Good shout," she said, trying not to sound too impressed by Will's coding skills. He was writing a rudimentary network enumeration of the remote server. What she would have done.

"Yeah. Before I got so rudely disturbed, I found a flaw in the applications set-up," he replied, not looking up from the keyboard. "Whoever built the system here was old-school. Plan is to launch an exploit and land me some code execution."

Spook pursed her lips. "Of course. With server misconfiguration issues we can easily get access."

"Jesus Christ, you two." Acid sighed from a few feet away. "Calm down with the sexy talk, will you? You're getting me all hot and bothered."

Spook gave Will a she's-always-like-this look. "Acid doesn't like me talking code."

He shot her a conspiring wink and set the program running, before turning around to Acid. "All this means is it's pretty viable we can get into their server and send a message. Tell the FBI, or whoever, where we are. What these asshats are up to."

"Why didn't you say that?" Acid sniffed. "How long will it take?"

"Not long. Fifteen minutes maybe." Will moved over to the middle screen, dragging the keyboard in front of him. "But look what else I found."

Spook positioned herself next to Acid as Will shut down a camera feed and opened up a new window. Clicking on a file, he twisted around to watch the women's faces as the document opened up on the screen.

"Bloody hell," Acid muttered

"Shit," Spook added.

The document showed a series of headshot photographs with a brief paragraph beside each one. Spook counted eight people in total. Most were in colour, but some had been greyed out, the word DECEASED written in bold red font over the image. Spook scanned down the list, her eyes falling on the photo of herself and then Acid, one above the other. She scanned the write-up.

Spook Horowitz. American. Age: 27

This meddling hacker is responsible for the brutal and unwarranted demise of Kent Clarkson and Sinclair Whitman. She is clever but weak and should pose no problem to any of our guests this weekend. However, do not underestimate her. She often travels with another of our targets, Acid Vanilla. The two together should be deemed dangerous, which is why they command the biggest score for this year's hunt at 50,000 points per head. Bag them both, and you'll be well on your way to this year's crown. *Please note, as always there is a double-points bonus for any target's inclusion in the closing ceremony*

Spook shivered, the sweat on her neck turning cold. She looked from Will to Acid. "Closing ceremony? What's that?"

"No idea," Acid mumbled, squinting at her own write-up. "'Once the deadliest female assassin in the world, now merely a sorry embarrassment that should be put out of her misery at the earliest convenience.' Caesar wrote that. Got him all over it. The hideous shit."

"At least we're the highest scoring targets," Spook offered. "Someone must still think you're pretty dangerous."

But the description had hurt, Spook could tell. And with that hurt came a renewed fire. It was evident in the twist of Acid's mouth. The look in her eyes. She wasn't going to let Caesar get away with that.

Sorry embarrassment? Not likely.

Spook smiled, feeling a little taller, a little braver. One of the things she found most exciting about being in the presence of this remarkable, scary, messed-up woman, when she got fired up, she really got fired up. Spook had endured a rather mundane existence before getting herself caught up in a global conspiracy and meeting Acid Vanilla, but if she was in any kind of scrape she knew, with Acid by her side, she had more than a fighting chance.

Turning her attention back to the screen, Spook surveyed the greyed-out photos, her eyes falling on the face of Grace Philips. Poor woman. She had a family, a husband at least, and she died here, alone, scared, on a strange island, and for what? So some evil prick could bag himself fifteen thousand points.

Man.

The realisation hit Spook in the chest and she let out a soft gasp.

"You all right?" Will asked.

"Just sucks," Spook whispered. "We're nothing but animals to them. Part of their sick, pointless game."

"Not entirely." Will moved over to the far screen and brought up a new document. "I also found the guest list and did a bit of cross-referencing. Looks to me like every one of the targets has been picked because someone rich and powerful has a beef against them. See this scrawny dude, Edward Menks? A few years back Grace Philips there was a prosecuting attorney that sent the old guy's son away for ten years. Tax fraud. Word is he was Menks' fall guy. His own son. And see here, this guy, Julian Bannerman. He's the legitimate face of a group of disaster capitalists whose database I recently wiped after finding a chink in their cyber-security."

"Oh, shit," Spook said, staring at the cold dead eyes of the man in the photo.

"Yeah. So I guess he's here for me. Ain't I lucky?"

"Don't worry," Spook told him. "You're with us now. If we stick together, we'll get out of this in one piece. Isn't that right, Acid? Acid?" Spook spun around to find her staring at the screen.

"Stupid wanker," she said. "Couldn't leave it alone."

"Who? What?" Spook followed Acid's eyeline to the next photo on the guest list. A fresh-faced man with side-parted strawberry-blond hair. He didn't look like a killer. Or even someone who enjoyed hunting. But then Spook's eyes fell on the name.

"Luther Clarkson," she mouthed. "Shit."

"Yeah, I was about to tell you," Will said. "Luther Clarkson is here. I believe you guys know his older brother Kent – ex-founder of Cerberix Inc. Ex-human being."

"We didn't kill him," Spook said. "I know that's what it says, but it was Acid's organisation – ex-organisation."

Will gave her a confiding smile. "Mr Clarkson is the guest of honour this weekend. He's put up a ten million prize for the highest scorer."

"Woah," she exclaimed, watching Acid's face illuminated in the glow from the screen. She hadn't blinked in at least a minute.

"Small change to him, though, right?" Will continued. "Since he inherited his brother's estate. Split between him and the younger sister, I believe."

Spook nudged Acid, who was still staring at the photo of Luther. "This guy isn't going to be a problem, is he?"

Acid chewed her lip. Spook tried again. "Acid?"

"What?" She shook away whatever thought had overtaken her. "I mean, no. Of course not. But we're still up against it, so let's not dawdle. How long until we can get a message out?"

"We should be inside any time now," Will said, moving over to the far screen. He stopped. An intake of breath. "Shit!"

"What is it?" Spook cried. "Oh no. Where is that?"

A new camera feed showed three men with large hunting rifles entering a grove of leafy banana trees. With concentration knotting his brow, Will boosted the image to full screen and clicked through a couple more camera options, cursing under his breath as he went. He turned to Spook. His sleepy eyes suddenly awake with fear.

"They're close," he rasped. "Real close. We need to move. Now!"

CHAPTER 16

Acid held the crossbow to her chest. She'd give anything for a handgun right about now. Nothing fancy, a light, dependable Glock would do it.

On screen the hunters were now moving apart, advancing on the cabin in a semi-circular formation.

"I can take these bastards," she said. "You two make a run for it, I'll hold them off."

"I need to stay," Will hit back. "Get the message out. It's our only chance."

"That's crazy." Spook grabbed him by the wrist. "They'll kill you."

"I'll be fine," he replied, followed by an unconvincing grin. "Look at these long legs. I can outrun anyone."

"You can't outrun a bullet."

Acid was only half-listening. Moving fast, she turned out the box of supplies, pocketing a handful of protein bars and grabbing up the flare gun, a single-shot Very Pistol in bright red, and a couple of spare flares.

"How long do you need?" she asked Will.

He turned his attention to the screen, at the status bar slowly moving past seventy percent. Seventy-one. Seventy-two. "Five minutes?"

"Okay, here." Acid handed him the flare gun. "Spook and I are going to slip out the side door, move into the tree cover. You get that, kid?" Spook nodded she had. "Will, the second we open the door, I need you to lean out and fire that flare gun directly at the nearest hunter. Once you do that, reload, same thing with the hunter on the far right – excuse the pun." She glanced between the two computer nerds listening so hard neither of them even registered the joke. Tough crowd.

"A flare gun won't hold them off," Spook said.

"It'll hold them off enough," Acid told her. "Whilst this is going on, I'll be taking them out, one by one. With the commotion and the smoke from the flares, I'm counting on them not realising what's going on until they're all dead."

"You fired a crossbow before?" Spook asked her.

She shrugged. "How hard can it be?" Then, seeing the expression of fear clouding the kids' faces, "Guys, seriously. This is going to work. Spook, when have I ever let you down before?"

"Never."

"Exactly, so let's show these sick fucks who the real 'sorry embarrassment' is." She nodded at Will. "You ready?"

Will held up the flare gun. Holding it like he'd never held as much as a water pistol prior to today. Her heart sank, but it was now or never.

"Just point it in their direction and pull the trigger."

"I got this," Will told her. "Now go, they're almost on us."

Acid and Spook moved over to the door. A second later Will grabbed the handle and, stepping around the front of them, swung it open. With a yell, he put his arm around the side of the door and shot the flare at the nearest hunter. The second Acid heard the pop, she grabbed Spook's arm and ran, pulling her out through the side door. Acid glanced over her shoulder, noting the positions of the three hunters as best she could through the fog of red smoke. Then she gestured to Spook and the two of them slipped into the undergrowth.

Staying in the trees and moving swiftly, the two women circled around the back of the cabin. Over to her left Acid could hear the hunters' shouts, directing each other through the already dissipating smoke. Will hadn't managed to take any of them out with the blast, but that didn't matter.

"Time to see what this cumbersome thing can do," she muttered to herself, coming to a halt behind the sinewy trunk of a tall eucalyptus tree and hauling the crossbow up to her eyeline. She scanned the area, finding her first target: a fat middle-aged man with a bright pink face and a flabby paunch hanging over the waistband of his too-tight chino shorts. This was Julian Bannerman, she realised, Will's disaster capitalist nemesis. She watched as he got nearer to the cabin, more hesitant now, but with no less impetus.

"Come on, Will," Spook murmured over her shoulder.

Her finger quivered on the trigger. Bannerman was still in her sights. The second Will fired the next flare she'd administer the steel bolt, straight to the temple.

The cabin door swung open and the hunters opened fire. The bats screamed across Acid's nervous system. Invisible wings fluttering against her heart. She held her ground.

One second.

Two seconds.

Another pop and the scene erupted with red smoke, the second flare bursting out from the cabin. It struck a tree and landed in front of the three hunters. As it hit the ground, Acid pulled the trigger, delighting at the sound. A vicious twang followed by the heavy *thunk* of metal splitting bone. Through the red mist she saw Bannerman drop to his knees and slump forward like a culled bovine.

"Good shot," Spook stage-whispered. "One down."

Acid shot her a look. "Yes, and two to go, so calm down will you."

Before the smoke cleared, she dropped the end of the crossbow to the floor and stepped on the cocking stirrup. Using both hands, she wrenched the rope back onto the firing mechanism and slipped a new bolt in place. Then, moving as silently as possible, only slowing briefly to check Spook was close, she continued on her trajectory, stopping at the edge of the clearing where she had a clear shot. Without too much thought she raised the crossbow and took down the second hunter with a perfect shot to the back of the head.

Two down.

One to go.

As the smoke from the second flare died away, Acid could hear the remaining hunter. "Are you men okay?" he yelled, in a pompous British accent. "Bannerman? Fisher? Can you hear m— Bloody hell!" He'd just seen the bodies. Quick as a flash, he moved to the side of the clearing, aiming his rifle into the undergrowth. "Who's there? Show yourself, you coward."

Acid hurried around to the side of the cabin, concealing herself amongst a patch of ferns. The leafy fronds brushed against her forehead as she knelt and lifted the crossbow for the final kill. The man was now moving around the space, leading with his hunting rifle. He seemed more angry than scared. He was in his fifties, thin but with bulbous cheeks that, coupled with his round glasses and piggy eyes, gave him the air of an overgrown schoolboy. Acid narrowed her gaze, vaguely recognising him as some figure in British government. Acid didn't follow politics. Never had. As far as she was concerned, they were all as bad as each other and voting only encouraged them. But the presence of this pink-cheeked muppet here on the island didn't surprise her one bit. She'd done enough hits over the years for the so-called good guys to know – there were no good guys.

She closed one eye over the barrel of the crossbow, lining up the shot. The man (Graves, was it? Michael?) was standing side-on to her just a few feet away. She could hear the awkward wheeze of his breathing as he peered into the jungle. A quick glance at the cabin and the door was shut. Will safely inside. The bats screeched their approval. They'd done it. Now all that was needed was for Acid to wrap this up and get them somewhere safe.

She moved her focus back to Graves. A throat shot, she was thinking. Straight through the jugular, let the miserable fucker bleed out for a minute or two. It wasn't a pleasant way to die. Horrible, in fact. But right now the bats were running the show. And they wanted blood. They wanted carnage.

Acid held her breath, readying herself, but before she had chance to even reload a fourth man stepped into the clearing. He was tall and slim with a shock of red hair and a self-important expression reminiscent of his brother. Luther Clarkson. He was accompanied by a weaselly little man who was hunched over a tablet, frantically tapping at the screen, and two much larger men dressed in combat fatigues and carrying military issue Sig Sauer MPXs. Acid stole a look at Spook. The kid's mouth was hanging open.

"What are we going to do?" she whispered.

Acid didn't reply. Truth was, she didn't have a clue. But she had to do something, and fast. Will was a sitting duck in that cabin. She leaned the crossbow against a tree. Even with time to reload she only had one bolt left and any shot would only reveal their whereabouts. She closed her eyes. Will still had one flare left. Could he see what was going on? Would he know what to do?

"One of them is in the cabin," Graves was telling Clarkson. "But there's someone in the trees too. They let off a smoke-screen, took these chaps out in the hubbub."

Clarkson gave the man a vague nod, before turning around and gesturing to someone out of view. Acid strained to see.

"What's going on?" Spook asked.

"Not sure. Just stay down."

But there was no time left. A second later Clarkson stepped forward, hoisting an MK153 anti-tank assault weapon onto his shoulder. A wide grin spread across his face.

"A rocket launcher?" Graves said. "What the hell are you going to do with that?"

"I'm going to have some fun," Clarkson bellowed. "Going to blow up these cretins."

Spook stifled a yelp as Clarkson aimed at the cabin and pulled the trigger. A loud bang reverberated around the trees and the cabin exploded in an eruption of fire and splintering wood. Exotic birds of many colours burst out from the trees as if from nowhere, filling the skies as they fled the harrowing sound.

"Will," Spook mumbled, as Acid flung a hand over her mouth, pulling her close.

Thick black smoke vomited out of a large hole in the front of the cabin, spiralling up into the pure blue sky. Acid held the young American to her chest. The blast had blown the roof clear off the cabin. Through the smoke and rubble she could see the interior was completely decimated. No one was walking out of that alive.

"Come on," she whispered, backing away into the depths of the jungle. "There's nothing we can do for him."

"But…"

"Spook, we have to go."

She grabbed the kid's arm and yanked her forward. With the hunters' self-congratulatory cheers echoing through the trees, they picked up the pace and got the hell out of there.

CHAPTER 17

Luther Clarkson handed his new toy back to one of the security team and surveyed his handiwork.

"Any survivors?" he called out to Jerry, his assistant-come-manservant-come-whipping-boy.

Jerry, standing in front of the large hole in the cabin, shook his head. "Not a chance. But I'm afraid to say it, I don't think you took out your top scorers."

"What the..." Luther exclaimed, striding over there and shoving Jerry out the way. He waved at the smoke drifting up from the glowing remnants and peered into the gloom. It was a real mess. Bits of machinery, lumps of concrete, a pair of Nikes in one corner. But as the smoke cleared, he saw one of the sneakers still had a foot inside, half a calf bone sticking out the top. "God-damnit. Who was this?"

"I believe that there is William Foster," Graves said, joining Luther at the side of the ruined cabin. "Bannerman's contribution to the weekend. An activist hacker type. Been a real annoyance for quite a few of my acquaintances the last year or so."

"Ah, gee. And they got Bannerman. That sucks," Luther growled, not looking at Graves. "Still, one dead loser, right?"

"Absolutely. Excellent work."

Luther turned and walked away. "Was he a good score?" he asked Jerry scurrying along in his wake.

"Not too bad," the assistant replied, scrolling down his tablet. "Twenty-five thousand. But I'm hearing reports now that Menks is dead. So that puts you back joint top."

Luther stopped by the side of the souped-up golf cart he'd arrived in, parked a little way from the edge of the clearing. "Menks is dead?" he mused. "How the hell did that happen?"

Jerry frowned at the screen, skim-reading while he spoke. "The report from the clean-up team mentions one of the prey getting hold of a rifle."

Luther took a deep breath, casting an eye over the area. He didn't like the sound of this. Engel had assured him, assured them all, there would be nothing and no one to fear on the island. That killing these meddlesome bastards was like shooting babies in a barrel. "I thought each rifle was personalised."

Jerry nodded, still hunched over the tablet. "Yes. Doesn't say how they did it. But it's certainly a concern. Especially with the two – your two – targets still unaccounted for…" Jerry trailed off, more than aware how he would react at the mention of those awful women.

He wiped the sweat from his eyes with his thumb and forefinger. "You think they did this? Killed Bannerman?"

"I don't know, sir. But they have form. My take is we get back to the resort, pronto. See what Mr Engel and Mr Caesar have to say."

Luther considered this for a moment and then called out. "Hey, Graves, I'm heading back. You want a lift?"

Graves, still picking through the remains of whatever was left of the cabin, looked over and held up a melted flare gun. "No thanks. I've got it in me now. I'm going to carry on the hunt for a while longer. I'll see you back there later."

"No worries." Luther clambered into the golf cart. "If not tonight, I'll see you tomorrow. The closing ceremony already. Time really flies when you're having fun."

Graves waved them away as Luther started the engine. He could feel one of his migraines coming on but he was damned if he would let it slow him down. Once Jerry was in the back seat, he turned the cart around and headed for the dirt track leading back to the resort complex. He needed some reassurance. Because whilst Luther enjoyed playing the tough guy, he was feeling uneasy. He'd come here, to this sweltering oasis, for one reason only. To kill the bitches who destroyed his brother. And to do so in the most sadistic and painful way possible. Only, with one day left to hunt, that had yet to happen.

He parked up outside the impressive main entrance of Engel's resort complex and hurried up the wide, marble steps, taking them two at a time.

"Where are we going, sir?" Jerry snivelled as Luther swung open the large glass door and marched through the entrance hall.

"Engel?" Luther yelled into the ceiling, aware the host had cameras and microphones everywhere. "Engel, I need to see you. Now."

Luther crossed his arms and waited as Jerry hopped from foot to foot. As usual, the pathetic cretin had nothing to offer but conspiring glances and a camp shrug of his shoulders. To take his mind off the blinding pain spearing him between the eyes, Luther cast his attention around Thomas Engel's vast vestibule. The entire space had been rendered entirely in cream marble, with two enormous chocolate-brown leather couches over in the far corner. Scattered haphazardly over the cold, marble floor were ten white tiger-skin rugs. Engel had delighted in telling his guests how one of his rugs, the largest one, had once been the last white tiger living in the wild. Bagged by Engel himself, apparently. Although Luther wondered if that was a little poetic licence on the host's part. It wasn't that Luther Clarkson didn't trust Thomas Engel, as much as he didn't trust anyone. His therapist called it 'severe OCD linked to past trauma', but as usual Luther dismissed the claim as horseshit. Quite simply, no one got the job done as effectively as he could himself. Which was why it irked him to think of those damn women still running around on the island. He should be the one to take them down. He'd paid a lot of money for the privilege.

"Mr Clarkson?" a shrill voice chimed across the room. Luther looked up to see a tall woman with blonde hair scraped back against her head, and wearing a long white robe. She smiled politely, revealing two rows of perfect white teeth. "My name is Fallon. Follow me, please, I shall take you to Mr Engel's suite."

Luther replied with a curt nod of the head before turning to Jerry. "Go to your room," he told him. "I'll call you when I'm done."

"Yes sir, and don't worry. We'll get them. *You'll* get them."

Luther shot him a wink that immediately felt awkward and only exacerbated the migraine. Punctuating it with a forced cough, he followed on behind Fallon as she led him through to the far side of the entrance hall to a steel-fronted elevator.

"How are you finding your stay?" Fallon asked, as they waited.

"Just fine," Luther replied, letting her friendly, slightly flirtatious demeanour drift over his head. "I have a few concerns that I'd like to bring up with Mr Engel. That's all."

"Of course," Fallon cooed. "I'm certain he can put your mind at ease. Ah. Here we are." The elevator doors opened. Fallon leaned around the side of the door and pressed a button on an internal panel. "This will take you up to Mr Engel. The elevator opens up directly in his suite. He's expecting you."

She stepped aside, brushing her breast against Luther's arm. She smelt of cinnamon and cocoa and the entire experience turned his stomach. Without another word, he stepped into the lift and stared blankly out as the doors closed and the chamber rocked into life. He used the short journey up to try and reset. He closed his eyes, channelling the deep rage into something more accessible. Like many younger siblings, Luther had grown up in his big brother's shadow. But that hadn't stopped him looking up to him a great deal. No one would ever have called them close, but that wasn't the point. No one would have called any of the Clarkson family close. But Kent's death (his murder, why not call it what it was) had hit Luther hard. The thought of those two women still alive tightened his jaw. But it was all still to play for. He'd get his revenge. That was inevitable. The hunt might not currently be going the way Luther had intended, but one thing about Engel's island, it sure was a great leveller. It didn't matter whether you were a trained killer, a Navy Seal, or Chuck Norris, without a weapon you stood no chance. The ridiculously named assassin and her pathetic friend were dead women walking.

The thought buoyed Luther. He opened his eyes as the steel doors of the elevator slid open to reveal a huge open-plan room walled entirely of glass and looking down on the tropical rainforest below. Pain Island.

"Luther, my man," a voice rang out. "Good to see you. Come. Join us."

It was Engel, reclining on a large black leather couch over on the far side of the room. In fact, most of the décor in the suite was black, the enormous desk that looked out over the treetops, the thick shag-pile carpet. Sat opposite him on a matching black couch was Beowulf Caesar.

"Been having fun?" Caesar growled as Luther sauntered over and perched on the end of the couch. "A shame Acid swerved the old rocket launcher. But don't worry. You'll get her."

Luther chewed on his lip. Still unsure of this Caesar character. After the mystery surrounding Kent's murder, Luther had hired a glut of private detectives to find out the truth. One name kept coming back to him. Beowulf Caesar, founder of Annihilation Pest Control. Luther had never heard the name before, but a little more digging told him they were best in the world if you wanted rid of someone without it touching you in any way.

"Here you are, son," Engel purred, handing Luther a glass half-full of amber liquid (or maybe that should be half-empty. Luther hated whisky. Hated all alcohol). "A fifty-one-year-old Macallan."

Luther sniffed the foul-smelling drink. Shrugged. He kept his eyes on Caesar; him grinning back, raising his glass once more. No, there was something not right about him. And it wasn't just the fact he was a pumped-up queer. A British one at that. The worst kind. Even in that first meeting with him, when Luther had demanded an explanation about his brother's death, he could tell Caesar was playing with him. He'd been apologetic of course, profusely so, insisting he'd done everything he could to help Kent. But then he'd dropped the bombshell. That it was his ex-operative Acid Vanilla who had killed him. He followed this by explaining to Luther how he desperately wanted to make amends and would be open to an idea. That's how Luther had first heard about the hunt and Caesar's plan for those who'd hurt his family. But at a price, of course. Luther had only been a billionaire for a short time, but he'd already had it spelt out to him many times. When you played ball with powerful people, there was always a price.

"How you doing, son?" Engel asked, sitting back down and throwing over a lugubrious look. "You seem a little tense."

"I am tense, quite frankly," Luther replied, putting his drink down. Swallowing his frustration. "I've paid a lot of money to be here. Put a big investment into the prize fund. And for that, I expected to bag those bitches myself. Just a little perturbed they got away today. Makes me concerned."

Engel frowned. "Why so?"

"I was informed that the prey were all sitting ducks. Yet I also hear from my assistant we have targets going rogue, guests being killed. Fuck. Someone took out Cornel Fisher and Julian Bannerman just now. And I hear Menks is dead. How do you explain this? Killed by sitting ducks, were they?"

Caesar chuckled to himself over the rim of his glass. "Don't bother yourself with all that, sweetie," he mused. "The important people are still here. Aren't we? And Tommy here has a narrative for the deaths, I'm sure of it. I mean, come on. Menks was about a hundred years old."

"Don't call me sweetie," Luther replied through gritted teeth. "And I'm glad you find this funny. But I'm here for one reason only. To avenge my brother. To kill those women. And that hasn't happened, and it now sounds like the hunters are becoming… you know…" He trailed off, steering away from the cliché.

Engel sat upright. "I'm a little insulted you think I don't have this in hand," he said sharply. Standing, he moved over to the side of the room and looked out through the glass. The sun was now on its decline, casting the late afternoon sky in glorious hues of lilac and fuchsia. "This isn't the first time we've had issues on the hunt, Luther. Accidents happen. You all signed the same contract, I'm sure you read the small print. The deaths of our guests will be handled professionally and the circumstances surrounding their demise will die with them. Mark my words, one doesn't run a grand scale event like this for over a decade and leave anything to chance."

"What about my prey?" Luther asked. "They need to pay for what they did."

"And they will," Engels said, turning from the window. "But believe me when I say, if they survive until tomorrow, they will meet a fate much worse than you could ever offer them."

Luther picked up his drink. Tried it. Regretted it. "How do you mean?"

"At first light my dedicated security team will do a sweep of the island, capturing and detaining all the remaining prey and bringing them here for the closing ceremony."

Luther sniffed back. He had been wondering, having heard rumours of the infamous ceremony. He placed his drink down and took a deep breath. Not being the one to kill his brother's murderers wasn't the way he wanted this to play out. But whatever way they went, it still was a result.

"Will they suffer?" he asked.

"Categorically," Engel purred. "Believe me, the best hunts are always the ones with a few prey left for the ceremony. Hell, we want survivors. It's much more fun that way."

He raised his glass, breaking out into a malevolent laugh that skirted far too close to hackneyed movie villain.

"Fine," Luther concurred. "We'll play it your way."

"Good lad," Caesar said, slapping him on the thigh. "You won't regret this. It's going to be a bloody riot."

Luther sat back, smiling to himself now, his migraine beginning to fade. He gazed out onto the island as the hot afternoon sun disappeared behind a row of palm trees. So, not the desired outcome, but a better one perhaps. This time tomorrow Acid Vanilla and Spook Horowitz would be dead. One way or another, Luther would get his revenge.

CHAPTER 18

If Acid turned around she could still see thick black smoke spiralling into the sky from the burnt-out cabin. Poor bastard. Didn't stand a chance. None of them expected some sicko with a rocket launcher to turn up, of course, but she couldn't help thinking, could she have played that better? Was she even doing any good? The list of people in her immediate vicinity who'd been hurt or worse recently was getting longer. This was why Acid worked alone. Preferred to, at least.

But on they both went, heads down, even Spook keeping good pace as they penetrated the murky refuge of the rainforest. Acid's thighs burned with fatigue and her chest was tight with exertion, all exacerbated by the close, sticky atmosphere. But they couldn't stop. Not yet. Not until she was certain they were safe.

Along the way, thick hanging vines slowed them down, as well as a gigantic buzzing cloud of black flies that got caught up in their hair and flew into their parched mouths. Palm fronds sprang out from the undergrowth like green demon fingers, scratching at their exposed skin and tugging at their damp clothes.

They'd been running through the dense jungle for ten minutes or more when Acid heard a familiar cry and spun around to see Spook sprawled on the ground, gripping her leg.

Shitting hell.

Not the time, kid.

"What is it?" she asked, going to her.

"My ankle." Her face contorted in a grimace. "I tripped over that damn root over there."

Acid touched her hand to Spook's ankle, ignoring her pained protestations. She felt around. It didn't seem broken. "Can you walk?"

Spook tried putting her weight on it. More cries. She shook her head. "Can we rest? Please. I think it'll be okay if we take five."

Acid breathed heavily down both nostrils, scoping out the area. Back the way they'd come were thick leaves and heavy tree cover. In front of them she could make out the edge of a low ravine.

"We can rest here a while," she whispered. "We'll shelter under that rubber plant over there. Can you make it?"

Spook took in the enormous plant a few metres away, a look of dread scrunching her button nose.

"Here, hold on to me." Acid scooped her head under Spook's shoulder.

"Acid, wait," she grumbled. "It hurts like a bitch. I think I've sprained it."

Acid laid her down gently beneath the rubber plant. The ground here was soft, recessed into a small basin where they could lie down. Above them leaves as big as golf umbrellas sheltered them from the late afternoon sun.

"This'll do," Acid said, lying back and pulling out two protein bars from her pocket. "Here you go. Energy."

Spook accepted the bar and the two of them ate in silence for a few minutes, listening to the sounds of the jungle: the gentle chirp of various insects accompanied with the occasional squawk of a Macau. It was almost relaxing. That was, until the ugly sound of a faraway gunshot pierced the calm.

"What if I can't walk?" Spook whimpered. "That's me done for. I'll never survive this horrible island if I can't walk. I'm screwed."

Acid tensed, fighting her own instinctive response as Spook fought back tears. She closed her eyes as the silent sobs rocked the ground between them.

"You will survive this," she said firmly.

"H-How do you know?"

"Because you're with me. And because we know who we're up against now and we will not let that pathetic prick win." She turned her head to look at the kid. "And because you're a lot tougher than you give yourself credit for."

Spook wiped a hand across her cheek. "You really think that?"

Acid resisted an eye-roll. Why was there always a follow up question? Why couldn't Spook just take the compliment and have done with it, she knew empathy and care weren't part of her wheelhouse. She might have hung up her assassin hat, but she was struggling to fit into the role Spook wanted of her. That of a concerned citizen, a compassionate friend.

"Yes. I do," she replied. "But you need to help yourself a little too."

"What's that supposed to mean?"

This time she couldn't suppress the eye-roll.

Spook clocked it. "Hey. I'm trying my best here. I know this is all my fault, but I said I was sorry, and I was only trying to… trying to…" She erupted in a flurry of tears, making Acid tense up even more.

"Don't, Spook." She placed her hand on the kid's arm. "I don't blame you. Okay? I mean, yes, you should never have gone after Raaz on your own. But I'm not pissed off with you. Shit happens."

"I didn't want you to kill her," she wailed. "She's not like the others, Acid. She's just Caesar's tech-person. She's not a killer."

"Isn't she?" Acid leaned back, brushing a low-hanging leaf from her face. "You ask me, she's as responsible as all of them. She has to die."

"Is this what your mum would want?" Spook asked. "Risking your life? More killing? More death? Why can't you just move on? Let it go."

She glared at the young American. "Let it go? Let it go?"

Spook stared back. Her eyes grew wide. Her mouth quivered.

Acid held onto her resolve for as long as possible, but it was slipping. "Fuck off. I know I sound like what's-her-name from bloody *Frozen*! Concentrate, will you?"

But it was too much. The tension was broken. A second later, they both burst into silly, giggly laughter that lifted the mood and for a brief interlude made everything feel okay.

"I'm sorry," Spook said, as more tears gushed down her face. "I wasn't making light of it."

Acid composed herself. Nodded. "It's fine. I get it. But to answer your question, no, I can't let it go. Because it's not just about my mum They betrayed me. Tried to kill us. On at least three occasions. I can't let them live after that. Any of them. It's a principle thing."

"Principles? Wow."

Acid sat upright. "You don't think I've got principles?"

"I didn't say that."

"Well, you kind of did."

Spook chewed her lip. "I know you have principles. It's just you seem to fight against them constantly. Like you don't want to admit you care about anyone. Like with Sofia back there. I had to beg you to help her. Yet you care. I know it."

Acid hugged her knees. "I haven't forgotten she's got my jacket. If I don't get that back, Spook, I swear I'll—"

She froze as the sound of a claxon echoed through the trees. It was far away, but the tree cover made it impossible to guess how far.

"What does that mean?" Spook whispered.

"Not sure." She squinted up through the trees. The sun had completely disappeared over the horizon, but dusk was still a way off. She turned to Spook. "How's your ankle?"

Spook sat up and bounced it gently on the floor a couple of times. "A little better." She scrambled onto her feet, crouching under the leaves. "Still hurts, but I think I can walk on it. If we go slow."

"I think we should keep moving."

"What the hell are we going to do, Acid?" Any humour was now absent from her voice. Her tone was soft, quiet. The sound of defeat. What Acid wouldn't give for the heightened panic of a few minutes earlier. Manic energy. It was what she knew best.

"Don't give up, kid," she told her. "I've got an idea."

"Yeah?"

"Yeah, but you're not going to like it." She reached down and scooped up a large handful of soft mud. As she talked, she daubed it around her face, down her arms. "We'll wait for nightfall, then I say we move on the complex, get inside somehow. There's got to be weapons in there. Weapons we can use. We can take them out one by one, easier in a place with corridors and corners." She grabbed up another handful of dirt and shoved it at Spook. "Here, we need camouflage if we're to get near."

Spook accepted the lump of black clay-like mud, staring at it suspiciously. She removed her glasses and tentatively applied a stripe of mud under each eye. Looked at Acid. "What?"

"For Christ's sake. This isn't a Hollywood movie where the pretty girl roughs it but only gets a little dirt on her face. You have to slap this shit on." She snatched the mud from Spook's grasp and pushed it into her face, smearing it across her forehead, down her cheeks, in her hair even. Spook squirmed and screwed her eyes shut, holding her breath as Acid applied the mud to her lips.

"Done?" she asked, placing her glasses back and pressing them down into the mud covering her nose.

Acid scoffed. "Kind of loses something with the specs, but you'll do."

Spook tried her ankle again. "What now?"

"From my reckoning, the complex is a good hour or two that

way," Acid said, gesturing over her shoulder. "We'll take it slow. You ready?"

Spook nodded. "Just one thing."

"What now?"

"Do you really think I'm a pretty girl?"

Acid glared at her. "Don't push it," she told her, but was glad to see Spook's mood had improved. For what came next, she needed her upbeat. Needed her ready for action. She turned and set off walking the way of the ravine. "Come on, GI Jane," she called after her. "These billionaires aren't going to gruesomely slaughter themselves."

CHAPTER 19

Moving slow and steady, Acid and Spook made it down the sloping side of the small ravine and found themselves in a dried-up riverbed that wound around the side of the island.

Acid paused, assessing the situation. "If we follow this track, it should take us to the foothills on the west side of the complex," she muttered, speaking aloud to better align her thoughts. "We'll stick to the trees on the far side."

Spook glanced up the steep side of the bank. "Can we keep to the flat a little longer?"

"We're pretty exposed here, kid. I'm not sure we should."

"Fine."

Taking it one step a time, and with Acid behind her, Spook made it up the far side of the ravine. The trees were denser here, the leaves thick and green, criss-crossing over each other to provide a web of cover. By following the dry river but hanging back a way, they should stay out of sight. If Acid's calculations were correct, they were near to the west of the island, some way from the centre. Her hope was there'd be fewer hunters around.

She stood on the side of the barren riverbank, peering over the tree tops. Up on her toes she could now see the high cliff on the northern tip of the island and the grand steel and glass structure of the resort complex. It was a good way off. Her estimation was now nearer three hours before they even reached the bottom of the cliff. With Spook's damaged ankle, more likely four.

"We'll get closer and take shelter for a few hours," she told Spook. "I'll make a move at first light."

"You'll make a move?" Spook asked. "Don't you mean *we* will?"

Acid threw up an eyebrow. "No, sweetie. I can't have you slowing me down. You'll be fine. We'll find somewhere safe for you to wait it out."

"Jesus, Acid," Spook said. "This is so typical of you."

Acid turned to face her, a million tiny bat fangs nibbling at her psyche. "What the hell does that mean?"

"You know what it means. Acid Vanilla: the one-woman army. The only person who can possibly get the job done. You know, it's okay to accept help once in a while. It's a good thing, in fact. No woman is an island."

Acid scoffed. "And what bloody good are you going to be, hobbling along like you are?"

Spook frowned, didn't reply. Didn't have a leg to stand on, did she? Or at least, she only had the one. Acid sneered and marched on. She was only trying to protect the kid. Why couldn't she damn well see that? And why did she have to make everything into a bloody therapy session?

Truth was, she had been managing her moods well lately. Sure, they were up and down (she'd never want to level out those times when she felt indestructible and super-creative) but it was good to be on more of an even keel. Even relatively speaking. Although, this recent stillness of mind had provided space for too much self-reflection. When that happened her reaction was the same as it always had been. Reach for a bottle of something strong. Drink until the bad thoughts went away. And sure, it was a Band-Aid on a knife wound, but it worked in the short term, and short term was all she could ever hope for. What she wouldn't do for a bottle of Chivas right now.

"Did you hear that?" Spook whispered, snapping her focus back to the present. "Up ahead. Listen."

Acid froze. Off in the distance there it was, a shrill squeal, halfway between a scream and a laugh. But it was human, she was certain. A human in distress.

"We need to help them," Spook said, pushing past and marching on ahead.

"Ankle feeling better?" she asked, taking a step back.

Spook turned and did that face. A scowl on top of a sulk. "Please, Acid."

"All right, but nothing changes," she replied. "I mean it, Spook. We have to step careful. Stick to the trees. Stay quiet."

"I'm not a complete idiot. Despite what you think."

Acid opened her mouth but thought better of it. She watched as the young American limped away, brushing fronds of foliage angrily from her path as she went. They had only known each other for eight months, but they'd spent a lot of time together in that period. Long enough for Acid to understand she shouldn't be too hard on the kid. She was being a prissy little bitch, but she was scared. Stress affected people in different ways. It wasn't always turned inwards.

She joined Spook amongst a grove of banana trees that stretched up to where the track turned into a rocky incline.

"They're on the other side of these rocks," Spook whispered. "They sound like they're hurt."

Acid listened, but couldn't hear anything. "Or they want you to think they're hurt."

"Geez. Not everything's a trap, Acid," Spook told her. "Try to trust people a little more."

She was off again, dropping bombs and hobbling away like she knew what the hell she was talking about. Acid sneered, cracking the dry mud on her face.

"Trusting people gets you killed," she replied, catching up with Spook as she weaved her way around the trees.

"I trusted you."

"You shouldn't have."

"What a dumb thing to say."

Acid didn't like this, Spook getting in her face. It wasn't the way their relationship worked. There was only room for one short-tempered bitch with a sharp tongue.

"Anyway, you're wrong about not everything being a trap," she replied, conscious of how much of a brat she sounded, but unable to stop herself. "It's just a matter of timescale. That's all. Love, marriage, work, friendship. It's all a trap."

Spook stopped at the bottom of the incline and slumped against a large boulder. "You really think that?"

Still going with the teenage angst, Acid shrugged. "Don't know. Maybe."

"Because I knew you were cynical but, shit, you really think friendship is a trap? Is that what this is all about, you treating me like this? You scared I'm going to hurt you?"

"I just want to get off this bloody island and find Caesar," Acid said, folding her arms. "I want to continue my mission." She looked away, feeling Spook's stare burning into her cheek.

"Fine." Spook sighed. "Best keep going then."

As if to highlight the point, another loud wail rose over the other side of the rocks. This time they both heard it.

Acid tensed. "Come on," she rasped. "Follow me. Keep low."

They made their way up the incline, keeping cover as much as possible, moving from rock to rock until they got to the summit. Acid grabbed Spook's arm and pulled her down into a squat behind a row of tall ferns. From this position they could see down into the clearing ten feet below where a short, stout woman was stooped over the lifeless body of a man. The wails were hers. And to prove it she went again, crying out like an ancient banshee. She beat the man's chest with her fist, shook him by the collar. But it was useless. Even from this distance Acid could see the large exit wound in his stomach, and his intestines pouring out like a grotesque squid trying to escape. Acid held her arm out, holding Spook back.

"We need to go to her," Spook whispered. "She needs our help."

"Does she?"

Acid squinted at the woman. The bats were rousing in her consciousness. Manic energy fizzing across her synapses. Something wasn't right. Acid might not trust people, but she trusted her instincts and her heightened senses to propel her through. The bats. They hadn't let her down yet.

From her vantage point, she watched the woman as she slowly got to her feet and brushed a strand of yellow-blonde hair from her face. The sweltering climate was on the wane now as dusk arrived, but the sweat was pouring off her. Her once-white shirt, now splattered with blood, stuck to the small of her back. Her black faded leggings were torn and dirty.

"What are we waiting for?" Spook asked, brushing Acid's arm away. "She's hurt. Upset."

"Not so fast," Acid said, not taking her eyes off the woman. "Could be a trap."

She felt Spook's glare even if she couldn't see it.

"You kidding me?" the kid whined. "This is exactly what I'm talking about. You're too cynical for your own good. You see the world through this frame where everyone's a bad guy. But that's not the case. It really isn't."

"So you're telling me there's no bad guys in the world? Hmm, weird that, sweetie. Seeing as we're here at the behest of a bunch of shits who want our heads hanging on the walls in their boardrooms. I'd say they were bad people, wouldn't you?"

"What's that got to do with us helping that poor woman?" Spook whined. "Yes, there are bad people in the world, which is why you need to help others a little more. The good ones."

Acid wasn't having it. She snapped her head back to Spook. "That's what you said about the journalist chick who stole my jacket. Remind me again, how did that turn out?" Spook looked away. "That's right. She fucked off. Ran away. And good for her. Because she didn't trust us. Because she was savvy."

"This is different. She's all alone. Distraught. One of those hunters could pick her off in a second."

Acid curled her lip, speaking through a snarl. "We haven't got time for this."

"Well, we need to make some time." Spook shrugged her away and set off, the pain in her ankle clearly taking a back seat to her anger as she traversed the dusty slope.

Acid made to call after her, but stopped herself. What was the point? Trusting strangers, helping people, they were both alien concepts to her. Not only that, she knew she was in the right here. Trusting people never worked out well. If you were lucky, they only broke your heart. But in Acid's experience, they could also get you killed. Or kill you themselves. Spook was different, of course. She was… well, Spook. Commendable, honest, lame but loyal. Annoying as hell, but kind of adorable too. Acid raised her head, watching as Spook reached the flat basin and approached the woman. Stupid kid. Too trusting by half.

Acid gritted her teeth and snarled into the sky.

"Fuck!"

She got to her feet and, moving at an angle, sliding her right foot in front of her and steadying herself with the left, hastened down the slope. She just hoped that she was wrong about this. Because if not, down there in the open there was nowhere to run, nowhere to hide.

CHAPTER 20

Getting closer to the woman, Spook could see she was in her early forties, and out in the real world (without this blistering sun and the horrors of their situation beating on her) she would have been a good-looking woman. Today, however, an unfavourable mix of sunburn and vast amounts of crying had made her face red and puffy. Her over-bleached hair was stuck up at all angles. Dry and frizzy in the tropical heat.

"Hey," Spook tried, speaking softly. "Are you okay?"

The woman looked up at Spook and froze, as though the fight-or-flight hormones were battling for supremacy in her system.

"Who are you?" Her accent was hard to place. Eastern European, perhaps.

"Question is, who are you?" Acid called, striding past Spook and going to the woman. She gestured to the body lying on the ground. "And who's this?"

From her current position Spook couldn't see the man's face, but she was glad of that fact. Before meeting Acid she'd never even seen a dead body in real life. Even at her parents' funerals it was closed caskets all round. It wasn't that she was squeamish, but being so close to death always cast a harsh light on her own mortality. Spook would still rather stick her head in the sand than face things head on. She knew Acid found her habit of disassociation in vital situations annoying at best (worrying at worst), but she was unsure how to change.

The woman looked Acid up and down. "This is Seb Logan, he was my friend. They killed him. Those bastards."

"Who killed him?"

The woman shook her head disdainfully. "I do not know their names. But they are guests of my boss. Thomas Engel."

"Engel is your boss?" Spook asked, stepping forward and holding her arms out in a show of peace. "Can you explain?"

The woman looked down at her friend and her face screwed up into more sobs.

Acid leaned into Spook. "We can't stand around while she mourns," she whispered. "Look how exposed we are."

Spook bit her tongue. "She's upset. Give her a break."

"You can't stay here," Acid offered, stepping towards the woman. "I understand you're upset, but there's nothing you can do for your friend now. We need to get away from this area."

The woman hunkered back a nostril of snot. "I understand. But where? They are everywhere."

"It's okay," Acid replied, looking at Spook as she spoke, throwing her an I'll-get-you-back-for-this look. "Come with us, you'll be safe."

The woman forced a smile. "Thank you. What can we do?"

Acid had already grabbed her arm and was guiding her towards the edge of the jungle. "We'll think of something," she said, beckoning Spook to follow. "Right now, we need to find shelter. My guess is the hunt's over for today, but that doesn't mean there aren't still hunters out there."

The three women hurried over to where the open basin met the edge of the jungle, finding themselves amongst a sea of bright red plants with tiny flowers that resembled yellow stars. Spook was musing how beautiful the flora on the island was when Acid grabbed hold of her shirt and pulled her into the gloom of the rainforest.

"Get in here. Quickly."

She gasped as the air quality went from being the freshest she'd ever encountered to something resembling the reptile house at London Zoo, heavy and wet and smelling of rotten fruit.

"What's the plan?" she asked as they traipsed deeper, winding around thick fibrous trees, brushing vines from their faces.

Acid didn't look at her as she spoke. "We'll find a spot to hide out, and then I want some answers from your friend. If Engel is her boss, she might be of use to us. Good work."

Spook gulped back a lungful of sour air, ready to tell her cynical companion how she was missing the point. That it wasn't just about being of use. That people had worth whether they could help you or not. But she stopped herself. It wasn't the time. Stay present, that's what Acid tried to drum into her. When people lost focus they made mistakes.

"Stop here," Acid called out to the woman, pointing to a circle of trees with large palm-like fronds that hung down low over the ground creating a tent-like structure. "We can rest for a while."

"Will we be safe?" the woman asked, looking at Spook.

"Safe enough," she replied, forcing a smile. "Acid won't let anything happen to you."

Acid brushed against Spook on her way past. "Let's not get ahead of ourselves, sweetie," she whispered, arching an eyebrow. "We don't know her story yet."

The three women moved under the cool shade, Spook sitting cross-legged facing the other two.

"My name is Spook Horowitz," she offered, once the woman had settled herself. "And this is Acid Vanilla. We're being hunted, like you. Do you know why you're here?"

The woman's eyes flitted from Spook to Acid and back. Her lips moved, as if rehearsing her words, but she didn't speak. Spook smiled and nodded, reassuring her as best she could. Difficult when Acid was leaning over to the woman, jabbing a finger at her.

"I don't remember seeing you on the list," she said.

"Excuse me?" the woman blurted. "What list?"

Acid was upright, one hand on the paring knife in her belt. "The list of people who've been brought here. To be hunted as prey. We saw the list earlier. You weren't on it."

"Wait, Acid," Spook said holding out her hand. "Are you absolutely certain?"

"I can explain," the woman said, hanging her head. "As I say to you before. I work for Mr Engel. Used to work for him. My name is Magda. I was a cleaner and cook for him. On this island, but mainly on Mr Engel's other island." The way she said 'other island' – nose scrunched up, clearly seeing things in her mind's eye she never wanted to see again – it made sense. Her story matched Sofia's description. Pleasure Island. Not pleasurable at all for those made to work there. Spook kept one eye on Acid. She was still fingering the knife handle, but she was listening.

"Go on, Magda," Spook whispered. "What happened?"

Magda shook her head as a solitary tear rolled down her cheek. "My friend back there. Logan. We worked together, making sure everything was to Mr Engel's liking. For him and his guests. I am not proud of this. We were never told exactly what happened outside the walls of the compound, but we knew. We knew, and yet we continued to work for him. What does that say about us?"

Acid seemed to relax a little, enough to let go of the knife at least. "You do what you have to. I get that."

Magda smiled through the tears. "The money was good. And Mr Engel treated us well, even though he made it clear we should never talk about our work with anyone."

"He threaten you?"

"Not in so many words. But then a few months ago another of Mr Engel's staff told me she'd been speaking with a journalist. Selling information on the islands."

"Sofia," Spook said, shutting up when Acid shot her a hard stare. "Sorry. Go on."

"A few weeks ago, I found out my friend had died. A break-in gone wrong, they said. But we all knew that wasn't true. After this I was distraught, Logan was too. Distraught and angry. But we kept our heads down. Kept working. Then a few weeks ago this journalist reached out to us. By email at first, using an encrypted address and a false name. I was stupid. I replied to her. We struck up a conversation, but Logan and I, we were conflicted. She asked us to talk about Mr Engel, about our friend too."

"And did you?" Spook asked, risking another look from Acid.

The woman shook her head. "I wish I had. Two days ago, Mr Engel came to our quarters himself and asked Logan and I to take a trip with him around the island. We were scared, but you don't turn down an offer from Mr Engel. No matter what it is. He drove us in his golf cart to the south shore and told us to get out. We did as instructed, and then I saw a side of the man I've never witnessed before. He was enraged. Shouting that we had betrayed him. That we were fools for replying to the journalist. And that we would pay with our lives."

"So he made you part of the hunt." Acid nodded to herself. "Explains why you aren't on the main scorecard, I suppose."

Magda sniffed back more tears. "We were terrified. But Logan protected me. As well as he could do. But you can only run for so long. Do you know there are cameras and speaker systems all over the island? They can see everything."

"Yes, we figured that," Acid said. "I take it Engel is only a creepy voyeur to the bloodshed, doesn't get his hands dirty?"

"That's correct. Also the hunters can communicate with other hunters and the resort, inform each other where prey can be found. We knew it was only a matter of time before a hunter found us. In the end it was a man called Jason Moss. Have you heard of this man?"

"No shit," Spook cried. "*The* Jason Moss? He's part of this? I thought he was a cool guy."

Magda turned her mouth down. "He shot Logan. Almost shot me too, but I managed to escape."

"Hmm. So how come you were with Logan when we found you?" Acid asked, with a frown.

Magda didn't flinch. "I couldn't leave my friend. I waited until Moss had left and returned to his body. He could have been still alive. But no."

"Fair enough. Who's Jason Moss?"

"A motivational speaker and author," Spook butted in. "Worth around five hundred million dollars apparently. Calls himself 'The Success Guru.'"

Acid made a sicking-up motion. "A self-help guru who's actually a self-serving piece of shit. Who *would* have thought it?"

"He is nasty man," Magda added. "They all are. Killing people for fun, for sport, for money. It is not right."

Spook glanced at Acid, who gave her a *don't start* kind of look.

"It was never for fun. Or sport," she said.

"So what now?" Spook asked. "Do you have any information that might help us?"

Magda cheered a little. "This is where Logan and I were heading before Moss found us. Towards the north-west corner of the island there is a path, steps that lead directly from the shore up to side of the compound." She looked Acid dead in the eyes. "From there you can take the service elevator to the roof. There are helicopters."

"I see," Acid replied, her perfectly plucked eyebrows knotting together over the bridge of her nose. "Sounds like a good plan."

"Really?" Spook asked. "Sounds dangerous."

"Okay, sounds like the *only* plan," Acid bit back.

"Yes, yes," Magda exclaimed. "Thank you. We can do this, yes? Escape?"

"We sure can," Acid replied, sticking out her chest. "What have we got to lose?"

Spook looked away and scoffed before she found her gaze resting on Acid's breasts. She took off her glasses and made a show of cleaning them on the underside of her t-shirt. A fool's errand, really, seeing as all it did was smear the lenses with a grimy mix of sweat and jungle juice. She placed them back on as Acid sat upright.

"Okay, here's the plan," she said. "We'll wait here until nightfall, then move over to the west side of the island. There seems to be fewer trees on that side, meaning we'll be more exposed, but with the cover of night we might make it to the steps undetected."

"Wow-wee," Magda cried. "I am extremely glad you found me."

Spook watched Magda, remembering back to her first encounter with Acid. How in awe of her she was back then. And terrified of course. Still was, truth be told. But like everything in life, the more you experienced something, the less edgy it became and the more you took it for granted. Seeing Acid through Magda's eyes, it gave Spook renewed hope. Because whether she liked it or not, Acid Vanilla was a formidable person. Someone you most definitely wanted on your side. A highly trained killer with a sharp, strategic mind and unprecedented levels of courage. Spook had been foolish all these months trying to domesticate this fiery individual. Acid Vanilla wasn't made for civilian life. She was a fringe-dweller. An iconoclastic original. Ready and able to do whatever was needed to survive. If those traits alone were enough to get them off this island, Spook wasn't sure. But right now, they were all they had.

CHAPTER 21

Way across on the opposite side of the island, Sofia Swann and Andreas Welles were still searching for a means of escape. Same as everyone. After the security alert they'd fled the scene, running as fast as their exhausted muscles allowed, keeping low and to the trees, not stopping until they'd reached the centre of the island. Now, knowing that they were being watched, it was easier to spot the cameras, easier to zig-zag around them and stay hidden. Sticking together, they'd moved across to the west coast in a wide arc and, knock on wood (not a problem in this damn jungle), they'd managed to stay out of sight from the hunters and island security.

Still, as time had ticked on, as the sweltering heat dropped and night seeped through the trees, Sofia found her plucky resolve wearing thin. Now, with the dark murky jungle stretching out forever on both sides, she began to drown in the ocean of her own thoughts. Seemingly from nowhere, a conversation she'd had with Mike a while back popped into her head, one of those silly intellectual discussions that they got into from time to time. A 'What would you do if...?' kind of thing. They'd been watching some war movie on Netflix. *Saving Private Ryan* perhaps, Sofia couldn't recall. It wasn't her choice, she knew that much. But their relationship was a modern, twenty-first-century concern, run like a democracy, and it was Mikey boy's turn to choose. But as the movie had dragged on, and she had grown tired of all that khaki and blood, she'd thrown one in the mix.

How would you cope mentally if you were fighting in a war?

Mike's answer had shocked her a little, but she had to agree it was the only choice. He'd thought about it for a while and then told her plainly. "I guess I'd get into the mindset I was going to die. It's the only way I could survive and make the right choices."

Sofia understood. He didn't mean it in a nihilistic 'What's the use, might as well end it' kind of way. But to get through that hell, you'd have to accept you were a goner. After that anything else was a bonus. Mike (an ancient history student when they'd met) had then gone off on a long-winded tangent about Samurai warriors and how they had a similar mindset of 'dying before going into battle'. Explaining how, by doing this, they could be present on the battlefield, not stuck in their heads worrying if they were going to die the whole time. Something along those lines. She had stopped listening. But being here now, on this hellish island, it all made sense. It was the only way through. So here she was, dead. Ready to do what was needed.

We are the dead.

We are the dead.

"Hey, how you holding up?" Welles asked, leaning into her as they strode on down a long dirt path that cut through a large area of dense vegetation. "You've gone a little quiet there."

She shrugged. "Was just thinking about some shit."

"Yeah, well, I advise against that, *chica*. Thinking about shit doesn't do any good. Not in these situations."

She was about to tell him she'd come to the same conclusion when they heard something ahead. A rustling coming from the trees.

"Move," Welles rasped, shoving her behind the trunk of a large fig tree and aiming his rifle up ahead. Calling out, "Who's there?"

Nothing. Sofia froze, not daring to breathe. She watched Welles' steely expression as he closed one eye over the barrel of the rifle. His entire body was rigid, sweat running down his face.

"Anything?" she whispered. From her hiding place, she couldn't see where he was aiming.

His eye twitched, but he didn't move from his position. "Nah," he replied finally, relaxing a little but keeping the rifle up. "Must have been an animal."

Sofia swallowed down a mouthful of thick rainforest air and moved around the side of the tree. "Should we rest awhile? Maybe take turns at some sleep? It's getting dark and I'm exhausted."

Welles didn't look at her. "No, we need to keep going."

"Going where? We're on an island. There's nowhere to go."

"Tell me again about the people you met," he said. "You think they're still alive?"

"Maybe. The English chick, Acid, she seemed pretty tough. I mean, she's a trained killer so…"

Welles nodded to himself, thinking. "We need to find them. Only way we have a chance against these motherfuckers."

"I don't know, man. Like I told ya, there was something weird about them. I didn't trust them. Hey…" She hadn't even finished talking when he set off, striding along the dirt path. "Wait for me, will ya?"

"You ever hear that saying, 'My enemy's enemy is my friend?'" Welles asked as she caught up alongside him.

"Erm, yeah, it's a pretty famous saying."

Welles threw her a side-eye. "Well, all right then. So it doesn't matter whether you trust this woman. We all want the same thing. Off this damn island."

As the sun disappeared and the sky turned a deep red, they trudged on same as before, keeping the track in sight but staying in the trees. They'd travelled another half mile before Welles stopped dead and once more hustled Sofia deeper into the cover of the rainforest.

"Quiet," he whispered. But she'd heard it too. Laughter. Coming from the other side of a small raised area up ahead.

She didn't move, her breath tight in her throat, her heart pounding against her ribs. What she wouldn't give to be back in Brooklyn. Hell, she'd settle for The Bronx, Queens even. Anywhere, as long as it had buildings, and roads, and places you could get a drink. As far away from this oppressive, sticky jungle as possible, with its bugs and creatures and men with hunting rifles waiting to kill you around every corner.

Welles held the rifle upright, gripping the barrel to his chest. He glared at her, trying to communicate with his wide, bloodshot eyes, nodding at the jungle, telling her to take cover. But she shook her head.

"Don't do it," she mouthed. "Too dangerous."

The laughter was growing louder and more distinguishable. Sounded like there were three of them. Men. Obviously men. Sofia didn't blink as she looked up at Welles. Don't be a hero, her eyes told him, we stick together.

Moving painstakingly slow so as not to make a sound, Welles unfastened the mag-clip on the rifle, pulling a face as though his team had just missed a three-pointer when he saw there were only two rounds left in the mag. He grabbed Sofia by the shoulder and moved his face down level with her own.

New plan, his eyes said. Follow me.

For once, she was happy to do as she was told. Stepping carefully, they moved deeper into the jungle where the trees grew tall with huge leaves. It was dark and eerie but that was a good thing, Sofia concluded. From everything she'd learnt about Engel and the hunt and his islands, most of the guests here were city types. The boardroom their usual domain. The stock market their weapon of choice. Not that they weren't dangerous (hell, they were armed to the teeth and trigger-happy, the lot of them) but they had no real experience in this sort of environment.

A little further and they'd be clear, she told herself.

And it was at that moment that she pushed through some low-hanging leaves and ran headfirst into the biggest spider web she'd ever encountered.

"Eugh! Shit! No!"

Sofia had had a fear of spiders from a young age. She didn't mean to yell out so loud, but instinct took over before her head got involved. If the web was this big, how big was the damn spider?

Welles spun around, a deep scowl furrowing his brow. "What the fuck?"

Sofia, frantically clawing at her face and flicking her hair about, exclaimed, "Is it on me?"

Welles stepped over and sternly shushed her. Once she was calm he raised his head, listening into the trees. His face was hard. His body tense.

She shot him a toothy grimace. "Sorry."

"No time for that," he said, as behind them they heard enthusiastic hollering, followed by the snap of branches and foliage being pushed aside. The men had heard her. They were coming. Welles grabbed her by the arm and pulled her into a run.

"What are we going to do?" she asked, as they ran through a display of huge white flowers that looked like they might eat a person.

"Just keep going," Welles told her. "I'm hoping we can outrun them. Don't stop until I do."

There wasn't any danger of that happening. The lactic acid in her system felt like it was cutting into her side, but Sofia didn't slow down for one second. How long she could keep this pace up, she wasn't sure. But if she ever wanted to see Mike again, if she ever wanted to see her friends, and her mom, and Brooklyn again, then she had no other choice. Behind her she could hear voices, the men barking instructions at one another.

Go left.

This way.

I can see them up ahead.

She risked a glance over her shoulder to see torch beams

slicing through the gaps in the trees. She screwed up her face. Pushed through the pain. She hadn't come this far to be killed by a bunch of Patrick Bateman wannabes. So she ran. With her head down and sweat pouring down her face. She ran. With her feet sore and her heart thumping. And those four words flashing through her mind.

We are the dead.
We are the dead.

CHAPTER 22

Andreas Welles leaned into a sharp turn as the sonic boom crack of a bullet whipped past his head at three thousand feet per second. Grabbing hold of a slim tree trunk for purchase, he swung himself around, making sure Sofia was still with him. She was. Her face white, distorted into an expression of abject terror, but she was still with him.

And so were the hunters.

Welles gulped for air, his chest tightening with every step. Despite eating well and visiting the gym three or four times a week, he was no longer a young man. A couple times since he'd landed on the island he'd almost uttered those immortal words, 'I'm too old for this shit', before stopping himself, realising how lame and clichéd it sounded.

"Welles," Sofia wheezed behind him. "Over there."

He followed her finger as she pointed over to a rocky cliff face that jutted out from the flat terrain. It was too risky to climb, but a hundred yards further along it levelled out. If they could get up there they might give the hunters the slip.

Welles slowed to a halt, waiting for Sofia to catch up with him before gesturing for her to go on ahead. "See where the trees open out? Head over there, we'll approach the raised level from the far side. I'll cover you."

She offered a curt nod and, with a reassuringly serious face, set off. Welles watched her go and turned back around. The trees here had grown close and were wound together in a way that would necessitate a single-file approach.

He raised the rifle to his shoulder and pressed his flesh-gloved finger to the trigger. "Let's see how brave you punks really are."

He didn't have long to wait to find out. A moment later he heard scattered movement in the trees, the sound of leaves brushing against bodies. The first guy through was only a kid. Mid-twenties, at the most. He was tall and broad with a chiselled jaw and that old-fashioned haircut favoured by a lot of young white men these days. Short back and sides, longer and swept back on top. He was wearing army-fatigue trousers and a green tank top. The full works. He'd even put a black streak of war paint under each eye. Shades of Arnie in Commando, Welles thought, in the split second it took him to pull the trigger and turn the guy's head into red mist.

The man's headless body dropped to the floor as his buddies appeared through the trees. To Welles they were like carbon copies of the guy he'd just wasted. Same height, same haircut, only with less cavalier expressions on their all-American faces. Met with the bloody remains of their friend, they halted, cried out in horror. Welles held his position, obscured from sight amongst a large bushy plant with huge red flowers as big as his face.

He thought about cranking another round into the barrel, but it was his last one, and there were two of *them*. Sure, with the amount of adrenaline and rage surging in his veins, he could take either one off these pretty boys hand-to-hand. But hand-to-rifle, hand-to-knife, he wasn't so sure. He remained still, his finger taut on the trigger.

"What do we do?" one of the men cried, making to lift his friend's body. "Pauly, help me."

"Who's there?" the other man, Pauly, yelled into the trees.

Welles leaned back into the undergrowth as he raised his rifle, scanning the area. He grabbed his friend by the shoulder and pulled him upright. "Come on, we need to get back to the complex. We don't know who we're dealing with."

"They've killed Rob," his friend yelled, voice breaking into a falsetto. "We need to find whoever did this and fuck them up!"

"No. That's not how it's done. You heard what Mr Engel told us at induction. Any fallen hunters must be reported immediately so the clean-up crews can take care of them." He took out a small device and held it up in front of his face. "Co-ordinates are forty degrees, thirty-six minutes, thirty-one-point-four seconds north. Let me lock that in."

"We can't just leave him here," the man said, his sorrow turning quickly to anger. "It's Rob. Whoever did this has to pay."

"Yes, and they will." Pauly grabbed his friend by the arm. "Don't you worry. The cameras will have picked them up. We'll find out who did this and tomorrow they'll pay. Closing ceremony, remember. Supposed to be a trip, bro!"

"But what about—"

"Forget Rob. Jesus, what do you want to do with him? He's got no fucking head. Come on. It's getting too dark to hunt anyway."

Welles held his breath as Pauly gave the area one last scope before slowly heading back the way they'd come. His friend, face still rigid with a mixture of rage and fear, raised his head, shouting into the trees.

"You're all dead! You hear me? Dead. So sleep well, you pathetic worms, because I'm coming for you. Tomorrow I'm going to destroy you. All of you. Just wait."

Welles let his eyelids fall heavy whilst tightening his grip on the rifle. The man was staring straight at him, hunting rifle aimed just below Welles' chin. If he saw him, at this close range he'd blow a hole in his chest big enough to climb through.

Another second passed.

And another.

But the man was looking through him. In the darkness, he couldn't focus through the thick tree cover. Finally, he turned and ran back the way he'd come.

Welles waited a beat. Time to get his heartrate under control. Then gently, quietly, he slipped out from under the trees and headed away to meet Sofia. Only one problem.

She wasn't there.

"Sofia?" he whispered as he made his way into the clearing. "You can come out, they've gone."

With the clearing providing a leafy light tunnel up to the night sky, visibility here was better. But there was no sign of her.

Scanning the trees, Welles noticed a camera up in a banana tree a few feet away. It was pointing away from him, the only one in the vicinity. Keeping one eye on its position, he headed for the raised upper level, moving in a wide arc to stay out of shot.

"Sofia, it's Welles," he tried, in case of any doubt. "Those guys are gone. We're okay for now. You here?"

Then he heard it. A low groan. Full of pain and sorrow. It was muffled at first, but grew louder as the sound enveloped his awareness.

"Down here. Far side of the clearing."

It was Sofia. But the far side of the clearing meant right in front of the camera. Resisting his first instinct, to run in the direction of her voice, he whispered over. "What happened?"

"Some sort of trap. A big hole, in front of the rocks. Can you see?"

Welles squinted into the gloom and there it was, directly in line with the security camera. A large pit, six foot by six foot. Man-made.

"It was covered with leaves and hessian," Sofia whimpered. "Bastards."

He edged nearer, still conscious of the camera. "Are you hurt?"

"Just winded. Could be worse. I thought I was going to end up on some freaking spike. But it's deep. Ten foot. Maybe more. I can't get out."

Welles was already searching for something to throw down for her. Would a vine hold? He glanced back up the path, wondering if he could fashion something from the dead man's clothes.

"Hang fire," he told her. "I'm getting you out."

But the words hadn't left his mouth when a shrill siren broke the air. Welles raised the rifle. One bullet left. But he'd make it count. He held his position as the siren reverberated through the trees a while longer, before slowly fading away. Another sound was now clear, carried over the night sky, a sound much more worrying. That of a vehicle engine. It was heading their way.

"There's someone coming," Welles yelled down.

"I hear them," Sofia replied. "You've got to get out of here. Save yourself."

"I'm not leaving you."

"Go, please," she said. "There's nothing you can do for me."

Welles side-stepped around the side of the hole. He couldn't see her from there, but any closer and the camera would pick him up. Not that it mattered anymore. He held the rifle high, calling into the hole.

"I can maybe overpower them, get us more weapons."

"Don't be a dick. It's suicide. I'm serious. Get yourself gone." Her voice was hard, a heavy resolve clipping her syllables. "You're a good man, Welles. If anyone can survive this, you can. So go, before they see you."

Welles lifted his ear to the night sky. Sounded to him like a golf cart or a small jeep. Closer now. Thirty seconds away. "All right, listen to me," he told her. "I'm going to hide in the trees over there and observe. I've got one round left, I won't let them kill you. If they take you I'll find you again. I promise. Whatever happens, don't put yourself in any unnecessary danger."

"Unnecessary danger? Geez, thanks, pal. I'll try not to."

Welles grinned into the darkness. Sense of humour was a good sign. "Stay cool," he whispered, before hurrying silently into the shadows. He found an old eucalyptus tree that had grown out of the ground at forty-five degrees and looked down on the pit from the higher ground. Positioning himself on the thick trunk, he had eyes on the clearing whilst keeping out of sight. He also had a clear shot if needed.

He lay the rifle out in front of him and got comfy behind the sight as a vehicle pulled up on the far side of the pit. Welles' estimation had been correct. It was a souped-up Willys-Overland Military Jeep, painted black with a silver and red logo on the door.

Island Security.

The engine was switched off and three men jumped out, all dressed the same. Black cargo pants, black boots, black undershirts, with the *Island Security* logo across the chest, same as on the jeep. With their blond hair and blue eyes, Welles would have guessed they were Eastern European, maybe even Russian. They looked almost cartoonlike in their size, with huge shoulders, and arms as big as his leg. Like three Ivan Dragos from *Rocky IV*. Welles held his nerve. Even if they hadn't been armed with Beretta PMX sub-machine guns, there was no way he could take them hand-to-hand. And with just one round left in the mag, it was looking bad for Sofia.

The men approached the pit, communicating to one another by looks and abrupt nods of the head. One of them, with spikey hair and a large snake tattoo on his shoulder, handed his weapon to his friend and sat on the edge of the pit before easing himself down into the depths.

Welles heard Sofia's screams. "What do you want? Leave me alone!"

The two men up top exchanged glances but their steely expressions remained fixed. As Welles watched on, enraged but impotent, one of them reached over the side and pulled Sofia out of the hole. Once clear she stumbled over on her side, remaining in a foetal position. She looked so tiny and frail lying there at the men's feet. Her hair was matted with sweat and grime and her already battered leather jacket caked in mud. She rolled onto her back and stared up at the men, big brown eyes wide in the moonlight.

"Please don't kill me," she said, as she struggled to her feet. "I'm getting married in a few months. And I promise, I'll never tell anyone what happened. I'll delete the article, never breathe a word of this. I—"

A swift backhander shut her up, almost knocking her back into the pit at the same time. Welles fingered the trigger of his rifle. The angle of the two men was such, he could almost do it. But even at this range he couldn't trust a round to make it through thick cranium bone and take out someone on the other side. Plus, Spike was now clambering out of the pit and slinging his Beretta PMX over his shoulder.

Not worth it. Bide your time, *tío*.

"Shall we search for her accomplice?" one of the men asked. "The male?"

Spike stood with his hands on his hips, regaining his breath. He wiped a hand over his forehead. "He's just some old guy, right?"

"Correct. A retired a cop, I think."

Spike's face hardened, deep in thought. "Leave him," he said. "He's no threat. Probably won't last the night. We'll log him as fallen. Save us coming back out."

"Are you sure, sir?"

"That's what I said, didn't I?"

Spike gestured to his cronies and together they grabbed Sofia up, one of them throwing her over his shoulder like she was a rag doll. She didn't struggle. She had no fight left in her. All Welles could do was watch as these giant blond thugs bundled her into the back of the jeep and set off back to the resort. He waited until he could no longer hear the low grumble of the engine, and then jumped down from his hiding spot.

From somewhere deep inside the rainforest came the screeching wail of an animal. It sounded insane and angry and he knew how it felt. He sniffed back and spat a ball of phlegm into the pit. The fact they'd got Sofia out of there, rather than staging an execution, meant they had plans for her. What those plans entailed was anyone's guess, but whilst she was still breathing, whilst he was too, Welles had a chance of saving her.

Old guy, huh?
No threat?
He'd see about that.

CHAPTER 23

Acid had spotted the cameras a while back, choosing to keep the discovery to herself rather than worry Spook, and she'd had one eye in the trees at all times. Now, moving along the shoreline close to the ocean, she was sure they'd be out of shot. With the ocean gently lapping against the shore on one side, and the soft chirp of insects rising from the sweet-smelling rainforest on the other, it was almost tranquil as they trudged onwards towards their destination. Towards their destiny. Every so often Acid would glance up at the resort complex that loomed ominously on the mountainside. A bright moon (almost full, but not there yet) hung benignly in the clear night sky above, casting the building with an eerie glow.

"Hey, guys," Spook called out after they'd been travelling a while. "Any chance we can rest?"

Acid spun around, ready to give the kid grief, before noticing how far she'd fallen behind. They'd been walking at a steady pace for the last hour, but the effort had clearly aggravated Spook's injured ankle. The limp she'd grimaced through earlier had developed into a painful hobble.

"Your foot is hurt?" Magda asked, going to her and roughly lifting the bottom of her leggings. "It is very swollen."

"It's really painful," Spook replied, glancing over Magda's shoulder, her eyes full of emotion and pleading. "Can we stop?"

Acid sucked in a sharp breath. They didn't have time for this, but she knew pushing Spook too hard would only have a detrimental effect. "Fine." She sighed. "Twenty minutes."

"Thanks," Spook said, sinking onto the soft sand and exhaling deeply.

Acid walked over to join the two women but remained standing, facing the jungle with her back to the ocean. One of them should stay alert.

A silent discord splintered her thoughts and her nerve endings burned with an intense prickly heat. But on the surface she was still. She sucked back a deep, conscious breath, slowing her heartrate and settling into a more productive mindset. One thing she'd learnt early in her career. It was vital she kept her focus in check. Her condition meant she often had ridiculous and dangerous ideas, insane flights of fancy that in the moment seemed a totally viable option. Whilst it could be said these notions worked out okay (the time she killed two colossal mercenaries armed only with a neck scarf and a high-heeled shoe, for instance) there were other times when this manic energy spilled over into recklessness. Like now. A big part of her wanted to leave Spook and Magda and storm the complex alone. Take her chances. The bats said she could do it. What's more, it'd be fun, they said. A real blast.

She looked down at the young American, who had taken off her trainer and was soaking her foot in the cool salty ocean.

Yeah, great. Let's see how far you get with one shoe if we need a quick getaway.

She kept quiet. But maybe this was the best idea she'd had. She'd slip away, get the job done before Spook realised what had happened. They didn't need to worry so much about escaping the island if every single one of the hunters and their security team were dead. Hell, they could even stay here a few weeks. A real tropical paradise away from the world. She glanced back at the complex. Another hour or two to get to the summit. Once up there it'd take her maybe ten minutes to get inside. At this time of night she'd catch them unawares, either asleep or having a nightcap. She assumed there'd be plenty of weapons up there. Lovely, shiny weapons. Knives. Pistols. Machine guns. Weapons she could use. The evil pricks would be like lambs to the slaughter.

"Acid? Why don't you sit awhile?"

The question snapped her back to the present. "Huh?" She turned to Spook.

"Sit," she repeated, tapping the sand beside her. "You need to rest."

"No," Acid said. "I don't."

"You are thinking of something?" Magda asked.

"I'm always thinking of something," Acid replied, still gazing into the darkness of the rainforest. "Aren't you?"

"Your face, I mean. It is very serious. Angry."

"It's a serious situation we're in. Don't you think?"

Magda let out a sigh. "Of course. But I am glad I found you when I did. I feel safer now. You are a brave woman, yes? Strong."

"Acid is a badass," Spook said. "A trained killer. If anyone can get us out of this, it's her."

"Oh my." Magda looked at Acid in that over-the-top way an aunt might do on hearing her favourite niece has just got into Cambridge. "You mean like a hit man?"

Acid side-eyed the woman. At the same time fighting the instinct to smack Spook around the back of the head. "Not anymore," she told her. "Nowadays I'm just... well... I'm just a normal person."

The words felt rotten in her mouth. *Normal person?* When had she ever wanted to be a normal person?

No. Not a chance.

Never, never, never.

So that settled it. Acid was going up there. Alone. She'd take these bastards down or die trying. Death or glory. The only way she knew.

"I'll be back in a minute," she told Spook, already heading for the cover of the rainforest.

"You okay?" came the concerned call from behind her.

She halted abruptly, hands slapping against her jeans as she turned to glare over her shoulder. "I need to take a piss. You want to come watch me?"

Spook's eye twitched and she looked away. "Keep a look out for the cameras, okay?"

"Yes, thank you," Acid murmured to herself as she set off again, trudging through the soft sand. "I am aware."

She got up to the edge of the rainforest and paused, noticing a camera up in a palm oil tree a few feet in front. It was best to assume they'd have night-vision capabilities, but after watching it for a while it didn't seem to be moving position. The current angle of the lens meant she could pass by undetected. Her plan now was to stick to the trees, get to the foot of the cliff face before Spook even knew she was gone. Only problem was she really did need to take a piss. She hadn't been since this morning, and the bottle of water drank at the cabin was making its presence known.

Damn it.

Moving further into the darkness, Acid positioned herself next to a large boulder and yanked down her jeans and pants. In a half-squat she relieved herself, leaning against the boulder to stop her tired legs from giving way, and keeping one eye on Magda. What was it about her that just didn't sit right? She'd done nothing wrong. In fact, being an ex-employee of Engel's, she was more than likely an asset. Yet something felt off. It was like she was trying too hard.

Of course, ask Spook and she'd say this was Acid's reaction to most people. To *all* people. She sneered at the thought, Spook's voice in her head telling her how she should let people in, accept help once in a while. But why should she? Give people enough time, they always let you down.

She finished off and was pulling up her pants, when a strange voice startled her. Quickly she fastened the buttons on her jeans and moved over to the edge of the rainforest, staying undercover of the trees. It was too dark to see that far, but the vocal tonality told her it was a man, approaching along the shoreline a few hundred feet from where Spook was sitting with her foot in the surf.

Acid held her ground. Was this a trap? Had Magda done this? *Now you see, little Spook, this is why I don't trust people.* Too much can go wrong. Assume everyone's the enemy and you don't get caught out. Assume they want you dead and you can strike first.

The bats were screaming now. Deafening, static voices, piercing Acid's consciousness. Leathery wings tearing at her psychology.

Should have trusted us sooner, they told her.

Should have trusted yourself.

Acid Vanilla raised her head. It was true. No one was capable of what she could do. No one else thought like her, acted like her. No one else could balance that knife-edge dichotomy of unfiltered energy and calculated focus.

And she was here.

And she was ready.

But the stranger was getting closer. Spook and Magda still looking the other way, seemingly oblivious to his presence. Another second ticked by and he came into view, silhouetted against the inky blue of the night sky. He was tall and broad and carried the unmistakeable outline of a hunting rifle. He called out again, his deep voice now distinguishable over the crashing waves and the gnashing bat-chorus in Acid's brain.

"Stay where you are," he called. "Or I'll shoot you dead."

CHAPTER 24

Spook noticed the man approaching as he raised the hunting rifle to his shoulder. She yelped, managing to swallow down her first instinct, to call out for Acid. Instead she dug her fingernails into her palm. Told herself, stay cool.

"Would you believe it?" the man growled as he stepped nearer. "There I was about to drive back to the resort with the rest of them when I thought to myself, 'No, Jason, it's a beautiful night, why not walk back along the ocean.' And I've got to say, ladies, I'm glad I did."

The man, now recognisable as Jason Moss, AKA The Success Guru, stopped a few feet from Spook and flicked the end of his rifle, indicating for her and Magda to stand.

"Can I put my shoe on first?" she asked.

Moss frowned. "Quickly."

Spook didn't need telling twice, keeping one eye on the rifle, she heaved on her trainer. Not so easy with a swollen foot wet with sea water. Magda was already on her feet, brushing the sand from her legs. She helped Spook up and patted her gently on the shoulder. She seemed remarkably calm considering the bolt-action rifle pointed at her head.

"Why are you doing this?" Spook asked. "I know you. You're a good man. Aren't you?"

Jason tilted his head from side to side. "Good. Evil. Who's to say what is and what isn't. If you ask me, goodness is in the eye of the beholder."

Spook scrunched up her nose. She could imagine Acid Vanilla saying something similar. Didn't stop being bullshit, however.

"Please, don't kill us," she pleaded. "It's wrong. You're better than this."

Jason Moss smiled his famous smile. All white teeth and dimples. "You ever heard of the shadow self?" he asked, his eyes twinkling in the moonlight.

Spook shrugged. "Doesn't sound too good."

"Oh, no. It's rather wonderful," Moss cooed. "A Jungian concept originally. He believed the shadow to be the primitive side of man's true nature, the side containing all the parts of our personalities we don't want to admit having. Only by fully acquainting ourselves with this darker element can we ever become whole."

Spook put her weight on her ankle, sending a shooting pain up her calf. No way she could run on it. She glanced into the trees. "So, what? This is you falling to the dark side, is it?"

"Perhaps," Moss continued. "You see, there's only so much grumbling one can hear. The world is full of imbecilic chumps who won't help themselves. It all got too much for me. Then a friend told me about this place, about the hunt. Said it'd be the perfect way for me to get to really know my shadow self."

"Geez." Spook sniffed. "You think?"

"I just want to experience every single emotion," he said, his voice lowering to a sinister whisper. "Every aspect of my personality. We can't fully appreciate life until we know what it's like to take one."

"What a load of crap," Spook yelled, feeling braver now. But there was a reason for that. In the midst of his pompous diatribe Moss had lowered his weapon. Now he was standing in front of her in full-blown motivational-speaker mode, eyes closed, beating the heel of his fist on his over-developed chest. Really into the sound of his own voice. So much so, he didn't hear Acid Vanilla approaching swiftly from behind. Before he was even aware of her presence, she'd smashed a rock the size of a giant's fist into the back of his skull, sending him staggering forward. Spook jumped out of the way as he crashed to his knees, a look of pained confusion distorting his perfect features. A second blow from the rock and he was out cold.

"You okay?" Acid asked them.

Spook didn't reply. Didn't move. Truth was, Acid's appearance had startled her. It was that look on her face, still slathered with thick mud but fixed in a mad pout, cheeks sucked in, eyes wide and unblinking. She breathed heavily down her nose. The muscles in her arms, the thick sinews in her neck, bristled with tension.

Spook had seen her like this once before, but it was still unsettling. This was Acid Vanilla in full-on kill mode. No thought. No feeling. Driven by pure instinct and the muscle memory of sixteen years as a deadly assassin.

"You are very good," Magda yelled. She pushed past Spook and leaned over Jason Moss's prone form. Spat on his back. "Fuck this man."

"He was the one who killed your friend?" Acid asked.

"Yes. Is he dead?"

Acid got a foot under Moss's upper body and rolled him onto his back before kneeling next to him and unbuckling his beige canvas belt. He let out a deep groan as she pulled it free from his cargo trousers and rolled him over onto his front. The groaning became louder, more frequent as he gained consciousness. Moving quickly, Acid yanked his hands up and behind his back and wrapped the belt around his wrists and ankles.

She stood, with her boot between his shoulders. "What's his name?" she asked Magda.

"Moss. Jason Moss."

"This is the motivational speaker guy? she asked, pressing her boot down harder. "How's that working out for you, mate?"

Moss struggled against the ties, but Acid leaned her full weight on him. A large gash in the back of his head was bleeding profusely.

"Let me go," he said. "You're making a big mistake."

"Hmm, not sure I am."

Spook glanced from the man back to Acid. "Shouldn't we get out of here?"

"Tell me about this closing ceremony," Acid asked Moss, ignoring her pleas. "What's it all about?"

"Go to hell," Moss said, the affected Cali accent slipping into something approaching Mid-Western. "You'll find out soon enough."

"I want to know now," Acid said.

She placed a boot on the back of his head and dug her heel into the wound. Moss thrashed around in pain, but his screams were quickly muffled as Acid leaned forward and shoved his entire face into the wet sand.

"Acid, no…"

Acid shot her an intense glare, mouthed, "What?" And not taking her eyes off Spook, relishing in her discomfort, she pressed down harder on Moss's head, drowning him in the slurry.

"What happens at the closing ceremony?" she yelled, finally taking her boot off his head.

Moss gasped for air. "I… don't… know," he managed, in between violent coughs. "This is…. my first hunt… I just…"

Acid pushed his face back into the sand.

"Drown the motherfucker," Magda cried, too gleefully for Spook's liking. "He murdered my friend."

Spook couldn't watch any longer. It was the screams that got her. Desperate muffled grunts of despair, like a tortured animal. She hobbled over to the shoreline and gazed out over the ocean. Putting some space between her and the torture.

"Tell me about the closing ceremony," Acid said again.

There was another whimper from Moss. More gasping for air. More pleading. But Spook was relieved to hear the sound of spluttering compliance.

"Fine… I'll tell you… all I know." He panted. "Please… I don't want to die."

"We'll see about that. Talk."

"I know only what I read in the pamphlet, and what I overheard in the bar last night," he said, speaking quickly now. "Each year they spare a few of the prey… I mean, those being hunted. So they can… unf—"

Spook spun around to see Magda kneeling beside Moss with a large blood-covered rock in her hand. The back of his skull was completely caved in.

"Oh, shit!" She looked away, swallowing back an acidic reminder of the protein bar from earlier.

"What the bloody hell did you do that for?" Acid yelled. "He was giving us information."

Magda yelled back. "He killed my friend. He had to die. You weren't going to do it."

"Yes," Acid said. "I was. *After* he gave us the information."

"How was I to know this? You tell him, 'We'll see.' What does this mean?"

Acid's voice had an edge to it Spook didn't like. "Listen, sweetie. I wasn't going to let that bastard live."

With her heart pounding out of her chest Spook stepped in between the two women. "We haven't got time for this," she told them. "He's dead. We're not. Now let's get moving before any other men with guns show up." As if to put a big fat exclamation mark on her point, a screech of feedback burst out from the trees.

"Security and clean-up teams to second quadrant," a robotic voice chimed. "Guest down. Repeat, guest down."

Spook gave Acid a firm stare. *See, I told you.*

"Fair enough." Acid sniffed, scanning the perimeter, looking for the source of the voice.

"This way," Magda told them, setting off at a pace. "We're not far from the steps. A little further, we'll be out of sight."

CHAPTER 25

The loud siren reverberated out through the trees. Over the top of the snaking, metallic din, Spook thought she heard a car engine, but she might have been mistaken. Or hearing things. She hadn't slept or eaten properly for the last fifty-odd hours and both her mind and body were shutting down.

As the black night faded to an inky dawn, the three women moved purposefully along the shoreline, going as fast as they could go. Which considering Spook's ankle was still giving her real pain, wasn't actually that fast at all.

Every so often Acid would glance over her shoulder, and Spook would try and meet her gaze, hoping for a reassuring smile from her inscrutable friend. Hell, at this point she would take an ironic smirk, one of Acid's classic eye-rolls. But no. Once satisfied they weren't being followed, her head was down, her expression fixed in the same harsh pout, and her annoyance growing more apparent. Spook could almost feel the brittle, nervous energy seeping out of her pores. She wanted blood. Wanted this done with. And once more Spook was the one slowing her down. Messing everything up.

They were in sight of the bottom of the cliff face, the steps a few hundred metres away, when Spook's ankle finally gave way.

She stumbled over onto the wet sand, swallowing the pain as best she could but letting out a cry all the same.

Magda was the first over to her. "You are hurt?"

"I'm okay," she said, sitting up and putting her feet out in front of her.

"Can you walk?" Acid asked, like a school mistress scolding an unruly child.

"Maybe we should rest," Magda said. "A few minutes. Let her regain some strength before we climb."

"Sorry," Spook said, directing the word at Acid. "I'll be all right in a sec."

Acid let out a loud huffing sigh. "Fine. Five minutes."

Magda sat next to Spook and nestled into her. A sign of solidarity, but it didn't help. A few feet away, Acid paced back and forth, kicking up small piles of sand.

"Your friend is hot-headed," Magda observed. "She gets you into trouble?"

Spook rolled her foot around the socket. "Yes and no," she said. "To be honest, I'm the one who gets her into trouble."

"No. You don't," Acid said, walking over and squatting in front of her. "You're just really bloody annoying."

The way she said it, there was no humour to her voice, but Spook saw a faint glimmer in her eye, a blink-and-you'll-miss-it moment, something she wouldn't have noticed if she didn't know Acid so well. But that glimmer, it buoyed Spook.

"Before you caved his head in, Moss was telling me about the closing ceremony." Acid fixed Magda with those penetrating eyes. "What do you know about it?"

Magda pursed her lips. "What do you?"

"That it's a big part of this sorry-go-round of a weekend. That there are double points for those taking part, whatever the hell that means."

Magda cleared her throat. "All I know, it is a closing party. I have never experienced it with my eyes, I am always in the kitchens. But there is lots of food, lots of drinking. It is a festival. A sick festival, I mean. The end of the hunt. How did you hear of this?"

Acid caught Spook's eye and raised her eyebrows, pursed her lips. A signal she wanted her input.

"We found a cabin in the middle of the island," Spook said. "Like a tech-store. There were computers that showed the guest list, information on the people being hunted, how many points we were worth, that sort of thing. It mentioned bonus points for inclusion in the closing ceremony."

Magda chewed on the inside of her cheek. "I see. But I do not know, I am sorry. But if we get up inside the compound we will kill these awful men, yes? The ceremony will not happen."

Acid peered up at the cliff face. A deep frown ridged across her forehead, cracking the dry mud. "You okay to walk yet?" she asked Spook.

"Think so."

Magda jumped to her feet. "Let's kill those bastard shits."

Acid squinted at her in the moonlight. "Where did you say you were from again?"

"I didn't say. Originally I'm from Russia. Siberia."

"I see. Well, Mags, you're going to need some of that Siberian spirit if we're going to escape this island."

"No problem," she replied, helping Spook up.

Acid took a deep breath. Puffed out her chest. "This is it then, ladies. You ready for the final push?"

"I am ready," Magda yelled.

"Me too," added Spook, though the silent evaluation she got from Acid was less reassuring. The wicked glimmer in her eye of a moment ago was now gone, replaced with a mixture of concern and unease that for once she was unable to hide.

"Just stick close to me," she told them. "One way or another, we're going to finish this tonight."

CHAPTER 26

Invisible bat wings fluttered across Acid's consciousness as the women scaled the craggy, uneven steps that led up the side of the cliff face. They had fallen silent a minute or so into the climb, better to conserve energy, but Acid's busy mind still buzzed with the usual cacophony of chattering voices and dark imagery as she flicked through a mental Rolodex of possible outcomes for when she reached the top. Ideas and notions flew at her like insects. Too many to focus on. She knew that in situations like this, overthinking was deadly. It slowed you down. Had you second-guessing yourself. If that happened you might as well give up. You were already dead.

From now on Acid's only driver was instinct. She might not trust people. Might not play well with others. But the bats were a different matter. Those pulsating impulses that lit up her nervous system like the Northern Lights. Experience (along with many broken bones and near misses) had taught her fighting the bats only made things worse. Like a ship negotiating stormy seas, you had to lean into the crashing waves, let the current take you where it wanted. Otherwise you ended up off course. Smashed on the rocks.

Easier in theory, of course. Different when every five minutes you had to stop to let your weaker companions catch up. Acid sat on a low ledge and puffed her cheeks out, watching Spook as she hobbled up the steps, leading with her good foot and dragging the other one painfully up to meet it.

Was it bad of her to think the kid was over-egging it?

And might she still convince them to wait for her somewhere safe, let her do the dirty work? In kill mode Acid was wild, feral, unable to account for what she might do. It was safer for everyone if she worked alone, allowed the bats and her intense bloodlust to take over.

She looked down at her hands, balled into two tight fists. What was it Spook called it when she got like this? Deep inner rage. Said Acid should see someone about it. But to hell with that. Right now it was what she needed. Besides, Acid knew there was only one cure for whatever was eating away at her: killing Beowulf Caesar. Avenging her mother's death.

"Before you ask, we haven't got time to rest," Acid said, looking out to sea as Spook gulped down a mouthful of air. "We need the cover of darkness, and dawn isn't far off."

"I wasn't going to ask," Spook said. "And who's dawn?" She hit Acid with a sly grin that only annoyed her.

Ignoring it, Acid looked over the side of the steps. They were over half-way up the cliff face, concealed by the curve of the mountain, but if she leaned out she could make out the edge of the shoreline and the dark shape of a vehicle. They'd found Jason Moss. Meant they'd be on their tail soon enough.

"Let's keep going," she said, turning her back on them and striding away up the steep steps.

Another thing about *deep inner rage*, why was it that people (civilians) always assumed anger was a destructive emotion? For Acid, anger was an energy. It was powerful. It got things done. Though of course, a lot of her training had focused on learning to step away from her emotions. All her emotions. Assassins were supposed to be cold, calculated, killing machines. Uncaring. Unaffected by death. Like a female terminator, Acid used to joke. Only thing was, she'd never really managed to completely step away. She assumed her emotions were too messed up to begin with (partly due to the cyclothymic disorder, but also because life had kicked her around for a good few years before she'd met Caesar). The way Acid saw it, after what had happened to her, she'd be crazy not to be angry. Mad not to be a little crazy.

So, yes, anger was an energy, anger was a good thing. And so what if it meant she was a loner and always would be? She didn't need help from anyone. Those who did were weak. Once they reach the top of the steps, a few minutes away now, she'd head off on her own, tell Spook that was the way it was. No discussion.

"Ah shoot, Acid, look."

She spun around to see Spook pointing at something above her head. She followed her finger to the top of the steps. Or rather, where the top of the steps should have been. It was only clear now after moving around the curve of the cliff face, but the last fifteen metres of the steps had crumbled away.

Shit.

Acid glared at Magda, biting her tongue both metaphorically and otherwise. "You didn't think to mention this, that the steps end a little premature?"

The woman raised her hands. "I knew the steps were here, but I have never used them before."

"Now she tells us," Acid sneered, under her breath.

"Could we use those ledges to get up?" Spook asked, gesturing to where a series of flat rocks, wide enough for two people, jutted out from the cliff face.

Acid considered the option. The rocks rose up at intervals a few feet between each one, with the top one around six feet from the summit. Jumping between them would be difficult, but not impossible.

"You two wait here," she told them. "I'm going alone. You stay safe. I'll come back for you."

"No!" Magda and Spook both yelled in unison. Magda adding, "I need to show you the way in. We all must go."

Spook looked over the side, widening her eyes at the steep cliff face and the large rocks on the ground below. "She's right," she muttered, rather unconvincingly. "We have to all go. That's how we do it."

"Come on, kid," Acid said. "Not the time for heroes."

"Check out the distance between that highest ledge and the top," Spook added, her voice more resolute. "You'll never reach it alone. We'll need to help one another up."

Acid closed one eye, surveying the distance. Damnit, she was right. "Fine. But once we're up there and inside, I want you to hide somewhere safe, away from danger. Understand?"

Spook stared back. Blank expression. She did this a lot, and it pissed Acid off. She was never sure whether Spook was being obstinate, thinking of something to say, or hadn't been listening.

"Do you understand?" she said, enunciating every syllable.

"What about you?" Magda asked.

"If I go on alone, I promise you, we'll all get off this rock a lot faster."

"Will you be careful?" Spook asked.

Acid winked. "You know me, Spooks. I'm always careful."

"Shall I go first?" Magda asked, already moving to the side of the steps and preparing herself to scramble over to the first ledge.

"Be my guest," Acid said, arching an eyebrow for Spook's benefit.

She stood aside as Magda tiptoed over to the edge of the broken steps and then with a guttural yell jumped for it. She reached the first ledge no problem. Once there, she steadied herself, looking back and giving a thumbs up.

Acid placed a hand on Spook's shoulder. "You next, doll."

"Yeah?"

"Follow Magda's lead. Grab hold of what you can for purchase. And don't look down."

"Wasn't planning on doing," Spook said, before looking down. Her whole demeanour wilted visibly.

"Be strong," Acid told her. "Don't think too hard about it."

"Easy for you to say." Spook sniffed, positioning herself at the edge of the steps and gripping onto a gnarled root that protruded from the rock.

"You can do this," Acid replied. "Believe in yourself."

Spook smiled. "You ever thought about being a motivational speaker?"

"All right, enough of the chat. Let's go."

With Acid close behind her, Spook rocked back on her heels and then leapt over the side. She reached the ledge easily enough and Magda grabbed hold, steadying her. Two ledges to go. The furthest distance they had to jump was over to the ledge a good two metres away, with the final ledge requiring a more vertical leap. Acid waited, focusing on breath control as she watched Magda jump for the far ledge. She got one foot on the rock, but as the other came down she slipped. Spook yelped. Time stopped. Tiny fragments of rock fell away as Magda clutched for something to stabilise herself. A root, a small rock. She found it in a small crack in the cliff face, big enough to get her fingers inside and pull herself forward. She was safe.

"Okay, it's you," Acid called over to Spook. "Take a run up if you need it. You've got space."

Spook didn't turn around but nodded all the same. She took a step back and then went for it. Every muscle in Acid's body tensed as the young American leapt for the far ledge, but she needn't have worried. Spook made it look easy. Magda made a grab for her once again, and pulled her onto the centre of the ledge as she landed.

Two down, one to go.

Now it was Acid's turn. She made the first leap easily enough, and once Magda and Spook had clambered up onto the final ledge, she shuffled up to the lip of the rock to study the distance. On level ground she'd make the jump with her eyes shut, but up here, in the half-light of early dawn, exposed to the high winds that rushed in over the ocean, it felt a big ask. She sniffed back. Reminded herself who she was. Who she'd become. Acid Vanilla wasn't just an old codename she'd hung onto. It was the persona that had saved her life. A mindset that allowed her to do what she did. Becoming Acid Vanilla had been a complete transformation for her, both physically and mentally. "If you can't kill someone, be someone who can." That was what Caesar had told her all those years ago.

If you were scared, be someone who wasn't.

She was Acid Vanilla.

And Acid Vanilla wasn't scared of anything.

She pushed off with her feet. Two steps, and she jumped for it, landing on the ledge easily enough, but as her foot went down she stepped on a loose rock and stumbled to one side.

"Shit."

With arms flailing, she grasped at thin air, desperately trying to shift her centre of gravity. Her heart turned over as the whole world spun. A chaotic swirl of green and blue and grey. The bats screeched. Over her shoulder, as if coming from another dimension, she heard the muffled screams. Spook, yelling her name. Tottering on the edge, ready to fall, Acid was able to get her fingertips to a bunch of coarse grass growing out the side of the cliff. Another second went by. Felt like an hour. Like a lifetime. She strengthened her grip on the long grass, managing to pull herself over onto the safety of the ledge.

"Acid? You okay?"

She glanced up at Spook, readying herself to give Magda a boost onto the summit. "I'm fine," she told her between gulps of air.

Once Magda was up on the headland, Acid jumped onto the final ledge to join Spook, who grabbed hold of her and gave her an awkward hug the second she was over there.

"I thought you were going to fall," she whimpered.

"Not a chance." Acid replied, pushing Spook's arms down. "Just showboating."

She rolled her head around her shoulders. Over on the horizon, a cusp of a new day's sun painted the sky with rich magenta and orange. In an hour's time it would be morning. The final day of the hunt, and the closing ceremony.

But not if Acid could help it.

"Here, take my hand." Magda appeared over the side, holding her arm out for Spook.

"Go on," Acid told her. "I've got you." She cupped her hands together as Spook stepped up with her good leg. With one hand on Acid's shoulder and the other gripping Magda's hand, they hoisted her up. Once her legs had wriggled out of sight, Acid stepped back, expecting Magda to return to help her.

"Hey," she hissed. "Can someone give me a hand now?"

Nothing.

Bloody amateurs.

It only vindicated Acid's belief: relying on others slowed you down, got in the way. She ran her attention up the side of the cliff. A coarse tree root hung down over the edge of the cliff that, if she got up on her toes, she could about reach. Without giving it a second thought she jumped for it, pulling herself up with a deep grunt. It was hard work, but she managed to haul her arms and shoulders over the cliff top.

"Come on, guys."

She was fumbling around for a foothold, when she looked up, alarmed to see Spook standing a few feet from the edge and her cute features crumpled with terror and regret. A small hunting knife was at her throat, held by Magda who stood behind her with her other arm wrapped around Spook's chest.

"What the fuck?"

"Stop right there," Magda yelled, the Eastern Bloc accent gone, replaced with West Coast American. "One move and I'll slit the bitch's throat." She pressed the tip of the knife into Spook's neck. Right over the jugular. She wasn't messing around.

"What are you doing? What do you want?" Acid asked, straining with the exertion of hanging there.

"Isn't it obvious?" Magda said. "I want to win. And I want to see you suffer."

"Magda, I don't know what they've said to you but—"

"Please, Acid Vanilla. My name isn't Magda. It's Karen. Karen Clarkson."

Spook gasped.

Acid grimaced.

"That's right. I believe you knew my big brother."

Bollocks. She had known something was off. "And Logan back there? Your friend?"

"That pathetic loser? I killed him, of course. Got me ten thousand points. I was about to head back to my room when I saw you off in the distance. So I hid my rifle, staged the whole thing." She licked a grey tongue across her teeth and grinned. "Not bad, hey? I used to do a bit of acting here and there. Girl's still got it."

"Commendable," Acid said dryly. "Okay, let me up, we'll do what you say."

Magda – Karen – sneered bitterly. "Oh no, Acid. You're far too much hard work. Can't risk it. I'm happy with this one." She pulled Spook backwards, pushing the knife into her flesh.

"You expect me to let you take her?" Acid rasped.

Karen's nostrils flared hungrily. "No, toots. What I expect is for you to regret everything you've done. But I'd suggest you do it fast." She threw Spook to the ground. "I'd say you've got about thirty seconds before you hit the rocks."

On the word 'rocks' Karen stepped forward and delivered a hard boot to Acid's face, bursting her nose open on impact. A blinding pain shot through her sinuses. Somewhere Spook screamed, drowned out only by the static crackle of the bats. Acid held on, groping desperately for purchase. But Karen went again, another boot, this time connecting with Acid's eye socket followed by a stamp on her fingers, grinding down with the heel of her boot.

Acid gritted her teeth. Screwed her face up. Tried to hang on. But the pain was too much. Her head was numb. Her system burned with adrenaline, the old fight-or-flight hormone trying its best. But she had nothing left. Nowhere to go but down. With one last gasp, she let go and fell.

CHAPTER 27

"Are you fucking kidding me?" Luther Clarkson yelled into Jerry's startled face. "She's got Horowitz?"

The meek assistant wiped a shaking hand across his cheek, before turning his attention back to the ever-present tablet. "I'm afraid so, sir. She's already registered the capture with the hunt co-ordinator."

"Goddamn it."

It was happening again. Despite Karen being two years Luther's junior (the youngest of the Clarkson brood) she always seemed to get one over on him. On grade eight piano whilst he was struggling to pass grade six. Captain of her softball team. Popular as hell at school. Even got into Kappa Alpha Theta at Yale, whilst Luther got himself mixed up in the damned Delta Kappa Epsilon scandal.

Not that Luther didn't love his little sister. He did. Loved her as much as he loved any member of his family. Which was to say, not a lot, but what irked him most about Karen was she always landed on her feet. No matter what. She wasn't even supposed to be here this weekend. She'd arrived late. Bought her way onto the hunt at the last minute. This was why she wasn't on any of the guest lists. But from what Jerry was saying, it was because she'd been missed off that she'd been able to bag herself Horowitz.

"So what happens now?" he asked, sitting on the edge of the enormous four-poster bed in the centre of his room.

Jerry squinted at the screen, scrolling down with a stubby digit. "She's being taken to the basement. There are cells down there. They'll keep her there until the ceremony." He looked up at his boss, trying to lighten the mood with the fakest smile you would ever see. "That's this afternoon. She'll get what's coming to her."

Luther lay back on the bed. "Yes, but I wanted to be the one to do it."

"You've still got a good score, sir. Three kills to your name. Pretty good."

"It's not about the damn score, Jerry." Luther sat upright. "I spent a lot of money to get Horowitz and Acid Vanilla on the island. It should be me avenging Kent's death."

He slid off the bed and marched over to the large window, looking down on the island. A soft haze muted the view.

"At least you kept it in the family," Jerry tried.

"What about this Acid woman? We have news on her?"

More swiping at the tablet. "Not a hundred percent certain, sir. There were reports yesterday she'd also been captured. But no positive ID as yet."

Luther stretched his arms and yawned. "Fine. If you can't tell me, I'll go ask Engel myself."

He strode over to the bed and grabbed up his silk robe, wrapping it around him as he made for the door.

"Should we bother him?" Jerry snivelled, following on behind as Luther strode purposefully down the corridor.

"Yes, we should damn well bother him. This is my hunt as much as his. I want to know what the hell is going on."

He reached the end of the corridor and stabbed his finger repeatedly on the elevator button. "Come on," he muttered, bouncing from foot to foot. "Jesus Christ."

"What the bloody hell is going on out here?"

Beowulf Caesar, sticking his head out of his room and into Luther's business. The last person Luther wanted to see. After his own sister, perhaps.

And wouldn't you know it, it was her bleach-blonde head that appeared next, from the room a few doors down.

"Lu-ther," she sang, like butter wouldn't melt. "What's wrong, hun? You seem sorta stressed."

Luther pursed his lips. "I'm going to see Engel," he said. "I'm sick of being brushed over."

"Now, now, dear boy," Caesar drawled, in those affected tones. "Why don't we all calm down. We're all on the same side, aren't we?"

He glided over to Luther and put an arm around his shoulder. Caesar was a big man. Overweight, yes, tall, broad, also, but it was more than that. He had a real presence about him. Oozed confidence. Made Luther sick.

"I don't want to calm down," he huffed, shrugging the arm away. "I'm being made a fool of. I paid you a small fortune to get those bitches here."

"Yes, and I'm delighted you got in touch," Caesar replied. "I was so glad to hear there were no hard feelings. But this *is* Mr Engel's event. His island. Come on, why don't you have a drink with us?"

Luther glanced up at him, taking in his bald cranium and thick-set features. "Isn't it a little early to be drinking?" he asked.

Caesar grinned, exposing his gold canine teeth. "It's never too early for a drink, dear boy." He placed a hand on the small of Luther's back, guiding him into his suite. Luther resisted at first. Didn't like Caesar touching him like that. Too sexual. But screw it, maybe a drink would help.

"You really need to chill out, Luth," Karen said, following them. "This is a vacation, remember? Supposed to be fun."

She strolled over and joined Caesar's lackey (some Arab girl Luther hadn't been introduced to) on a large white leather couch.

"Fiery Hot Boy?" Caesar asked, appearing over Luther's shoulder and handing him a frosted martini glass full to the brim with bright red liquid. "One of my own inventions."

Luther took a sip and pulled a face. Placed it down on the low coffee table. "Why are we sitting around here?" He sighed. "Aren't there targets still out there?"

"Apparently not," Caesar said. "Your sister here was just telling me how she'd done us all an enormous favour."

"That's right," Karen said, placing an arm over the back of the couch. "Got Horowitz for the closing ceremony and sent the weird girlfriend to her death."

Luther sat up when he heard this. "You got them both?"

"Sure did."

"And you're absolutely sure Acid Vanilla is dead?" Caesar asked, sitting down on the arm of the couch. "Because I've made that mistake myself. Don't underestimate that girl's ability to survive."

"She's dead all right. I saw her bounce off the ledge below and disappear down the side of the cliff face. No one could survive that fall. No one. I imagine right now her broken body is being ripped apart by scavengers."

Caesar grinned, showcasing those gold teeth again. Except there was something else behind his eyes, Luther noticed. Not sorrow exactly, but he wasn't as happy as this outward display might suggest.

"All we have to do now, is enjoy the closing ceremony," Caesar said, real energy behind his smile now. He raised his glass in the air and Karen and the lackey did the same. Obligingly, Luther followed suit.

"To us," Caesar bellowed. "And to the closing ceremony of this amazing hunt. From what I've heard, it's going to be a real bloody treat. With emphasis on the bloody."

CHAPTER 28

It was true. Acid Vanilla had hit the stone ledge hard. The violent momentum of her fall sending her tumbling over the edge.

But she wasn't done just yet.

With Spook's screams ringing in her ears, she plummeted down the steep cliff face, her fingers grasping desperately at the rock. Something to hold on to. She was almost half-way down when her hand touched on something woody. A meagre vine protruding from a crevice in the rock. Her fingers closed around the fibrous plant. But she could already feel the roots giving up the ghost. It did however slow her velocity enough that she could right herself a little, shift her body around so she was sliding down the steep cliff with her back to the rock. A few feet below her the incline levelled out a little but not enough to halt her any. The jagged rocks at the bottom of the mountain were approaching fast and if she didn't do something she was dead. She pressed herself back against the sharp unforgiving cliff face, skin torn and bruised, hands, feet and arse all applying as much friction as she could handle. Assessing the distance between her and the ground, her and a nearby cluster of tall trees, she gave it a second. And another. Then using the last strength she had she pushed off from the cliff face and launched herself into the air.

Shit, not far enough.

Her eyes blurred with the wind rush. Where was up, where was down? Where were the rocks? Arms flailing in a vain attempt to catch her fall, she braced for impact. Braced for death. Pain tore through her side, something slapped at her face. Not rock. Trees. She thrust out her legs and arms, star shape. Squeezed her eyes shut against the branches poking and scraping at her skin. Still falling too fast, still bracing for impact, every part of her tense, every part frozen in fear.

This was it.

This was really it.

Her eyes flew open in the second before she hit the ground. A quick and hard impact. A sudden stop that forced the last molecule of air from her lungs.

She had landed on her back. Unable to move. Fighting to breathe. A black veil seeping its way insidiously across her vision.

Sleep now, it told her. Be at peace.

Acid wanted nothing more than to shut her eyes and submit to the soft depths of unconsciousness, but the bats had other ideas. They screamed at her.

On your feet...

This is not the end...

This is not the end...

Easier thought than done. Acid turned her awareness inside, scanning her body. Nothing felt to be broken, but as she raised her head she saw the deep wound in her side, snaking around her torso like a cruel smile. The acknowledgement delivered an intense stabbing pain that crippled her. Her face ached from Karen's boot. Her head throbbed, a mixture of dehydration and where she'd banged it on the ledge on the way down.

"Shitting-bastard-mother-Christ."

She rolled onto her side and pushed herself up to a sitting position, before carefully peeling up her torn shirt and inspecting the damage. The branch had gone in just under her lower rib on the left side, torn a chunk of flesh two inches long. It looked worse than it was. But hurt more than it looked. She felt at the skin around the gash, couldn't feel any foreign objects, but there was all sorts of dirt and bacteria in there. It needed cleaning out if nothing else.

With growing discomfort as more injuries became apparent, and with a lot of creative cursing, Acid got herself upright and on her feet. Slowly and painfully, holding onto trees to stay upright, she travelled deeper into the rainforest. As they'd walked along the shoreline earlier, she'd noticed a small stream that wound out from the trees and met with ocean maybe a kilometre away. Her only thought now was to find that stream. Hydrate her parched, broken soul. Clean her wounds. After that, who knew? One step at a time.

Broken, tired and sweating profusely, Acid lumbered on through the heady undergrowth. The close, sticky air more oppressive than usual, the flies hungrier. She swatted them away as best she could but soon gave up. Let them go to work on her. At least something was getting sustenance. Her eyes were growing heavier with every step. The deep slash in her side pulsated, as though pumping out gallons of much-needed life force. A few more steps and she stopped, removing her hand from where she'd been clutching at her side. The wound was still bleeding, but not as much as she feared. Over in the distance she could hear running water. Only faint at first, as though she might have imagined it, some kind of aural mirage, but as she carried on it became more apparent. The gentle bubble and gurgle of running water. Fresh water.

Lifted by the sound, she staggered onwards, bouncing from tree to tree as though in a pinball machine, but eventually finding herself at the side of the stream. She fell to her knees and leaned in, putting her entire face into the cool water. It roused her immediately. She came up for air, scooping handfuls of the refreshing liquid into her dry mouth. Once hydrated, she carefully removed her top and flushed out the laceration with the clean water. The pain took her breath away, but she kept on, pouring water into the cut until it was clean. Next she removed her bra and twisted out the under-wiring from the left cup. The metal wire was thicker than she'd hoped, but it was all she had. With all the force she had she bent it straight over a rock and then, squeezing the wound together with the fingers from her other hand, punctured the skin with the wire, shoving it firmly through both sides.

She screwed up her face. Leaned into the pain as she threaded the wire through and then using the same rock, bent it back over itself. It wasn't easy, especially with her hands sticky with blood and one eye swollen shut, but it'd hold the wound closed for a short while.

Exhausted, she had another long drink from the stream before lying back on the soft ground. Strange beetles climbed into her hair, tiny feet itching her skin. She closed her eyes. Once the water had sufficiently revived her system, and the immediate threat of death had subsided, her focus spread beyond the moment, bringing with it a deeper pain. One of regret.

Spook.

How the hell was she going to get her back?

Of course, that question relied on the fact the poor kid wasn't already dead. If she was… well… Acid didn't want to consider that.

"Bloody hell," she murmured to herself. "How are you going to get out of this one?"

Acid knew Spook blamed herself for them being here on the island (and in many ways she should; if she hadn't gone looking for Raaz in some ridiculous attempt to reason with her, then none of this would have happened), but she had let the blame lie solely at the kid's feet, and that wasn't fair. Truth was, Acid blamed herself. Like always. (When you won't accept help from anyone, who else was there to blame?) If she hadn't been so bloody-minded about her vendetta, Spook would be safe and well. They both would.

She let out a deep sigh. Maybe it was time to give up. Stop the chase. Caesar wouldn't stop looking for her until she was in the ground (and after killing most of his best operatives she couldn't really blame him for that), but he was keeping it in-house, hadn't declared open season on her. Whether that was out of deep-rooted loyalty or just him managing his brand, not wanting the world to know one of his best operatives had gone rogue, she wasn't sure. But it meant she and Spook still had a chance to disappear. For good. They could change their names, move to South America. Start living life. In peace. Whatever that meant.

She tried to sit up, but the pain pushed her back down again and she let out a mournful cry. A wail of deep despair rising from the pit of her soul.

Because who the hell was she kidding?

It was over. She wasn't going to South America, or anywhere. She was going to die here. On this island. Either from a bullet or an infected wound, but one way or another, Acid Vanilla was done.

Her mind drifted back over the last few years. To all the choices that had led her to this point. Perhaps it was time for her to go. She'd be doing everyone a favour, especially Spook.

Sorry, kid.

Acid's heart sagged at the thought of her up there. What she was going through. She'd be terrified, of course. But the worst thing was, she'd still have hope. That was Spook all over. She'd be telling herself Acid was coming to save her. Only she wasn't. She couldn't even sit upright. She was broken and useless, and she'd let her friend down.

Her friend.

If she wasn't already lying on her back, the words would have floored Acid. As it was, they just punched her heavily in the heart. It was the first time she'd thought of Spook as her friend. It was the first time she'd thought of anyone as her friend. Since she was a young girl at least.

She bit her lip and dug her elbows into the soft ground. With a grunt of effort, she pushed herself upright and looked around, seeing the area with renewed focus. Clenching her jaw through the pain, she got to her feet. First thing you do in the field when something unexpected trips you up: get off the X. Move away from the scene as quickly as possible. In high-pressure situations, standing still gets you killed faster than an infected wound.

A quick scan of her surroundings and an assessment of the morning sun's position told Acid the shoreline was over to her right. A few hundred metres, give or take. Going up the mountain the same way as before seemed like her only option.

Brushing heavy leaves from her path, she headed towards the shore. She'd only been walking a few minutes when she entered a small clearing, surprised to see an empty jeep parked up along the side of a dirt track. She blinked, like a weary Bedouin mistrusting the sight of an oasis. But it was real, all right. What's more, attached to the inside of the door on the passenger side was a green metal box with the white square and red cross insignia of a medical kit. Bandages. Stitches. Antiseptic spray. With a gasp of relief, she stepped cautiously towards the jeep. She had her hand on the door handle, ready to yank it open and grab up the box when she heard the snap of a twig. She spun around. Greeted with the sight of an immense man with blond, swept-back hair and an expression of pure hatred spreading across his tanned features.

"Wait," Acid said. "Please, I can—"

The heavy butt of an AK-47 assault rifle connected with her jaw. She went down like a sack of shit, her head spinning with the force but remaining conscious. The man advanced and she shuffled away, scuttling backwards until her spine hit the wheel of the jeep. Nowhere left to go. She looked up into her assailant's face as his thin lips twisted into a cocky sneer. He was wearing a black uniform with a red logo on the chest. Part of Engel's security team.

"I see we still have vermin running around the island," he snarled, in a thick Eastern European accent.

"Fuck you," Acid said.

"I don't think so." He knelt beside her, leaning in close. "You almost got lucky. The reports said all the prey was accounted for. I was doing one last sweep before the closing ceremony, and here you are. But maybe you are already half-dead though, huh?"

Acid turned her head, his rancid breath hot on her cheek. "Get it over with," she rasped.

"Oh? We've got a tough one here." He got to his feet, shaking his head at her prone form. "But I like that. It is much more enjoyable when the prey fights back. Or try to, at least. But you must realise by now. You don't get to win at this game."

Acid sniffed, tasting blood at the back of her throat. "Do it," she whispered, keeping her head down.

"I'm sorry. The time for the easy option has passed. Stand up." Acid didn't move. The man stamped his foot, shouting now. "Stand up."

"I'm not playing." She glared up at him, her eyes wide. The bats screeched in her ears. "You're going to have to kill me. So go on, do it."

The man paused, a quiver of uncertainty playing across his brow. He raised the AK-47 and aimed it at Acid's head. She closed her eyes and waited. It wasn't the first time she'd been in this situation, but she couldn't remember a time when she'd felt this helpless and hopeless. She'd heard it said that before you die your entire life flashes before you, and had often wondered what it felt like. She'd seen the terror in people's eyes as she'd pulled the trigger herself. Never seemed like a pleasant experience. But now, lying here facing her own mortality, Acid felt nothing. The bats had deserted her and, in their place, a quiet stillness. It wasn't unpleasant, just not what she'd imagined. She heard the trigger being pulled back. This was it. The end.

"Do it," she repeated.

Do it.

Do it.

She wanted him to do it. It was all she wanted.

The wet spray hit her face a split second before she heard the gunshot. She opened her one good eye in time to see the security guard staring down at her with what might have been a confused expression. Difficult to put one's finger on exactly what he was thinking, when the entire right-hand side of his face, from his temple to just below his lower jaw, had been blown away. He dropped the assault rifle to the floor and stumbled forward. Acid had just enough strength left to push him to one side as he collapsed on top of her.

From out of the trees' darkness, a second man came forward. He glanced around the clearing before stepping over. "My name is Andreas Welles," he told her, holding out his hand. "I'm on your side."

Acid was dizzy with fatigue and pain. Her eyes closed of their own accord. She tried to open them again but couldn't. "I'm done," she told him. "Just leave me here. It's over."

"Not a chance," he said. "You hear me? I know who you are, and I need your help. Because, miss, this is far from over."

CHAPTER 29

The sound of a key turning in the locked door revived Sofia Swann from a fitful sleep. She sat upright on the large double bed in the corner of the room and rubbed at her eyes, surprised and rather annoyed with herself that she'd drifted off.

How in heaven's name could she sleep?

At a time like this?

As the lock clicked open, she swung her feet onto the cold marble floor and looked around the room, shaking off the last fog of sleep from her consciousness. She'd slept in her clothes, still wearing the jacket Acid Vanilla had loaned her, but she had taken her shoes off. They were over on the other side of the room. A pair of Converse, once white, now caked in mud and algae. Probably the worst footwear one could choose for trudging through a tropical rainforest, but Sofia hadn't intended on doing that when she got dressed three days earlier.

She hurried over and slipped them on before moving into the centre of the room, ready to deal with whoever was coming through the door. Those pricks from yesterday had been respectful, by and large, in so much as they hadn't tried anything (after the short drive back to the resort, they'd brought her straight to this room and locked the door behind them), but that didn't mean they weren't coming back. She'd seen how the tallest of the three had been looking at her. Made her feel sick.

The door opened to reveal one of the guards, silhouetted against the stark white corridor. His huge hand gripped the arm of a small, sobbing figure, wearing thick-framed glasses and covered in dirt. With a squeal, she was shoved into the room and the door slammed shut.

"Spook?" Sofia moved over and knelt beside her. "Are you hurt? Did they touch you?"

Spook didn't lift her head, hiding behind her bangs. She wept quietly before removing her glasses and rubbing at her eyes. A stream of tears cut through the dirt on both cheeks, like an inverse of the classic mascara run.

"Acid," she wailed. "She's... They..."

"Ah, shit. You mean she's..."

Spook raised her head and met her eyes. "Kent Clarkson's sister. She was a late sign-up or something. Wasn't on the list. She tricked us. Kicked Acid off the cliff."

"Oh babe, come here." Sofia grabbed Spook and hugged her tight. It didn't seem to do either of them any good, but it was what people did in these situations.

Jesus.

Like this was a situation anyone had ever had to deal with before.

But then, they had, hadn't they? She and Spook were here precisely because the hunt existed, and had existed for many years. In the last decade, groups of rich men (and women, let's be fair) had congregated on this island for the single purpose of killing other human beings. Bunch of sick fucks. Although even now, having been here since that first claxon horn sounded, having seen what she'd seen, it still felt too vile and surreal to be true.

"What are we going to do?" Spook sobbed. "We're screwed."

"We don't know that. I met a guy out there. He's a cop. FBI. He might still be alive. Hell, your girl might be too. She seemed tough."

"She is," Spook blubbed. "But not invincible. She's only one person, despite what she makes out."

"Got to have faith, kid."

"You sound like her," Spook said, attempting a smile through more tears. "You're similar, you know that. Not just in how you look."

Sofia smiled. "Not sure that's a compliment, but thanks. So if you think that way, you know *I'm* tough, right? Brooklyn born and bred. I ain't going down without a fight. Neither should you."

But Spook was inconsolable. "There's no way she survived that fall. She's gone and they're going to make us part of some horrible ceremony."

Sofia gave up on the hug. "Yeah. I heard them talking about it when they brought me in. You know what happens?"

She shook her head. "Karen Clarkson said it'll make me wish I was already dead."

Sofia curled her lip to one side. That's what she was afraid of. She moved over to the bed and considered Spook. With her torn clothes and face covered in mud she looked like a crazy woman. Her thick Asian hair was matted and damp, stuck to her face on one side.

"You want to clean up?" Sofia asked, nodding over to the door in the far corner. "There's a bathroom and shower unit."

Spook glanced over at the door but didn't move. "What's the point?"

"Might make you feel a little more human."

"What, just in time for them to kill me like an animal?"

Sofia pouted. Fair point.

She wracked her brain, hoping some words of encouragement might manifest themselves, but nothing came to her. It would have been pointless anyway, as a second later a key turned in the lock and the door swung open. She hurried over to Spook as a short man wearing a cream safari suit and far too much fake tan marched into the room. Thomas Engel. Following on behind were three tall and muscular women dressed in white flowing robes. Two brunettes, one blonde. Each one exuded a serene beauty, but which clearly belied a cold cruelty. The effect was bizarre and jolting. No doubt exactly what Engel was aiming for. The blonde carried with her a small tablet, which she was already swiping at, engrossed in whatever was on the screen. The brunettes carried machine guns, held upright, close to their bodies. Once in the room they stood guard on either side of the door, staring forward.

"Good morning, ladies," Engel purred, holding out his arms beatifically. "My name is Thomas Engel. Welcome to my island."

"Fuck you," spat Sofia.

"Oh dear. That's no way to talk to your host." He moved around the side of the women, making a show of looking them up and down. He stopped next to Spook and placed his hand on her shoulder. "Stand for me, will you?"

Sofia sneered. "You won't get away with this, you piece of shit. I've still got the article saved on my cloud storage. If I disappear my fiancé will find it. You'll be done for."

Engel let out a low chuckle and walked over to stand beside the blonde with the tablet. "I see. You're the journalist." He turned to the women, speaking in hushed tones, but loud enough for Sofia to hear. "I thought these were both Luther Clarkson's prey?"

The woman didn't look up from the screen. "We thought so too," she whispered. "This one is for certain. Spook Horowitz. She's a top score this weekend. Her capture for the ceremony has put Ms Clarkson in the lead."

"So where's her friend? I'm confused."

More swiping, more frowning at the screen. "Acid Vanilla. Currently, we have her down as unaccounted for. Presumed dead." Her face dropped. "Oh."

"Balls. What now?" Engel asked through a fixed toothy grin sent Sofia's way.

"It's nothing, sir."

"Dalilah? Out with it."

"One of the clean-up team has gone offline. An hour ago." She narrowed her eyes at the screen as Engel leaned over to look. "It's probably nothing. A signal error."

"Either way, we need everyone accounted for," Engel rasped under his breath. "If there's prey still out there, they need taking care of. There's been too many problems already this weekend. I've got the narrative team working overtime covering for all the fallen guests. Get it sorted. Now. I want clarity, but keep it on the lowdown. I don't want any of the guests getting wind of this. The ceremony is in three hours, for Christ's sake."

He turned his attention back to Sofia and Spook, hitting them with a bright, all-American smile.

Sofia met his gaze square on. "Sounds like you got a few problems, slick?"

She didn't take her eyes off Engel as he twisted his mouth from side to side. A show of mock worry. "Nothing we can't deal with."

The blonde with the tablet left the room as two more women appeared, wearing the same white robes as the others. One was holding a bowl of water with two sponges bobbing on top, which she placed at Sofia's feet. The other had armfuls of large green leaves and bits of foliage.

"What's going on?" Sofia asked.

"You'll see." Engel smirked, walking backwards towards the door. "I'll leave you to prepare." He gave her a lascivious wink as the two women moved over to Spook and began to undress her.

"Get the hell off of me," Spook yelled.

Sofia watched, open-mouthed, as they tore the clothes off her and began washing her with the wet sponges. "You fucking sick creep," she called after Engel as he backed out of the door.

"There's no use fighting it, my dear," he cooed. "You must

look your best for the ceremony. You don't want to meet your maker covered in all that mud and grime, do you?" He closed his eyes, smiling that toothy smile of his. The one which made Sofia want to be sick. "Don't be mad, ladies. The closing ceremony is always such fun, and you're the main event. The stars of the show." With one last grin and a wave of his hand, he disappeared around the side of the door.

CHAPTER 30

Acid was imagining herself on a beach somewhere. Above her a wash of cloudless azure, spanning all the way to the horizon. She could almost feel the gentle waves lapping benignly at her bare feet as she sipped on something long and colourful and incredibly alcoholic. She screwed up her face, desperately trying to hold on to the imagery, casting herself in this idyllic setting, free from worry and pain. Difficult when you were sitting on the hard bonnet of a jeep with someone pulling sharp wire from out your flesh.

"Bloody hell. You almost done?" She opened her eyes and peered down to see Andreas Welles remove the last of her makeshift stitches.

"Worst is over," he grumbled, not looking up. "Just keep your shirt held up so I can clean it."

"You know what you're doing?"

"Yup."

Acid raised her eyes to the sky, focusing her attention away from her injury. "So what's your story, Andreas Welles? What brings you to this little piece of paradise?"

The man sniffed. "I'm FBI. I was investigating one of the

people involved in this weekend. Guess he decided he wanted rid of me in the most fucked-up way possible."

"FBI? I see."

"Don't like cops, huh?"

Acid rolled her head to one side. "To be honest with you, I've never had much to do with them. I'm a good girl."

She watched Welles as he moved over to the first aid box and selected a small vial of brown liquid. Iodine. What was he saying about the worst being over?

"Well, well," he mused, unscrewing the cap. "I guess my journalist friend back there must have been mistaken."

"You mean Sofia?" Acid asked, throwing up an eyebrow.

"Yeah. We were together for a while."

"Definitely Sofia? Sofia Swann?"

"Pretty girl, about your height. Same hair. In fact, you've got a look of each other."

"Yeah. I don't see it." Acid sniffed. "But you were with her? What happened? Is she…?"

"No. At least I don't think so. A security team showed up and took her back to the resort. I was on my way to find her when I bumped into you." He positioned himself beside her and held up the vial. "Brace yourself."

She puffed out her cheeks as Welles poured the unforgiving liquid into the laceration. Not the kind of alcohol she'd been hoping for. "Bloody bastard shit."

"*Now* the worst is over," he said. "Here, hold this to it." He handed her a pad of cotton wool gauze and returned to the first aid box.

"Did she tell you she ran off on us?" Acid asked.

"*Sí*," Welles said, not looking up. "Told me why, too. Unless, like I say, she was mistaken about it all."

Acid nodded to herself. He knew who she was. What she was. Not a great mix, an ex-assassin and an FBI agent. But here they were.

"So you think she's still alive?" Annoyed at how shaky her

voice sounded, she coughed. "I mean, is it even worth trying to get up there?"

Welles stared at her with an expression half-way between disdain and disappointment. "You serious? Of course we have to try. Why do you think I'm patching you up? Sounds to me like you're a lady who might help me."

"I'm no lady."

"Apologies. Old habits. You know what I mean." He stood, holding up a tube of Dermabond and an open pack of Steri-Strips. "These should do the trick."

He got to work, squeezing the sterile glue into the wound before closing it up with the Steri-Strips. Acid watched him work, tilting her head to one side to keep her hair out of his way.

"I let my friend down," she told him. "She wouldn't be here if it wasn't for me."

There it was again. The F-word.

Welles finished off with the Steri-Strips and glanced up at her. "You can still make this right. Help me."

"Do you really believe they're alive?"

"I don't know," he growled, standing upright and squinting up at the resort complex. "But if they're not, I want to get up there and take some of those assholes down."

Acid fought back a bitter laugh. Sure, the guy was talking her language, but a heaviness had descended on her shoulders these last few hours. "If I'm going up there, I'm going alone," she told him. "I appreciate the patch-up, but I don't work well with others."

"I see. So, what? It'll be you against all those hunters? Not to mention the security teams. I don't know if you saw the dude who attacked you just now, but they all look the same. Like fucking Olympic athletes."

She shrugged, a hint of petulance twisting her pout. "I'll take them out or die trying. We aren't getting off this island, are we? Got to accept that."

"No. I don't accept it. There's got to be a way. What's up with you, kid?"

"Kid? You're calling me kid? I'm thirty-four years old."

Welles beat a fist against his chest. "Try sixty-five. I'm an old cop, a few months away from retirement – means I've got a target on my back – but I'm not giving up. Together we can do this. We'll rescue the girls *and* kill those motherfuckers."

Acid slipped down from the bonnet of the jeep. "Sorry, my head's all over the place. It wouldn't work."

"What the hell," Welles yelled. "You're not serious?"

"Yes. I am. So leave me alone and let me do what I need to do."

"You won't a stand a chance. But together we—"

She spun around. "I can't work with a bloody cop. Are you serious?"

Welles stepped forward, pointing a finger at her. "Bullshit. You think I've spent forty years as a high-ranking officer to not know when someone's lying to me?"

"Forget it," Acid yelled, throwing her arms up. "I don't need this shit." She reached into the jeep and lifted out the AK-47, gave Welles a wide, manic grin.

"You're crazy," he scoffed.

"Now you're getting it," she told him. "I am crazy. I'm fucking crazy. So stay away from me, okay? Or I might… You'll…"

"What?" he yelled back. "What might you do?"

"I might get you killed. All right?"

"You kidding me?"

"That's what I do. I put people in danger, and they die. Which is why I have to do this alone. I can't trust you, and you certainly can't trust me. I promise you that."

Acid gasped as tears fell from her eyes. Welles looked away, uncomfortable, but that made two of them. The unexpected rush of emotion startled Acid, but she was on a roll. It was a release, of sorts.

"My friend Spook, she thinks I'm angry at her," she went on.

"That I blame her for us being here, but I don't. I just let her think that way because I was angry. At myself mainly. You see, I'm not a good person. *I* should be the one being used for whatever grim shit goes on at the ceremony. I should be dead."

"C'mon. Don't talk this way."

"It's true. Look at me. I'm fucked. My eye won't open. I've got this rip in my side. Plus my head and heart feel like they're going to explode. So, forgive me, Mr Welles, if I don't feel too confident we'll save the day and all live happily ever after."

He shook his head. "I never said that. But we have to try, goddamn it."

"It's a suicide mission," she hit back. "So let me go alone. I don't care anymore. I'm no good for anything else. I—"

Acid shut up as Welles stepped close, the tip of his nose centimetres from hers, his breath on her face as he balled her out. "Stop that. Now," he scolded. "I imagine, doing what you do, you've got a lot of experience in these high-risk, high-pressure situations. But guess what? So do I. I've done bad things. Real bad things. And I'll tell you something else. I don't care who you are. I don't care what you do, or did, or even if I live or die. All I care about is taking out as many of those rich punks as I can. So let's be a team. Let's get up that mountain and kill those evil motherfuckers."

Acid rubbed her thumb into her palm. She didn't look up, but in her peripheral vision she saw Welles straighten his back. He didn't take his eyes off her.

"How? We've got one AK with half a magazine left," she whispered, when the silence between them had grown too heavy. But then it struck her. "Hey, wait a second, you were using one of their hunting rifles. But they're locked."

She turned to Welles to catch him grinning proudly. He held up his hand, and she noticed for the first time the glove he was wearing was made of human skin. Blackened and crispy and gnarled at the edges, but skin all the same. Complete with fingerprints.

"You bloody genius. Why didn't I think of that?"

"See?" he told her. "Not just a pretty face. I got skills, baby. You don't have to worry about me. So, are we doing this?"

Acid squinted up through the trees at the resort complex. The morning sun had now found its place over the far side of the island, reflecting off the glass and metal structure. It was going to be another hot day.

"All right, you win," she said, throwing the AK-47 over her shoulder. "We're doing this."

CHAPTER 31

House rules in Engel's resort complex clearly stated that no one, guests and staff alike, should run anywhere. To even walk at pace was frowned upon. The way the enigmatic billionaire had explained it to his guests at the elaborate drinks reception, was the resort offered a tranquil and serene experience. Free from bluster and stress. The perfect antidote to the madness and gore of the hunt. It was, he told them (employing that flawless smile of his), like experiencing heaven and hell all at once. Damnation and paradise. They could spend the day living out their most base animal instincts and at night castigate their sins in the various spas and saunas on offer, and even, if they so wanted, receive a visit from one of Engel's famous Pleasure Maidens.

These rules, of calmness and composure at all times, endured throughout the entire complex. The corridors of the upper floors were the same as the grand entrance hall and the lounge areas. No running. Minimal noise. But that didn't stop Raaz Terabyte from panting loudly as she raced from her own meagre room, down two flights of stairs, and along the lengthy corridor that wound around the side of the complex towards her boss's vast suite.

She banged on the door with the heel of her fist. "Caesar?" she whispered, remembering the house rules at last. "Are you in there?"

There was no response, but she could hear movement. Finally, the door opened ajar and the boss's bloodshot eye peered around the side.

"What time is it?"

Raaz swiped open the tablet in her hand and checked. "A few minutes after ten."

Caesar let out a groan. "Wait there a moment."

He closed the door, leaving Raaz bouncing from foot to foot. She was excited and had been awake since before eight. She had news. Good news. Annihilation Pest Control would finally be rid of those meddling women. And all without Caesar having to get his hands dirty. Raaz had long suspected the boss still harboured a soft spot for Acid Vanilla. This was one reason why - when she'd heard about the it from a contact in the US - she'd thought the hunt to be the perfect way for them to kill three birds with one stone. Acid and Spook being the first two birds, the third being the fact that bringing them here reaffirmed Annihilation Pest Control's position as the go-to organisation for the rich and powerful who had troublesome pests they needed rid of.

Because whilst the finger of blame had never been explicitly pointed Caesar's way, Raaz had seen the jobs dry up somewhat since Kent Clarkson's death and the chaos surrounding Acid's defection. But not for much longer. After this weekend all would be forgotten. Acid Vanilla and Spook Horowitz would be dead, and Caesar would once more take his place as the head of the most elite assassin network in the world.

Raaz paused, hearing movement behind the door. Voices. "Hey boss, I… Oh."

She stepped back as a tall blond Adonis-like security guard scuttled past her and headed off down the corridor. She watched Caesar watching the man leave, his well-defined eyebrows twitching wantonly.

"Sorry about that," he purred. "Just making use of the facilities one more time before I get ready for the ceremony."

He stepped aside to allow Raaz to enter, his silk kimono (floor-length, she was glad to note) swishing elegantly as he beckoned her into his suite. One step inside and Raaz was wishing she'd asked to meet downstairs in the lounge. The air was thick with the stench of sweat and sex and spilt alcohol. Empty bottles and brightly coloured sex toys, along with various knives and other bits of weaponry, had been strewn around the room. Raaz headed for the couch over on the far side of the room, averting her eyes as much as possible.

"Sit down," Caesar told her, positioning himself on the opposite end and crossing one leg over the other. "What have you got for me?"

Raaz brushed a questionable-looking magazine to one side and perched on the soft cushion. She held up the tablet. "We've got them," she said. "Best of all, they're going to be part of the ceremony. You know what that means."

Caesar's face didn't move, but Raaz noticed a slight tremor at the corner of one eye. She'd been watching for it.

"Both of them?" he asked.

Raaz nodded, brushing past the boss's hesitance. "Yes, sir. What a day it's going to be. It's been a long time coming."

For Raaz, this was the understatement of the year. She bit her lip, thinking of her fallen colleagues. Those Acid had killed since she screwed the organisation over and went rogue. Banjo, Barabbas, Hargreaves, even. Not to mention Davros and Spitfire. Why the boss wasn't absolutely ecstatic over the news got to her. But it was what she'd come to expect whenever Acid was involved. Which was why she'd orchestrated it so her imminent demise was no longer Caesar's call.

"Didn't Karen say Acid was at the bottom of a cliff?" he asked. "I did wonder. I told Engel he should be careful. That he underestimated Acid at his peril. But he just shrugged it off. Thinks he's untouchable. Well, we both know how that turns out." He looked away, out the window.

"You're not regretting this, are you?" Raaz asked. "You do understand we need them dead. It's the only way we can rebuild, both in terms of our reputation and future recruitment. I had some strong contenders lined up for our vacancies. But they've gone elsewhere. Because of her and her vendetta against us."

"Yes, I am aware, Raaz," Caesar bellowed. "Don't confuse my thoughtfulness with weakness. Or me going soft. Don't you forget it was my idea to blow Acid up that night. I wasn't simply sending her a message. I wanted her dead and I still do."

Raaz sat upright. "Apologies, I spoke out of line. But don't worry, by the end of today she'll be no more. Look."

She tapped on the tablet screen and brought up a video. Footage she'd ripped from Engel's closed-circuit camera system. The camera angle wasn't great, and the quality grainy, but she'd recognise that leather jacket anywhere.

"And there she bloody well is," Caesar growled, leaning closer. "Along with Spank Hornybitch, or whatever the pissing fuck she's called. Where is this?"

"Engel has cells on the lower level," Raaz told him. "They're being held there before the ceremony. This footage is from earlier."

Caesar sat back, allowing the kimono to ride up, exposing a huge flank of white thigh. "Karen Clarkson still thinks she's killed her."

"Well Karen Clarkson is wrong. Sir."

Caesar closed his eyes, head rocking slowly back and forth. "So here we are. I'll get to see it. The death of Acid Vanilla. Well done, Raaz. We'll be back in business in no time. In fact, after this weekend I'd say Annihilation is only going to go from strength to strength. Engel has already mentioned he may have a job for us. Luther, too. Outstanding work."

Raaz stood. "You'll be coming to the ceremony?"

"Try and stop me. But I need a shower and a pick-me-up of

some kind." He glanced about him. "Send someone up with a jug of strong coffee and one of Engel's special injections, will you? Have you had one yet? Absolutely spaffing marvellous. I feel like a new man. In fact, bring me one of those as well."

Raaz frowned, clutching the tablet to her chest. "Excuse me?"

Caesar waved her away. "Never mind. I'll see you later. Come get me before everyone leaves. We'll travel to the ceremony together."

Raaz clicked her heels and hurried past the seedy detritus in the room. But as she got to the door, she paused and turned back to her boss.

"We did it, sir," she said. "I mean, you did it. Annihilation Pest Control are back where we belong. At the top."

"That we are," Caesar bellowed, throwing his arms over the back of the couch. "That we bastard-well-are."

CHAPTER 32

A few doors down from Beowulf Caesar's suite, Luther Clarkson was examining the label on a well-chilled bottle of a 2009 Dom Perignon. Then, holding the bottle at the prescribed forty-five degrees, he twisted out the cork, letting the gassy build-up send it flying across the room with a satisfying pop.

Karen rolled her eyes at her brother's gaucheness (only idiots and poor people sent the cork flying off like a pop gun) but held her glass up all the same, biting her tongue as Luther poured out the sparkling wine.

"Thanks, Luth," she said. "We drinking to me? The undisputed champion of this year's hunt?"

"Whatever, Karen." Luther said, concentrating on filling his own glass and making a real mess of it, the foam rising up over the rim. "You got lucky, that's all."

"Oh, dear. Jealous much?"

"Not at all. To be honest with you, I'm glad it's over."

"And glad those bitches are dead, right? Or will be soon." She raised her glass as Luther did the same. "So here's to Kent Clarkson, may he rest in peace."

They chinked glasses and drank. The bubbles tickled Karen's

nose. She wasn't a big drinker. Eggnog at Christmas, a glass of fizz on special occasions, that was it. She looked about the room for inspiration, something to talk about. Luther wasn't a great conversationalist at the best of times but this morning he seemed particularly stoic. She was still grasping at straws when there was a knock on the door. Thank god.

Luther frowned. "Are we expecting someone?"

"Not me."

"Hello," her brother called over. "You can come in. It's open."

The words had barely left his mouth, when the door swung open and Thomas Engel bounded into the room followed by two female guards. They were all wearing the same long, flowing white robes.

"Well look at you, all fancy," Karen cooed, flirting a little as she took in their host's attire and the gold ceremonial garland hanging around his neck.

"Why, thank you," Engel said, spinning around so they could get the full effect. He held up the garland. "This once belonged to an actual Mayan priest. It's ceremonial. Worn when making sacrifices to the sun god. Kind of fitting."

"Indeed," Luther told him. "Drink?"

"Not while I'm working."

Karen moved closer. "So you're an integral part of the ceremony, I take it?"

"Of course," Engel said, clapping his hands together. "I love it. Favourite part of the weekend. You'll see."

Karen drank back her champagne. "And have we finalised the scores? I think it's only right one of the Clarksons win this year. Seeing as we've put up most of the prize fund."

"Let's not talk money," Engel purred, his face crumpling around the edges. "But I do hope you and your brother know how grateful we are you've joined us this weekend. It's been an interesting year for the hunt, but with your input especially, Ms Clarkson, it has once again been a triumph."

"Well, all right then," Karen said, her cheeks burning as Engel threw a wink her way. "You're very welcome. Isn't he, Luth?"

Her brother, ever the petulant middle child, shrugged. "I suppose. I got my fair share of hides out there too, you know. I'm not sure it's entirely fair Jenny Come-Lately here is allowed to take part."

"Ah, save it," Karen scolded, but smiling for once. "We've all had a good time, and we achieved what we wanted from the weekend."

"Exactly," Engel beamed, raising his arms in a self-conscious Christ-pose. "So why don't we now vacate to the arena basin and take our seats for the final act of the hunt. The closing ceremony." He placed an arm around Karen, sliding his hand down to the small of her back and guiding her out of the room.

"Did your men get confirmation on Acid Vanilla?" she asked him.

"Please don't worry," he told her. "All is taken care of."

But the way he said it, followed by a pensive glance at one of his guards, made Karen uneasy.

"She's definitely dead?"

Engel swallowed, his face melting into a colossal grin. "Absolutely," he told her. "Couldn't be more dead."

"Well, good. Make sure she's added to my score." Karen turned around so Luther could hear. "I want it on record it was me who took down both of Kent's killers. Both bitches."

Luther screwed his nose up at her. Mouthed, *Fucking loser*.

Karen turned her attention back to Engel, the unease dropping away, revelling now in the attention. "You know, Tommy, I was a little tired earlier, but I'm really looking forward to this ceremony of yours. I've heard good things about it. Very good things."

At this Engel stopped and turned to her, taking in Luther as well. A supercilious smile curled his full lips. "Oh, my dears," he whispered. "You have no idea. No idea at all."

"What, it's really that special?" Luther asked.

Engel smirked. "All I'll say for now is, if you thought the hunt was fun, if you thought it pushed certain… boundaries, shall we say – then just you wait until you see what's coming next."

CHAPTER 33

"So you're really an FBI guy?" Acid asked.

The question hung pointedly in the air, breaking the hour-long silence that had fallen between her and Welles as they climbed the uneven stone steps leading up to the resort complex.

"FBI Guy?" Welles mused. "I like that. Sounds like the title of an old disco track or something."

Acid rolled her eyes at the blue sky above. Nice reference. Shame it was fifty years out of date. Behind her Welles began singing to himself, the way he thought *FBI Guy,* the disco song, might go. From Acid's reckoning it was pretty much The Village People's *Macho Man,* but with the different lyrics.

F-B-I-I Guy…

She huffed loudly and made a show of shaking her head. Thankfully it had the desired effect. Welles shut up.

"Just trying to lighten the mood," he told her. "But to answer your question: yes, I've been at the Bureau for twenty years now. Before that, I was a detective. Downtown LA, mainly."

"I see. I suppose you've been in worse situations than this then?"

He gave a gruff chuckle, but there was no joy to it. "Let's just say, Lincoln Heights in the late seventies, early eighties, wasn't the nicest of places. Lot of drug use, people killing each other. And that was just the cops." The laughter grew louder, turning into a wheezing cough.

Acid turned to face him. "Do you need to rest for a minute?"

Welles regained his composure and shook his head sternly. "No time for rest, miss. We gotta get up there."

"You can call me Acid, you know," she told him, carrying on up the steps. "I don't really respond to *miss*."

"Apologies, old habits, like I say. Not sure I'll get used to calling someone Acid, though. That your real name?"

She tensed. "It wasn't the name my mother gave me, if that's what you mean, but it is now. The person I was died a long time ago. Acid Vanilla is all that's left."

"I see."

Silently she cursed herself as she went on with the climb. It was one of those moments when you experienced yourself through the eyes of someone else and realised you sounded like a complete wanker. Or a pretentious weirdo. But then again, maybe Acid had already made peace with the fact she was both those things.

"So can I ask you – as an *FBI Guy* – you ever heard of Annihilation Pest Control?" She glanced back over her shoulder, but Welles' face was blank.

"Doesn't ring any bells. Should I have?"

"No, you shouldn't."

It always surprised her how clever Caesar had been, keeping the organisation off all law enforcement radar for the past twenty-five years.

"So I take it Sofia was right?" Welles asked. "You are a hit man. Sorry – hit woman."

"She told you that?"

"Is it true?"

Acid tensed. Spook's voice in her head. *Trust people.* That old shit again.

She looked Welles up and down. He was getting on, and life had clearly toughened him, but he still had a twinkle in his eye. She liked that, and he seemed a decent enough guy, but what the hell did she know about decent guys? And he was a Bureau guy after all.

She threw her gaze back up the mountain side. They were almost at the point where the steps crumbled away.

Sod it.

In the current situation, what the hell did she have to lose?

"I was a *hired killer* for sixteen years," she told him. "Since I was eighteen. Until six months ago."

"What happened six months ago?"

"I met someone who made me see there was a different way."

She swallowed down a sigh. The thought of Spook up there scared and alone rocked her. Poor kid. She could be annoying as hell sometimes but she was good to have around. Acid didn't tell her that enough. And now she might not have the chance.

"I'd been wanting out of the game for a while," she went on. "But I don't think I'd really articulated it to myself properly. Spook made me realise I could take control over my future."

She moved aside as Welles joined her at the last step. They stood in silence, considering the three ledges they'd need to scale to reach the summit.

"We're going to get them back," he whispered. "Don't you worry about that."

Acid nodded. "You going to be okay making this jump?

He raised his head. "Piece a cake."

"You want to go first or second?"

"I'll go first."

Acid was surprised and rather impressed with the old guy's agility. After over-egging the first jump and almost stumbling off the far side, he took the next two in his stride and made getting up the final six feet look like a walk in the park.

She, of course, knew the pitfalls already and followed his lead as swiftly as possible, much easier now without the addition of that toxic sow and the boot to the face. Once on the final ledge she grabbed for Welles' arm and he pulled her up onto the headland.

"Over there," he said, pointing to a small door in the side of the complex, half-hidden behind a cluster of rocks and a row of decorative fig trees. "Looks like a staff entrance. Hopefully means it's unlocked."

They moved over to the door in haste. Welles got there first and waited for her before trying the handle.

"We need to do this as stealthily as possible," she whispered. "The last thing we need is the entire security team bearing down on us."

"Agreed," he rasped, gripping the door handle and easing it open. "Ready?"

"Ready."

Acid held the AK-47 to her chest and slipped through the door, followed close behind by Welles. Once both inside, he gently closed the door, plunging the long steel-wrapped corridor into darkness. Acid blinked into the gloom, aware at once of how cool the air was in here. A shock to the system after the heady, sticky heat of the island. Moving together, they got to the end of the corridor and found another door. Welles did the honours once more, Acid leading with the assault rifle. Through the door and they were in what looked to be an entrance hall, a large white room with high ceilings and enormous windows placed at intervals along the wall opposite. There was no one in sight. Slowly, tentatively, Acid moved into the space, keeping her aim high.

"It's clear," she whispered.

Welles was beside her in a moment. "Okay, first step. We need to find me some firepower."

Acid agreed. Over by the far wall in front of one of the windows, a small lounge area had been set up comprising of two cream leather couches, which were so huge in scale they could have been modern art pieces. Beyond the couches, in the right-hand corner of the room was another door. Without a word they made their way over there, Acid walking backwards as they got closer, covering them.

"Looks like stairs. Going up," Welles whispered, peering through the glass panel half-way up. He eased open the door and she hurried through, taking the steps two at a time.

They reached a small L-shaped landing with another set of stairs on the far side and a door with a small metal sign, top centre: *Main Vestibule.* Attached to the wall to the left of the door was a bright red fire extinguisher.

Acid waited by the door for Welles to join her and gestured for him to take it. "Might come in useful," she added.

"You want me to drown them in foam?"

"If you want," she replied. "I was thinking you'd use the blunt end to smash someone's skull in, but either way."

Welles shook his head but took the extinguisher all the same. He held it with two hands, like a battering ram. "Through here," he told her. "I reckon this will give us access to the rest of the building."

Acid put her back to the door. Holding the assault rifle in one hand, she pushed down on the door handle and leaned against it. The door eased open no problem and she spun around, her trigger finger taut and ready, but once more the space was deserted. Over to her left she noted the main entrance. An impressive cut-crystal chandelier hung down over the space whilst on either side of the enormous doorway, two fire pits burned aggressively, encased in elaborately carved marble surrounds. In the centre of the room lay an expansive white fur rug, doing its best to soften the hard marble floor. Off to one side, two more modern-art-sized couches were positioned in a U-shape around a low table, on top of which was stood a large antique vase, spilling over with stark white lilies and pink orchids. Opposite this seating, at one end of the room, Acid spotted a steel-fronted elevator and a wide, open doorway with brightly decorated urns standing guard on either side, each one as tall as Welles and twice as wide. Through the doorway, a wide corridor rendered in cream marble led off from the main space before disappearing around to the right. Thomas Engel, it seemed, was a real fan of marble. Which was lucky for Acid and Welles, as it carried the sound of distant footsteps down the corridor long before whoever it was came into view.

"Over here," Acid rasped, hurrying over and positioning herself around the side of one of the urns. Welles copied her on the other side and they waited, poised with fire extinguisher and assault rifle.

The footsteps grew louder. Female, it seemed. The distinct click-clack of heels on a hard surface. Acid sucked in a deep breath, holding it in her lungs for a three-count before releasing. Next she did the same with the muscles in her arms and legs, tightening for three, then releasing. It was a way of grounding herself in her body, readying herself for action. She placed the assault rifle on the floor by her feet, careful not to make a sound. She'd meant what she'd told Welles. This was a stealth mission. No need to get messy and chaotic if she didn't need to, no matter how much enjoyment it might fleetingly provide. She closed her eyes, listening as the click of the heels fell out of time with the clack. Meant there was two of them. Behind the urn on the other side of the doorway, she could make out the top of Welles' head. Could she trust him to do what was needed?

She pressed herself against the cold porcelain urn as two women marched past her into the main space. They were each well over six foot, with icy blonde hair dragged back into a tight bun. Guards on patrol, although the uniform of white flowing robes was an odd choice. As they shimmied into the room, the soft silk hugged their athletic frames, revealing the unmistakeable shape of a holster and pistol strapped to their hips. Jackpot.

Staying low, Acid crept out from behind the urn. A glance to her right told her Welles was following her lead as she padded towards the nearest guard, approaching in a semi-circle and not taking her eyes off her. The woman had a good few inches on Acid, but that wasn't a problem. She'd taken down bigger and uglier many times before. A quick nod to Welles and she went for it, leaping up onto the guard's back and wrapping one arm around her neck. The woman clawed at her, tried to scream, but Acid was applying enough pressure on her throat it came out as a confused grunt. At the same time, Welles was on the second woman choking her out the same way. Most people (civilians) think a choke hold is all about cutting off the person's air supply, but that's a messy way of doing it, and can take up to a minute to render someone unconscious. You want to knock someone out in under ten seconds, then you go for the carotid artery in the side of the neck. You get that right and you cut off vital blood supply to the brain. Acid held on tight, riding the tall guard and applying more pressure. One last gasp and she collapsed to the floor. Acid jumped free in time and composed herself before rolling the fallen guard onto her back.

"Now that's more like it," she purred, lifting up the robe and removing a Taurus PT111 from the woman's belt. She held it up, feeling the reassuring weight in her fist. She looked over at Welles. "You good?"

"Yeah," he said, getting to his feet and holding up a matching pistol. "No sweat."

"Cool. Let's go. The elevator."

Before Welles had chance to respond, she was already over there and stabbing her finger on the round silver button displaying an up arrow.

"You sure about this?" Welles asked as the doors sucked open and they stepped inside. "What are we gonna walk in on?"

"No idea." Acid shrugged. "But screw it. What have we got to lose?"

CHAPTER 34

As the elevator doors glided shut Acid scanned the control panel, opting for the button marked *Viewing Platform* and jabbing at it a few times for good measure. As the metal box shuddered into life, she glanced at Welles.

His face said it all.

What the hell have I gotten myself into?

Who is this crazy woman?

Acid knew the expression well. She'd seen it on the face of pretty much everyone she'd ever worked with. Man and woman. One more reason she preferred working alone. But regardless, she was enjoying herself. Taking down those guards just now had hit every one of her pleasure receptors. She felt powerful, unstoppable, and she wanted more. Even if a part of her knew this was all part of her condition. Millions of chemical equations erupting across her nervous system, making her feel invincible.

If she had time to consider her current heightened state from a logical perspective, she might tell herself to slow down. To step careful. She knew from experience that being this way was a double-edged sword. On one hand, the manic energy surging through her system allowed her to take insane risks, do things no one expected of her. But on the other hand, it made her take insane risks, do things even she didn't expect.

Either way, the bats were in charge. They were ready, and they wanted blood. As the elevator slowed to a stop, she raised the Taurus, put one in the chamber. Next to her, Welles got into a firing position.

Time to go to work.

The doors slid open and they vacated the elevator swiftly, leading with their pistols and moving around the space, covering the area from both sides. It took them all of three seconds to discover the room was empty. Acid lowered her weapon, taking in the huge open-plan room. Part of it had been set up as a lounge area with high-backed leather seats and round dark mahogany side tables. The seating area had been positioned so it faced a large glass wall, and beyond it the lush greenery of the island. On the opposite wall, a marble-topped bar displayed an extensive selection of expensive liquor bottles and buckets of ice. Acid's eyes grew wide at the sight of it all.

"Not the best of ideas," Welles said, reading her mind.

"Just a little one?" she pined, holding her finger and thumb up to exemplify the tiny amount she was considering.

"You serious?"

She let her shoulders drop defensively. "I don't know. Probably not. Half the time even I can't tell whether I'm joking or not."

Welles didn't reply, but the look he gave her said it all. Same look he'd given her in the elevator. Maybe it was time for Acid to stay quiet and let her actions do the talking.

Leaving the pull of the liquor bottles behind, she moved over to a high table on the adjacent wall. It was made of the same dark mahogany as the other tables. On top was a pile of cards coloured a pale yellow. Acid picked one up and scanned the page, her lip curling with anger as she did.

"What you got there?" Welles asked, coming over.

Acid held the card up so he could see. "Scorecards," she told him. "Sick bastards."

Each card pertained to a different member of this year's hunting party. The one Acid had hold of belonged to a Peter Van Tam. Never heard of the guy, but no doubt he was another of Engel's nefarious billionaire acquaintances. He was also dead, if the large red stamp reading DECEASED was to be believed. At least that was something. The people they'd brought to the island, those being hunted, none of them had gone down without a fight.

"Let me see." Welles took the card from her, shaking his head incredulously as he read. "Shit. It really is a game to these people." He chucked it back on the tabletop. "You know, I wish I could say it was a shock, that happens. But it's not. Not really."

"And people say my old line of work was bad." Acid sniffed, her eyes scanning the names on the other scorecards. "Yet the people I killed – corrupt politicians, despots, cartel bosses – you ask me, they always deserved it."

Welles didn't look convinced. "That what you tell yourself? Because—"

"Oh, spare me the fucking speech," she said, rolling her eyes. "I haven't got time for a lecture."

She was already striding towards the elevator when it shuddered into action, the light display above showing it coming down from an upper level. They darted towards it and splayed themselves against the wall as the elevator doors slid open.

A short man wearing a terrible outfit of oversized board shorts and a light blue polo shirt wandered aimlessly into the room. His thick brown hair was sticking out at all angles, as though he'd only recently got out of bed. Acid shot Welles a confused glance. Got an over-the-top shrug in response. The man was standing in half-profile a few feet from her, his face illuminated by the tablet he was furiously swiping at. He looked to be in his late twenties, maybe younger, if the smattering of puss-filled spots around his mouth was any sign. Though as he nervously touched his fingers to his chin, she reasoned it was likely this tick, rather than adolescent hormones, that was responsible for the repellent red and yellow display.

Welles widened his eyes at her. *What do we do?* But Acid had already decided. Gripping the Taurus handle tight, she strode over to the man and pushed the gun muzzle into his cheek.

"Make a sound and you're dead," she told him.

The man let out a squeak and held his hands up. "Don't shoot," he whimpered. "Please."

"Who are you?" she asked.

The man looked at her feebly and pulled a face. "J-J-Jerry," he stammered. "Jerry Mankowitz. I'm Luther Clarkson's personal assistant. Please don't kill me."

She adjusted her grip on the gun as Welles stepped over to join them. He flapped his hands, making a silent whistling motion. Doing that annoying thing people did when they were trying to calm a situation. The effect was it only wound her up more. The bats were screaming.

"Where is everyone, Jerry?" Welles asked, keeping his tone steady and his voice friendly. A typical cop.

Jerry looked frantically from Welles to Acid and back again, perhaps assessing who the leader was. To help him with his decision, Acid raised the Taurus and smacked him on the top of the head with the barrel.

"He asked you a question, dickhead."

"Okay, okay," Jerry said. "But if you're here looking to save those girls, you're already too late."

"What does that mean?" she asked him. Another answer like that and Jerry was going to get his brains painted all over the elevator doors.

He gestured meekly out the window. "You can see for yourself."

Acid shoved the kid at Welles. "If he moves, kill him."

With Jerry whimpering in her wake, she marched over to the window. Down below a trail of jeeps leaving the complex and driving down a wide track that ran around the side of the island. There were four people in each jeep. A driver, two passengers and an armed security guard hanging out the back. The fact the guards were poised with assault rifles and scanning the surrounding area told her they weren't there for show. They knew Acid and Welles were still alive, and they weren't taking any chances.

"Where are they going?" she asked Jerry, not turning from the window.

"Don't you know?" he replied, a twinge of peevishness undercutting his whine. "The closing ceremony starts in one hour."

Acid narrowed her eyes at the last jeep leaving the complex. Along with the security guards, there were three women onboard. In the front seat, a tall woman dressed in a white robe, blonde hair tied up in a bun. Same get-up as the guards downstairs. But she wasn't the reason Acid's breath caught in her throat. On the back seat, huddled together, were sat two smaller women with dark hair. Despite the weird, leafy outfits and bizarre headdresses, Acid recognised them straight away. She watched the jeep disappear around the side of a large rock formation before moving her attention back to Jerry.

"Where is it held?" she demanded. "How do we get there?"

"I don't know."

"You don't know? You don't bloody well know?" In a beat, Acid was on him. She grabbed the snivelling wretch by the collar and flung him over her hip. He landed on his back and didn't have time to catch his breath before she was straddling him with a knee on each arm, the muzzle of the Taurus into the middle of his forehead.

"I'm just an assistant," he cried, any hint of bravado now gone. "I'm only here because Mr Clarkson sent me to fetch his scorecard."

"Yes, we've seen them."

"Well, you've also seen that my name isn't on one. Take a look. Jerry Mankowitz. I don't have one, because I've not killed anyone. I would never. I swear."

"But you're here. With them. Enabling them," Acid rasped, spittle flying from her lips. She screwed the gun into his skull.

"That's as good as guilty in my book. So talk, or *I* swear, I'll kill you."

She sensed Welles beside her, silently judging her, but she didn't care. He had his values. She had hers. She'd kill him too if she had to. She leaned over Jerry, her finger twitching on the trigger. There was no idle threat here. Right now she wanted to kill him more than anything she'd ever wanted in her life. But the intensity of her stare, the ferocity of her demeanour. It also had the desired effect.

"Fine. Fine," Jerry spluttered, not taking his eyes from Acid's. "The ceremony is held in the arena basin over on the south-east of the island. You can get to it by driving along the track that runs down along the east side."

"Driving?"

"There's a big garage on the lowest level," he said, screwing his eyes shut and sending tears cascading into his hair. "There's a bunch of jeeps. There'll be extra, I'm sure of it. Take the elevator down to the entrance hall and then go along a corridor which leads to another elevator down."

"Do we need codes? Any access issue?"

Jerry shook his head. Tried to, at least. Difficult with the gun pressing down hard. "No. Mr Engel is pretty relaxed about that kind of thing. I guess you can be when you own the island and have a security team like he has. They're dangerous, you know?"

"Yes? So am I," Acid told him. "Thanks for that, Jerry. I guess you're now surplus to requirements."

"Oh shit. No," he wailed, appealing to Welles. "Man, I don't want to die. I'm just an assistant. I'm not one of these people. I make less than fifty grand a year, for fuck's sake. I just got caught up... I never..."

Acid didn't move. Her trigger finger was white with tension. She heard Welles say something to her, but the words swam into the ether before they registered. The bats though, she could hear. Kill him, they told her. He deserves to die. Think of Spook.

Spook?

It might have been Jerry's wounded expression, or that look in his eyes, a mixture of confusion and fear – it might have just been his nerdy, thick-rimmed glasses – but in that moment Acid saw her friend staring back at her.

Bollocks.

She glanced up at Welles.

"Hey, you do what you have to do," he told her.

Great. Not what she wanted to hear. She turned back to Jerry, her hand quivering on the trigger of the Taurus.

Do it.

Do it.

She lifted the gun, the muzzle leaving a fleshy indent on Jerry's forehead. "You're bloody lucky I've got a cop with me," she said. "Otherwise you'd be dead."

She spun the pistol around so she was holding it by the barrel and smashed it around the side of the kid's head, knocking him out cold.

"He got off lightly," she told Welles, ignoring his arched brow as they raced over to call the elevator. "Now let's get down to those jeeps. We've got a closing ceremony to crash."

CHAPTER 35

Spook leaned into Sofia, lowering her voice in case the other passengers heard. "Do you really think he's still out there? Your friend?"

Sofia looked straight ahead, her head rocking inadvertently from side to side as the jeep negotiated the uneven terrain. "He ain't my friend," she whispered back. "But he seemed legit. A Bureau guy. Knows what he's doing."

"So we've still got a chance," Spook told her. Told herself. She gripped Sofia's upper arm in way of reassurance. This too done more for her own benefit than that of the gruff New Yorker. "Acid's tough as hell," she added. "I don't believe she's dead."

Sofia let out a loud sigh. She might as well have said, *Don't be so ridiculous. It's over.*

Because it was. Wasn't it?

Spook could tell herself whatever she wanted, send herself crazy with a bunch of empty words and gestures, but deep down she knew the truth. She was going to die today. Here on this island. And for what? So a group of braying billionaires could have a good laugh at her expense.

She peered out at the dense jungle that spread out over the mountainous landscape. Above them, the hot sun was already making its presence felt. She had a passing thought to mention how the journey was reminiscent of Han and Luke being taken to the Sarlacc pit in Return of the Jedi, but she thought better of it. That was her disassociating again, and she'd promised herself she wouldn't do it. Even when, by rights, it would most definitely help. Take away this tightness in her throat. The shakes in her hands. The other reason she didn't say it, was she suspected Sofia wouldn't get the reference. No one did these days. But that was Spook's generation for you. Millennials. Even Acid Vanilla would get a Star Wars reference, and that was saying something.

She sat back, fiddling with one of the large leaves that made up the dress skirt she was wearing. "Please, Acid," she whispered. "Please be alive. Please save us."

Beside her Sofia took a sharp intake of breath. "Motherfucker."

"What is it?" Spook asked, but as soon as the question had left her mouth she knew what Sofia was referring to.

In another hundred yards the track sloped down to a large clearing. Spook's old geography knowledge told her this was once a lake. The flat surface giving it away. The grass here had been cut back uniformly. Short and tidy, like a football field. Around the outside of the basin were two rows of seats, with a small wicker table set up beside each seat all the way along. A set of binoculars and a decanter of water on each table. A little way from the seating in the centre of the arena, a small stage had been set up, no more than ten metres wide with rich purple velvet draped over the entire structure. On each side of the stage (more like an altar, come to think of it) stood marble plinths holding flaming torches, grey, wispy smoke spiralling into the blue dome above. It was an imposing sight, but not the reason for the goose bumps or the shiver of icy fear coursing through Spook's body. Because behind the altar, towering at least twenty foot over the arena basin, was a large wooden totem pole, chilling in its grandness.

"What the hell?"

Spook took in the wooden structure. The top section had been carved into the head of a goat, painted white with devilish red eyes. It leered down on them with a ghoulish grin as the jeep got nearer. Underneath the goat, Spook made out the carvings of two human heads, ugly and distorted, one on top of the other, and identical except for the paint work. One pink, one brown, with insane, rolling eyes that dripped with cartoon tears. Spook gasped back a sharp breath as she noticed the heads were hollow and the eyes small windows about the size of her head. A small door hung open at the side of each of the heads revealing the space inside. Big enough for a person. The final section of the totem pole was an actual devil, classic, macabre, and painted bright red, with a forked tail wrapped around the grotesque squat body. A large hooked nose hanging over two rows of sharp yellow teeth completed the look. The entire structure was unsettling, but it was what had been placed around the devil's feet that made Spook cry out.

"Sofia," she said, turning to her fellow prisoner. "They're going to…"

"Yeah. I know," she replied, not taking her eyes off the bundles of straw and dry timber. "They're going to set fire to that thing. With us inside."

Spook's stomach back-flipped as the jeep came to a stop in front of the imposing monolith.

"End of the road, ladies."

Spook looked over her shoulder and was met with the yawning mouth of a large rifle. The guard holding it gestured towards the door where Sofia was being dragged out by one of Engel's female security team. He snarled at Spook, "Get out."

Without a word she shuffled along the bench seat and followed on behind Sofia. Now, under the vigilant watch of more armed guards, they were shepherded around to the front of the jeep where they stood side by side, arms folded over the ridiculous, leaf-covered bra-tops they'd been forced to wear. More jeeps were arriving now, people taking their place in the seating area.

"Get them into position," a voice ordered.

Spook's breath caught in her throat as a man stepped into view carrying a wooden ladder. He placed it up against the malevolent carved structure and backed away.

"You first," the female guard said, pointing a rifle at Sofia.

"What you going to do?" Sofia said. "Shoot me? Well go for it, hun. What the hell have I got to lose?"

The outburst got her a backhand across her face, the force sending her stumbling over onto one knee before a rifle butt around the side of the head finished the job. She fell to the floor unconscious.

"Sofia," Spook yelled, but shut up quickly as the cold end of a rifle was stabbed into her kidneys.

All she could do was watch as a burly male guard grabbed up Sofia's limp body and flung her over his shoulder. The fact he made a joke of smacking her ass as he walked her over to the ladder sent waves of impotent rage shooting up Spook's spine. The effect was emboldening, but just like always, her pathetic, useless timidity took over and left her with no clue what to do with that feeling. The frustration and anger only grew inside of her as Sofia was placed inside the top head and the door tied shut with a length of thick rope.

The guard slid down the ladder and eyeballed her. "You're next," he told her, with a glint in his eye. "You want to do hard way or easy way?"

She shuffled quickly over to the bottom of the ladder as he positioned it alongside the lower door. She hated herself for being so subservient, but she hated the idea of being smashed in the head with a blunt instrument more.

The guard laughed at her as she climbed up the rickety ladder. Difficult when your entire body was shaking with an uneasy mix of adrenaline and trepidation. After pausing on a middle rung to compose herself, she managed to climb the remaining three feet and haul herself inside the hollow head. Through the eye holes she could see out across the arena basin. Back at the holding cell, the older and more sour-faced member of Engel's wardrobe department had wanted to remove Spook's glasses. They detracted from the overall look, she'd said. But luckily (or unluckily, depending on your point of view) she'd been talked around by her colleague, who'd argued the guests would want to see Spook as they remembered her, and to enjoy her terror when she saw with sharp clarity the horror that awaited her.

"Spook, you down there?" It was Sofia. Her voice sounded shaky, but she was awake. She was alive.

"Yeah, I'm here," Spook called back. "You okay?"

"Am I okay? You serious?"

"All right, you're not okay. You know what I mean. Your head."

Sofia grunted. "It hurts like hell and I've got a lump forming. But hey, look on the bright side, won't last for long."

Spook didn't know what to say, so she said nothing. Instead, she moved closer to the window and peered out as more guests arrived.

"Look at them all. Fat pigs," Sofia whispered. "See the Clarksons, sat over on the left?"

"I see them."

"I recognise a few of those old guys from somewhere, too. Congress, maybe. Wouldn't be surprised."

Spook leaned her forehead against the carved wood. "Why are they doing this? All that money and they still want to inflict pain on people."

"You don't get to be a billionaire without hurting people," Sofia replied. "This hunt, it's just an extension of what those pricks do every day. Screwing over the little guy, removing anyone who gets in their way, by any means necessary. It's boardroom aggression taken to the nth degree. The urban jungle transformed into a real one." She huffed loudly. "What a story. I could have really hit the big time—"

"You might still," Spook butted in. "There's a chance."

"Come off it," Sofia said, her voice cracking with emotion. "We're done for. No one's coming, Spook. The bad guys win. When there's money behind them they always do."

Spook frowned, searching her bewildered mind for a response. She wanted to tell Sofia she was wrong, but her heart wasn't in it. The minutes ticked away. Hot, sticky sweat poured down her face. There was no air inside the carved wooden heads. Like being in a sauna. Or an oven.

Or a bonfire.

Startled by the hyper-real ominousness of her plight, Spook scanned the crowds once more, hoping, praying she might catch a glimpse of her. Acid, coming to the rescue. But what she saw instead sent her spiralling even further.

"Caesar."

"What's that?" Sofia asked.

"See that bald guy wearing the lime-green safari suit? That's Beowulf Caesar. Acid's old boss. The head of Annihilation Pest Control."

"The big guy? I see him. Who's the broad next to him, with a face like a slapped ass?"

Spook swallowed back a mouthful of bile. "She calls herself Raaz Terabyte. She handles all the comms and tech for the organisation. And she's a fucking bitch."

"I see. You not a fan of this Raaz chick?"

"This is all her fault," she replied.

"How do you mean?"

"She's a techie. Like me. And yes, I'm aware she works for an assassin network, but she's never killed anyone. I didn't think it was cool she should have to die like the rest of them. I mentioned this to Acid, but she's got tunnel vision as far as her old organisation is concerned. All as bad as each other. All have to die."

"I can see her point."

"Yeah, well, I went looking for Raaz. It sounds dumb, but I figured if I could talk to her, I could convince her to leave Annihilation. To disappear. Save herself."

She paused. She could sense Sofia shaking her head in disbelief.

"And that didn't go to plan?"

"She knew I was coming. She used me as bait to get Acid there too."

"I take it that's why Ms Smiley-Personality wasn't too happy with you?"

"Yep." Spook leaned against the side of the wooden cell and slid to the floor.

"Sorry. I don't mean to be a bitch," Sofia told her. "Or use past tense. Because who knows, right, maybe she survived that fall. Maybe she's going to come storming through the trees and save us."

"You think?" Spook asked, unable to draw the strength to even sound optimistic.

"Weirder things have happened. We're not dead yet."

She was trying her best, Spook knew. Her words a vain attempt to keep both their spirits up. As this was usually the role Spook assigned herself, she appreciated the gesture. But then Sofia let out a desperate sigh from deep inside of her that negated all sense of hope, false or otherwise.

"What is it?"

Spook got to her feet as excited mutterings ran through the crowd. She peered through the window in time to see a lone figure striding over to the centre of the stage. Thomas Engel. The host of the hunt. The owner of Pain Island. Like many of his subordinates he was wearing a long flowing robe in white silk, but with the addition of gold ceremonial garland, resplendent with dark rubies and bright turquoise embedded in the metal.

"Look at him up there. Horrible fucker," Sofia rasped, as if reading Spook's thoughts. "Thinks he's a damn god or something."

Spook couldn't take her eyes off Engel, parading around the stage with his arms outstretched, smiling at the spectators as they settled down to watch. Young fresh-faced women sashayed between the seats, delivering drinks and small silver bowls containing unidentified snacks.

Engel let his hands drop and a silence fell over the arena.

"My exalted guests, welcome to the final day of the hunt and what many believe to be the most gratifying part of the weekend." His voice boomed out from unseen speakers, hidden in the trees that circled around the perimeter of the arena. "The ceremony will begin in a few minutes. But before then my girls will come around to deliver drinks and take any orders. Also, whilst you are aware that phones and any photographic equipment is banned from both my islands, some of you have had clearance for communication equipment. Please, let me reiterate the information that was on the contract you all signed. No recordings of any kind must be made of this ceremony."

Spook scanned her eyes over the seats, taking in the faces as they drank and ate and guffawed like noxious swine. They were loving this. Excited to be part of something so exclusive. So poisonously above the law.

"I also ask that you don't talk to anyone about your experience this weekend. Not only is it a little incriminating for all concerned, shall we say?" He paused as a murmur of laughter rippled around the crowd. "But we don't want to ruin the surprise, do we? So, whilst I encourage you to recommend the hunt to anyone you believe will be open to the experience, please do not breathe a word of what the weekend entails. Is that clear?"

A flurry of chattering movement drifted around those watching, a nodding of heads and utterings of agreement. Satisfied, Engel clasped his hands together and two women appeared carrying long batons of wood. They glided elegantly over to the side of the stage and faced the audience with the batons held high in the air. It was more pomp and ritual, but Spook guessed what those batons were for. The situation was getting tense.

"This don't look good for us," Sofia rasped. "You tried your door?"

Spook pushed at the heavy wood, already knowing the answer. "Yeah," she said, meekly. "Won't budge." She moved back to the window and pushed her face through the hole as Engel moved to the front of the stage.

"Listen up my friends," he told the crowds. "I know you're all desperate to get going with the revelry and debauchery. But if you will indulge me for a while longer, I need to check something with my people. I'll be back in a few minutes to say a few more words about the weekend, and to toast our fallen brothers and sisters. Then the fun really begins. We shall hand out the prizes for the weekend, reveal our top scorers, and then the moment you've all been waiting for." Here he put his back to the audience and gazed up at the totem pole. "We light the ceremonial totem and rid ourselves, both metaphorically and actually, of the wretched vermin that have threatened to undermine our important work."

As Engel's voice fell silent, Spook heard a soft wail from above. Sofia sobbing to herself. "This is so unfair," she whispered. "My poor Mikey. I'm so sorry, baby."

"Sofia, stop that," Spook said, finding something inside of her she didn't even know she had. "Don't give up. Not until you have to. I've been here before. There's still time for... something to happen."

"We're dead," Sofia cried. "*We* are the dead. We have to accept that. We have to. They're going to burn us. They're actually going to burn us."

Spook leaned against the cell wall and folded her arms. A part of her wanted to respond, to tell Sofia she was wrong, but the words weren't coming to her and maybe there was nothing more to say. Sofia was right, they were screwed. No one was coming for them. Acid Vanilla was dead, and dying with her was any chance Spook might have walked away from this in one piece. Give it another ten minutes and she and Sofia were toast. Quite literally.

CHAPTER 36

Acid slipped out the elevator before the doors slid all the way open, swiftly making her way along the steel-lined corridor that led to the main space of the complex's lower level.

"You know where you're going?" Welles asked, hurrying along in her wake.

Acid didn't answer. She was heading for an open doorway, half-way along the corridor on the opposite side. Once there she waited for Welles to catch up before giving him a knowing nod and gliding silently into the room. The Taurus PT111 led the way as she moved around sticking close to the walls. Empty.

"Some sort of holding cell?" Welles mused, walking over to the bed. "Are these…?"

"Yes, the clothes they were wearing." Acid hurried over and rifled through the dirty jeans and grass-stained shirts. She found what she was looking for and pulled it from the pile. "Thank god."

She held the leather jacket to her, the smell of it elevating her disposition significantly. To most people it was a fetid combination of stale beer, old perfume and a lifetime of blood, sweat and tears. But for Acid, it was the smell of her past. The smell of home.

"You all right?" Welles asked through a frown.

"That I am," Acid said, slipping her arm into the sleeve. "Your journalist friend stole it from me. It's good to have it back." She pulled it on and checked for damage. It was fine.

"Chicks and clothes. Can we go now?"

She ignored the comment, scanning her eyes over the room. Nothing else here. A basin of water, sponges, a few twigs and leaves. She moved back to the doorway and put her head around the side.

"All clear."

They vacated the cell and hurried along the corridor. At the end it opened out into a large room with a high ceiling and spaces marked out on the concrete floor for thirty vehicles. On the far side, the floor ramped down to an open hatch twenty feet across, through which could be seen the exotic greenery of the island. Just two jeeps remained over on the far side of the space, and hanging on the wall on the same side was a long gun rack. It had been emptied of most of its bounty, but three assault rifles remained.

"Over here," Acid yelled as she hurried over to the rack. "It'll be nice to arrive prepared."

She grabbed the nearest rifle, an M16, and held it up, testing the weight of it. It would never have been her weapon of choice. In her line of work, stealth and secrecy were more vital than heavy artillery. But what had Caesar drummed into her all those years? That a successful assassin must adapt to the situation? She pulled another rifle off the rack and flung it at Welles.

"Good spot," he growled, pulling it out of the air. "It's almost like they want us to spoil their fun."

Acid threw up an eyebrow. "Makes you think, doesn't it? Reckon it's a trap?"

"Not much we can do about it either way." He sniffed. "I'd say we're pretty much committed. But, no. You ask me, they're a bunch of arrogant bastards who don't stress the detail. They think they're untouchable."

"I hope you're right," she replied, hurrying over to the nearest jeep and jumping in the passenger seat.

"I'm driving?" Welles asked, climbing in beside her and fingering the keys already in the ignition.

"If it's all the same with you I want to keep my hands free," she said, positioning her rifle over the side of the vehicle. "Keep it steady, okay?"

"I'll try my best," he replied, firing up the engine and shoving the stick into gear.

The hot sun hit Acid in the face as they trundled down to level ground and Welles opened up the throttle. Even with the gentle breeze coming in from the ocean, the heat was oppressive. Sweat formed on her skin as she blinked a few times, adjusting her eyes to the brightness.

They drove in silence, the jeep speeding along the dusty track that looped around the side of the island. Welles leaned into each bend, not letting up on the gas and sending huge plumes of dust and dirt flying up in their wake. Acid sucked in her cheeks, gripping the rifle tight. They followed the track curving around a large mound strewn with rocky boulders and lanky ferns that quivered and bowed as they drove past. Once at the other side, the ground levelled off considerably and the ferns gave way to a copse of tall fig trees.

From this point on, the sounds of the jungle became engulfed with human noises. Engines. Laughter. The boom of a PA system. And then, as they continued past the line of fig trees and swept around the side of the island, keeping to the outside of the track, they saw it. A huge carved totem pole, painted in striking colours and standing ten feet higher than the trees.

"Oh shit," Welles said. "You see that thing?"

Acid narrowed her eyes. Of course she'd seen it. But that wasn't all she'd seen. "Spook and Sofia," she mouthed to herself. Then as they moved further down the track and the tree cover fell away, she saw the flaming torches, the bonfire built of straw and timber around the base of the structure. "Shit, Welles. They're planning on setting fire to that thing. With them inside."

Welles put his foot down, keeping them away from the crowd's sightline by driving alongside a series of tall sand dunes close to the shore. Now Acid could hear the PA system more clearly. The voice booming out over the relative calm of the island, punctuated every now and again with an electric crackle of feedback. She couldn't see who was talking, but her guess was Engel, speaking in a pompous droning tone, an attempt at an English accent that failed miserably. He was speaking of the hunt being in its thirteenth year, how it was going from strength to strength. She curled her lip as she listened, staying conscious of where she placed her focus. The last thing she needed was her anger bubbling over into the red and clouding her judgement. Highly stressful situations such as this required a light touch and an ability to stay centred. Get too tight around the matter, get up in your head and you make mistakes. From now on, Acid knew, every mistake was a death knell.

As Welles slowed the jeep and circled around the back of the arena, Engel's voice grew louder. Talking about how his island was the perfect antidote to the pressures of modern life for high-class individuals. And that by removing the troublesome blights they were doing society a favour. It was a cull, he said. Survival of the fittest. Them helping nature along.

"You hear that shit?" Welles growled as he shut the engine and rolled the jeep to a silent stop amongst a group of tall ferns that stood back from the lip of the basin. "These people, man. What's scary is they really believe it."

Acid swallowed. She didn't like it any more than Welles, but if she was honest with herself, she'd said similar things in the past. Not about innocent people, of course. But you kill people for a living, you have to justify it somehow. The line she'd always gone with was, people didn't get those kinds of prices put on their heads without being nefarious and dodgy bastards themselves. But there were always exceptions, the ones like Spook, who came and went (by Acid's hands) over the years. The ones she didn't like to think about.

She shook her head as a way to disperse these intrusive thoughts. Not the time.

Once the jeep came to a full rest and the engine was silent she got out. Staying low and out of sight she moved over to the edge of the arena.

"What are we dealing with here?" Welles whispered, lying down alongside her as she watched through the fronds of a large fern. "We stand any chance at all?"

Acid took a deep breath and held it in her lungs. From this position the imposing totem pole structure stood between them and the small stage where Engel was still waxing lyrical. She could see now he was dressed in something like priest attire, waving his arms around gregariously as he spoke, the long white robes flapping about him.

"They're all here," she replied. "Luther Clarkson. The bitch who kicked me off the mountainside. Graves. Engel. And – ah, might have known."

"What?"

"Beowulf Caesar. My old boss. Along with Raaz Terabyte. Well, well, today might not be so bad after all."

Welles jostled for position beside her and squinted through the leaves. "How are you figuring that?"

"Let's just say I've got a little vendetta I'm working my way through."

Welles shook his head and huffed out a gruff laugh that had little humour on the other side of it. "Well, I'm glad it's all working out for ya." He lowered his head, thick eyebrows knotted together. "Poor girls. They look terrified up there."

As Acid pulled her attention back to the totem, the macabre heads stacked one on top of the other, she could make out the sorrowful faces of Spook and Sofia. They watched on helplessly as one of Engel's large, blond-haired security guards began pouring the contents of a metal canister – liquid paraffin at a guess – around the base of the structure.

"Shit. We got a strategy here?" Welles murmured.

Satisfied with his handiwork, the guard walked back to the side of the raised seating area and placed the canister next to three similar ones. Acid gripped the M16 to her chest, her finger tightening on the trigger.

"I wouldn't exactly call it a strategy," she replied, hitting Welles with a devilish grin. "But I reckon with a bit of luck, and a lot of bluster, we might just pull this off."

CHAPTER 37

Caesar leaned into Raaz and huffed pointedly. He'd been looking forward to Engel's infamous closing ceremony all weekend, but like a lot of things in life, he mused, the more you anticipate something the worse it seems.

"No wonder he doesn't like people talking about it," he whispered at Raaz. "No one would bloody come if they knew it was just him waffling on. Like's the sound of his own voice, doesn't he?"

Raaz smiled politely but didn't respond. She faced forward, her arms crossed and her expression rigid. Caesar eyeballed her a while longer before tutting impetuously and leaning back in his seat.

"Get a bloody move on and light it up, will you?" he muttered.

Beside him, Raaz cracked a smile finally. "Wonder what she's thinking up there."

"Probably shitting her knickers," Caesar bellowed in her ear. "Well, good. You know I've often heard being burnt alive is the worst way to go."

Raaz's smile grew wider. "Yes, I believe that's true."

"Did you ever see the evidence footage Davros took of him

setting fire to that chap over in the Congo?" He nudged Raaz boisterously. "The screams that came out of him. Bloody hell."

"I remember. Took him a while to die. I imagine that's going to be the same today. What a shame. Poor Acid Vanilla and her pathetic little friend."

Before Caesar could respond, the surrounding audience erupted into applause, drawing his attention back to the stage where Engel was now reading from a scroll of paper.

"We come to the point in proceedings where we recognise our fallen brothers and sisters," he bellowed, his voice dropping an octave or two. "It is true, there have been too many of the wrong kind of deaths this year, but we will learn from our mistakes. My team are already putting procedures in place to ensure none of the targets can ever go rogue again."

A murmur washed over the crowd. Cries of "Good to hear it" and "About time".

Engel raised his hands for quiet. "My team is also hard at work on the death narratives for those who have died. Once ready they will be circulated to the more genial members of the world's press. As far as anyone will ever know, the lives lost this weekend will be the result of boating mishaps, riding accidents, other wholesome activities. The ones we can't cover up in these terms will be signed off as heart attacks or strokes. I have medical teams at my disposal who take care of all the legal paperwork."

Sat on the other side of Caesar, Luther Clarkson turned and patted him on the arm conspiringly. "We lost some good men this weekend," he sneered. "But we wiped out plenty more bothersome ones."

On hearing, Karen Clarkson leaned over. "Did you see I got the top score of the weekend? Four kills, plus bonus points for bringing in that pathetic Cerberix employee up there." She waved her hand at the totem. "And I signed on late. Not bad going, huh? My brother here is in a real stink with me for beating him."

She broke out in high-pitched, snickering laughter that made Caesar lament ever sitting near this gauche duo. Karen and

Luther were nothing like their charismatic brother. Yet, Caesar had to admit, the weekend had been a tremendous success. Not only was he getting rid of Acid Vanilla, but brokering her and Spook's presence here, mixing with the likes of the Clarksons and Engel, it had cemented his position alongside the top echelons of, not just the rich and powerful, but those shadowy beings behind the rich and powerful. The *actual* rulers of the world.

"Okay then, here we go," Karen cried excitedly, as two of Engel's Amazonian-looking female guards advanced on the totem pole carrying flaming torches.

"And now we shall experience the last act of this year's hunt." Engel's voice echoed around the basin. "The sacrifice of the damned."

Caesar chewed at his bottom lip as the guards knelt at the feet of the large wooden devil, praising the totem before lowering the lit batons onto the pile of sticks and straw. The fire burst into life immediately, the paraffin spreading the blaze around the base and sending flames licking up the wooden structure in a matter of seconds. Caesar heard screams coming from the two wooden heads, but they were quickly drowned out by the enthusiastic jeering from the audience.

"So long, Acid," Caesar mumbled into his drink. "You brought it all on yourself."

Beside him, Raaz was restless. "Wait a minute," she said, tearing her attention from the burning tower and addressing Karen Clarkson. "You mentioned you got double points for the Cerberix employee, Spook Horowitz, yes? What about Acid Vanilla, the one who... who killed your brother?"

Karen flicked a strand of luminous yellow hair from her face. "Why, honey, she's already dead."

Raaz glanced up at Caesar, who met her eyes with a frown. "Yes, so you thought," he said. "But we saw her in the cell with the Horowitz. She's up in the top head."

"No way, José," Karen said. "That's some slutty journalist who was trying to expose Engel. I guess they look alike. But your Acid Vanilla, she's dead. Killed her myself."

Luther Clarkson shook his head. "Only she didn't get the points for that one, did you, sis? They didn't recover the body in time, so no points awarded. Means my dear sister didn't make the all-time leader board. Such. A. Shame." He stuck out his bottom lip in mock sorrow.

"What do you mean? There was no body?" Raaz asked. "Is she dead or not?"

"Of course she's damn well dead," Karen yelled. "I kicked her off the top of the mountain. I told ya, there's no way anyone could survive that fall. If you ask me, it's just Engel and his old boy's club not wanting a woman being on the leader board."

Caesar sat upright in his seat as Karen's words spun around in his head.

No way anyone could survive that fall.

The problem was, Acid Vanilla wasn't just anyone.

She was tough. Determined. She had more guts than sense most of the time. But if Engel's goons hadn't found her body, Caesar had a troubling suspicion she wasn't dead. And if that was the case, she was still out there. And she'd be coming for him.

CHAPTER 38

It took the sight of the flames climbing up the side of the totem pole to spur Acid into action. She ran back to the jeep, yelling over her shoulder for Welles to follow her.

"You take the wheel," she told him, clambering into the passenger side and positioning herself with one foot on the leather seat and the other on the dashboard. Standing upright, she raised the M16 to her shoulder and leaned the small of her back against the headrest. "Let's do this."

Welles twisted the keys in the ignition and gave Acid a reassuring nod as he shoved the stick into gear.

"Hold on," he told her as he manoeuvred the jeep through the dense patch of ferns, then through the line of trees. They dipped violently over the side of the arena basin and, once in sight of the ceremony and on level ground, he put his foot on the gas.

Acid braced herself against the dashboard as they sped onwards towards the totem pole, hoping they weren't too late. The flames were really taking hold. Black smoke rose up the sides and spiralled up into the clear skies above.

"Get us as close as you can to that thing," she yelled.

"Got ya."

The security team had spotted their approach, but Welles

steered them out the way of the first flurry of shots. A hail of bullets peppered the ground alongside them, sending clouds of sand and earth into the air.

"Stay in line with the totem," Acid told him. "Keep it between us and the stage."

"Yeah, I'm trying."

Another few metres and Welles slowed the jeep. Enough that Acid could jump out, stopping briefly to call back. "Get up there and free the girls. Climb up on the hood if you need to."

Moving around the side of the totem Acid brought up the assault rifle. She had the outline of a plan, but for it to work she needed three things: oxygen, fuel and a spark. Two of those would be easy enough to come by, the third not so much. But this was her only option.

Stepping out from the cover of the totem she raised the M16 and squeezed the trigger. The buffering recoil of the rifle took her by surprise and the first shots went high. She fired again, steadier now and enjoying the crisp sound of the rifle fire as she zipped a line of bullets towards the three paraffin canisters that had been left at the edge of the audience. She heard a series of pops as the bullets punctured the thin metal and clear paraffin gushed out onto the ground.

That was her fuel.

But she still needed the spark. Despite what the movies might have you believe, a bullet wasn't going to do it for her. But the tall female security guard, standing a few feet in front of the canisters and holding a flaming torch, she was a different matter. A bonus and a blessing all rolled into one. Plus she was already in high alert, glancing around, confused, unsure where to run. Acid kept her finger depressed on the trigger and slew a line of bullets her way, tracing a trail of red holes across her legs and torso, chopping her down. The woman screamed and stumbled backwards, dropping the fiery baton.

And there was her spark.

With a whoosh and a flash, a gigantic explosion decimated the audience on the far side, sending chairs and body parts flying into the air. Acid saw the burning torso of Graves hit the side of the stage and bounce onto the grass, his bloated, pompous face twisted in a deathly rictus.

Acid smiled to herself as chaos and confusion rained down on Engel's grim parade. People were screaming and running in all directions, knocking one another over in the melee. As the smoke parted Acid saw the blast had taken out a good portion of Engel's security team. But not all of them

The surviving team members moved quickly to red alert, running to cover the guests whilst yelling instructions to each other. Twenty feet away a blond security guard turned and locked eyes with Acid. His face twisted into a cruel sneer as he aimed his rifle towards her. But before he could pull the trigger she squeezed off a trail of rising shots that exploded up the centre of his chest. She ran towards him, leaping over his lifeless body and it slumped to the floor and continuing on her trajectory.

The bats screamed across her synapses as she zig-zagged around more shots coming from the far side of the arena. She returned fire, taking out another security guard and skidding for cover behind the back of the stage. A quick glance over to the totem pole and she saw Welles was fighting against the blazing fire. With the end of his rifle he'd managed to undo the rope tying Spook's door closed. As Acid looked on, the door swung open and Spook's limp coughing form stumbled out into Welles' arms. She was free. But it was far from over.

"Hey, watch out," Acid yelled over, before taking out a female guard who was on her way over there with an M16 slung over her shoulder. She got her one in the stomach, one in the chest, two crimson roses bursting out from the long white gown.

Spook, on her feet now, must have seen the woman fall because she snapped her head Acid's way and waved.

"Keep it together, kid." Acid raised her hand. "Don't do anything stupid."

She turned her focus back to Engel and his cronies. A group of security guards had formed a human shield around the last of the guests and were scanning the area, guns raised and ready.

But not ready enough.

With a banshee scream, Acid sprang up from the cover of the stage and sprayed the group with a torrent of hot punishing metal rounds. The security guards flailed and cried out as bullets ripped through their chests and abdomens, the cruel shrapnel blossoming inside of them and ripping through bone and major organs. Acid kept her finger pressed down on the trigger, an intense inner rage spurring her on as she chopped down more guards and a few of the frailer members of Engel's guest list. But there were still more of them. Shifting into peripheral vision, she noticed two female guards over to the right of her, robes billowing behind them as they took aim at her.

"Not a chance." She shifted her aim, trailing a path of bullets their way, before sensing an alarming looseness under her trigger finger and hearing the discouraging *chk-chk-chk*. She looked down at the rifle, then back to the two women now smiling smugly at her.

"Shit."

Acid hit the deck as the women opened fire, the unforgiving rounds tearing across the plush velvet flooring and splintering the wooden stage underneath. They advanced on her as she pulled the Taurus PT111 from out of her waistband and checked the mag. Seven of the thirteen rounds left. She'd make them count. She popped her head over the lip of the stage and risked a look. The women were close. Another few seconds and they'd be around the side of the stage with a clear shot at her.

It was now or never.

Acid raised herself up from behind the stage, just in time to see both women jerking to the beat of a high-powered machine gun. Eruptions of red plasma polka-dotted their robes.

"Acid."

It was Spook. She and Sofia running her way with Welles

covering them, the M16 used to take down the women guards still on his shoulder.

"I thought they were going to kill you," Spook cried, grabbing Acid's arm and dragging her behind the cover of the stage.

"Yes, well, there's still time." She nodded at Welles. "Thanks for that."

"Not bad for a cop, huh?"

She allowed him the hint of a smile. But there was no time for pleasantries. Over on the other side of the arena, she saw Caesar and Raaz heading for the row of parked jeeps. She looked at Welles. He understood.

"You girls, wait here," he told Sofia and Spook, pulling out his pistol. "Either of you used one of these before?"

"Spook has," Acid told him. "She's a good shot."

"Okay, cool." Welles handed Spook the gun, ignoring her pleas to the contrary. "If anyone comes near, shoot them. Aim for the chest, just below the neck. That'll give you a good range for a kill shot. Don't worry, we'll be back soon."

"Where are you going?" Sofia asked.

"I'm not letting that bastard get away," Acid said. "Not again. Come on, FBI Guy."

She set off, moving in a wide arc and throwing her aim from side to side as she went, shifting her focus from macro to micro as she homed in on Caesar. Being a big man, he never moved fast. In fact, Acid couldn't recall a time when she'd ever seen him run, not even in the early days when he too had worked in the field. That he was now lurching ungainly across the arena buoyed her somewhat. It meant he knew she was coming for him. And he was running scared.

She was almost on him and lifting the pistol to take a shot when out of nowhere something heavy smacked her off balance. She staggered, her head spinning and a shooting pain spreading out from her cheekbone as another blow to the back of the head floored her. With tunnel vision comes a decrease in awareness, and a decrease of awareness in chaotic situations is often dangerous. Acid rolled onto her back in time to dodge out of the way as Karen Clarkson swung a pair of metal field binoculars at her head.

"I'm going to kill you," she said, leaping onto Acid's chest and pinning her arms down with her knees before grabbing her around the throat.

Acid shoved her hips upwards, trying to throw her assailant off, but Karen was heavier than she looked and her hands were squeezing down tight. Despite the chaos she reasoned she had ten seconds before she passed out. Before Karen Bloody Clarkson killed her.

Wasn't going to happen.

Beside her she saw Welles fall to the ground with a thud, himself engaged in a vigorous struggle with Karen's brother. Pinned down as she was, she couldn't see what was going on entirely, but from the sound of it Luther was pounding the shit out of the ageing cop. With a grunt, she dug the heels of her boots into the ground and shoved off again, this time shifting Karen a little higher up her torso. Enough so she could manoeuvre the pistol so it was pointing awkwardly at her attacker's ribcage. The position of her hand in doing so sent a blistering cramp shooting down her wrist. She stroked at the trigger but the tendons in her hand were so tight it was a struggle to put any strength behind the action. Above her, Karen's face was bright red, tightening her grip all the time as she squeezed the life out of her. Acid had one chance at this. She closed her eyes and focused all her energy into her hand. The bats screeched. The world faded to grey.

Pull it.

Pull the trigger.

A sonic crack fractured the air as all the anger wiped from Karen Clarkson's face. In its place fell a look of pure confusion that turned quickly to dread. Her fingers slackened on Acid's throat, enough she could wriggle free and throw her off. A carefully placed bullet in the middle of her forehead put the witch out of her misery before another took care of her pathetic sibling.

"Good work," Welles said, getting to his feet and helping Acid up. "The motherfucker blind-sided me."

She nodded, her breath frozen in her chest. But she had no time to compose herself. Caesar had commandeered one of the jeeps and, with Raaz beside him, was pulling it out of the parking lot and heading for the complex.

Acid gave chase, racing over there with a speed that belied the pain in her muscles and the numb hollowness rising in her soul. He had to die. Today. For the memory of Louisa Vandella, her poor, innocent mother. But also, she realised, for the memory of Alice Vandella, the young girl Caesar took under his wing all those years ago and made into a cynical, loveless killing machine.

She was over there and clambering into a jeep of her own when she heard the cry. Welles, shouting her name. She glanced over to see him pointing over to the stage where Thomas Engel and two enrobed females were dragging Spook and Sofia into a waiting jeep.

"We got to go after them," Welles said, running over to the jeep and jumping in the rear.

"But Caesar," Acid replied, watching powerlessly as her old mentor disappeared around a mound of trees. "He's getting away. I can't... I can't..."

"Acid. There'll be another time," Welles told her. "But right now we have to save the girls."

Acid turned away, but she'd already accepted the choice. She started the engine and reversed the jeep into a skidding turn before shoving it in first and slamming her foot to the floor.

"You got ammo left?" she asked, as she leaned into a tight turn.

Welles checked the mag of his rifle. "Some. You?"

"Five rounds, tops."

"We can still do this," he told her. "Keep the faith."

She stepped on the gas, pushing all her weight down and leaning forward in her seat as if the action would make them go faster somehow. In front of her she could see Spook's face, staring forlornly out the back of Engel's jeep whilst next to her, Sofia, still with some fire in her, struggled with one of Engel's female guards. A second guard was positioning herself on the back seat and aiming a hunting rifle at Acid.

"Shit," Welles yelled, as Acid swung the jeep off to one side, putting a line of eucalyptus trees between them.

The surface here was uneven, with every bump and pothole felt, but the trees provided some cover as shots ricocheted off the road in front of them.

"Can you get alongside them?" Welles asked, lifting the rifle over the side of the vehicle and taking aim.

"I'm trying," Acid replied. She leaned forward, her knuckles white on the wheel. "You got a clear shot?"

"Not yet."

A quick glance and Sofia was still struggling with the female guard. They were standing up in the back of the jeep. As Acid watched, the guard loomed over and smashed a fist down on the top of Sofia's head. But it also left the tall woman exposed.

"Take her," Acid yelled, but Welles had already pulled the trigger.

A split second and the guard's head jerked to one side in an eruption of ruddy mist. She fell forward onto Sofia, driving them both over the side of the jeep.

"Ah, shit."

Acid pulled the wheel violently to one side, driving through a gap in the eucalyptus trees to re-join the main track as Engel sped off ahead. Her first instinct was to keep going, to get Spook back whatever. But as she drove alongside Sofia another part of her (the part that, ironically, sounded a lot like Spook) won out and she slammed on the brakes.

"Get in, quick," she yelled.

"You hurt?" Welles asked, grabbing Sofia by the forearm and pulling her into the passenger seat.

"I'm fine," she said. "But we need to hurry. There're choppers waiting for them. And Engel has already engaged something called Endgame."

"Endgame?" Welles repeated, as Acid pulled the jeep back onto the track and the pursuit continued. "What do you think that means?"

"Well, I don't want to pull rank on ya, Mr Bureau," Sofia said, throwing a side-look Acid's way. "But I'd say it's pretty easy to decipher. The crazy freak has some kind of contingency plan. A way to cover his tracks. And I'd say we've got about fifteen minutes before this whole island goes up in flames."

CHAPTER 39

The words had barely left Sofia's mouth when an enormous explosion over in the centre of the island rocked the jeep. Acid held the wheel steady and dropped down a gear as the dirt road rose up in front of them.

"Hang on," she yelled, applying more gas and steering into a sharp turn that took them all the way around the side of the island.

In front of them they could now see the imposing steel and glass structure of the resort complex. Engel had already pulled up outside and was heading for the main entrance, followed by his remaining guard. But not before she'd grabbed Spook by the waist and flung her over her shoulder. The three of them disappeared through the enormous glass doors as Acid skidded the jeep to a stop.

"Shit," Welles said, shaking the M16 and throwing it down. "I'm all out of ammo."

Acid shrugged. "Like you said, boss. We can still do this. Keep the faith."

Not waiting for the others she jumped out of the jeep and ran across the marble-paved concourse towards the entrance. She had one thought on her mind. Save Spook. Kill Engel. (All right, two thoughts.) The bats screeched across her consciousness, her eyes burned with unblinking intensity. Every muscle in her body seared with pain and fury. But she was doing this. She had to. Win or bust. Death or glory.

She got up to the doors and shouldered open the heavy glass before dropping to her knees and scoping out the room with the Taurus 9mm at arm's length in front of her. She'd been expecting more guards, but the vast, open-plan space appeared to be empty.

As Sofia and Welles arrived behind her, she got to her feet and the three of them moved deeper into the complex. They stepped cautious, moving steadily along the edge of the large room, with Acid and Welles flanking Sofia and keeping their aim high. But Acid knew cautious and steady didn't get the job done. Not when you were up against the clock. As if to highlight this point another explosion rocked the foundations of the complex.

"Crazy bastard," Welles said, grabbing Acid's arm. "He really is blowing the place up."

They darted over to the corner of the room where they now had eyes on the landing area opposite and the elevator to the upper levels. Engel was there, desperately pressing the down button, his other hand gripped tight around Spook's wrist as she struggled to get away. Acid was reassured to see she still had some fire inside of her.

Spook spun around to see Acid approaching. "Wait," she called. "It's a trap."

She hadn't gotten the last syllable out before Engel's guard sprung out from her hiding place behind one of the large urns and opened fire.

"Move," Acid yelled, throwing herself at Sofia and Welles and jostling them behind a large marble plinth. A huge modern art sculpture, rendered in marble (naturally) stood on top, spiralling up towards the high ceiling like a gargantuan strand of DNA. It was well made, but not Acid's taste. Meaning she felt no remorse as a moment later the entire lower half of the sculpture was destroyed in a hail of bullets. Tiny splinters of marble cascaded over their heads as the remaining half of the double helix fell forward and smashed noisily onto the floor. Acid seized the moment, leaping to her feet and firing as she went. She took out the guard with a perfect shot, just left of centre. Right in the heart. The woman went down, but not before she squeezed off another flurry of shots. Acid dived for cover, cutting her face and hands on remnants of modern art as the bullets pinged off the walls and ceiling.

Sofia and Welles ran over and helped her up in time to see Engel and Spook stepping into the elevator and the doors sliding shut in front of them. Before they closed, Acid raised her head, making eye contact with Engel as he raised a hand in a farewell motion, his arrogant leer smacking up against Acid's malevolent snarl.

"Hang on, Spook," she yelled as the elevator doors closed. "I'm coming."

She got over there in a few strides and jabbed over and over at the button, watching breathlessly as the guide-light showed the elevator ascending to the roof terrace. It wasn't coming back down anytime soon.

"The stairs," she growled, already on her way over to the small door over in the opposite corner. She burst into the back stairwell without slowing her pace any and took the steps two at a time, dragging herself up with the railing's help. Engel was heading for the helipad, that much was clear. It was three flights up, not far, but her lungs ached and her legs were seizing up. Three days of no rest and little food finally catching up with her.

"Keep going," she grunted to herself. "You can do this."

But could she? Acid had no idea what to expect when she reached the roof. Engel already gone, taking Spook with him to god knows where? More armed guards? She hadn't been counting, but she must only have one or two rounds left in the Taurus. Not the best odds in the world, but she'd done well with less.

"Hey, you okay?"

She glanced over her shoulder to catch Sofia's concerned look.

"What? Apart from the obvious?"

The journalist looked down briefly, then back up through her long eyelashes. "Listen, for what it's worth, I'm sorry. I just wanted to say, that, before… you know. I should have trusted you. Shouldn't have run off."

Thanks for the sentiment but bad timing, sweetie.

"It's fine," Acid told her. "It's what I'd have done."

"You're a tough cookie, I'll give you that, Acid Vanilla. I'm glad I've got you on my side."

Not letting up the pace, Acid flicked a glance back at the woman panting to keep up behind her. Maybe she could see the similarity now._Same cheekbones. Same pout. But whether she could handle herself like Acid could was a different matter. So, what, she was from Brooklyn? Well so was Woody Allen. The girl might talk a good talk, but in Acid's experience that rarely meant much in the real world. Welles too, he'd proven himself along the way, but the guy was tired out and clearly past his prime. Whatever happened next. It was down to her.

Another few steps and she reached the top level. She paused to catch her breath, allowing Welles and Sofia to catch up so she could tell them, "Stay here, out of sight. It's best if I do this alone."

"The hell you talking about?" Welles asked. "I'm coming too."

"Don't be ridiculous," Acid told him through gritted teeth. "You're unarmed. It's too dangerous. Stay put, I'll come back for you."

"Not a damn chance," Welles said, resolution deepening his voice. "We're in this together now, Acid. I know you ain't too big on teamwork, but tough shit. Anything I can do out there to help, I'll do it. Now let's go."

Sofia was nodding in agreement, although not quite as convincingly. On the other side of the door, Acid could hear the distinct whirr of rotary blades. She put her shoulder against the door and grabbed the handle.

"Fine." She held their one remaining weapon aloft. "But don't blame me if this goes tits up."

CHAPTER 40

The downdraft from the helicopter blades, coupled with the extreme heat, was reminiscent of a hairdryer being blasted in her face as Acid eased open the door and stepped out onto the tarmac. She blinked, forcing her eyes to become accustomed to the change in light from gloomy stairwell to bright sunshine. Over on the far side of the roof, a raised mezzanine level was strewn with tables and chairs, sun loungers, and a well-stocked bar area. From there a short flight of stone steps led down to the far helipad where a chopper waited, fast filling up with the remaining guests, falling over each other to clamber inside. Acid spotted Jerry, Luther Clarkson's hapless assistant, squashed in the back seat with his face up against the glass. She'd let that one go. For Spook.

Spook.

She scanned her eyes across the roof top, her focus snapping to the far side of the complex where Engel was standing in front of a second chopper. His tanned forearm was gripped tight around Spook's neck, and he had a gun pressed to her temple.

"Stop right there or your little friend is dead," he yelled, on seeing Acid. He backed away, moving onto the outlying helipad.

Acid raised the Taurus, training it on a point just below Engel's over-plucked eyebrows. "It's over," she told him.

"Not a chance. You miserable cretins might have ruined my fun this weekend, but you won't ruin me." His eyes bulged with rage and his cheeks shook as he screamed, "I am Thomas fucking Engel and I decide who lives or who dies. I make the rules."

He dragged Spook towards the waiting chopper, the kid gasping for air, clawing feebly at the arm pressing against her throat.

Acid kept her aim up. "Let Spook go."

Engel laughed a deep, bitter laugh. Then stopped immediately. "Oh, you're actually serious. But, no. Sorry darling. She's coming with me. Call it an insurance policy."

Spook's eyes widened, her face red and pleading. "Acid," she groaned. "Please. Just shoot him."

Acid's finger tightened on the trigger but she was fading fast. Could feel the fatigue washing over her. She gripped the wrist of her gun hand to steady it. The manic energy of the bats was still strong, but she could sense the darkness enveloping her from the inside.

"Acid?" Welles whispered as Engel stepped closer to the chopper. "You got the shot."

"Just about."

But she couldn't, wouldn't, risk it. Not yet. Not like this. Acid was a crack shot. Had been. On a good day at least. But all it took was a centimetre or two in the wrong direction and Engel would survive the shot long enough to take Spook down with him. They were almost at the chopper now, but Engel's next step was uncertain. He'd have to take his eyes off Acid to open the chopper door and get inside. But he wasn't going to risk that. His only other option was to push Spook into the cockpit first. But again, that left him exposed. Acid could take the killer shot. She swallowed. Her throat was dry.

"Put the gun down now," Engel called over. "Or I swear, I'll kill this bitch."

She lifted her chin. The guy wasn't stupid. He'd assessed his options and was doubling down.

A bead of sweat ran down the side of her face as another explosion rocked the complex. Behind her she sensed the growing agitation coming off Welles and Sofia. Another explosion like that and the whole place would start crumbling. They were on borrowed time. Acid knew it. Engel knew it too. But that was the problem. She took a deep breath, keeping her aim up. All she needed was for him to drop his concentration for one second.

"Put the gun down, you crazy bitch."

"Not going to happen. Let her go."

No one moved.

One second.

Come on, you bastard.

Over on the far side of the roof she sensed more commotion, a flurry of activity out the corner of her eye. Then she heard the shouting. The distinct and affected tones of Beowulf Caesar.

Acid tensed, breathing heavily down both nostrils. This was the closest she'd gotten to him since Germany. She had a real chance now, to avenge her mother. But he was getting away. She shifted her position a few inches, still with the gun on Engel but able to watch as Caesar barged his way over to the departing chopper.

Do it, the bats screamed at her.

Forget the damn kid.

This is what you're here for.

This is who you are.

Kill him.

Acid gulped down a lungful of air and her aim faltered a touch. Welles saw it too. "Keep on this one," he growled. "I'll take care of Cueball over there."

"Welles, wait," Sofia cried, but he'd already set off.

In her peripheral vision Acid watched as the big old cop, no doubt a force to be reckoned with in his younger days, ran towards Caesar, ready to tackle him to the floor.

Only he never got there.

Caesar saw him coming and with a leery sneer pulled a small handgun from out the pocket of his safari suit. Acid saw it. Sofia's high-pitched yelp told her she saw it too. Welles certainly saw it as he skidded to one side to remove himself from the situation. But it was too late. A flash, a crack of gunfire, and Welles fell to the ground.

It was all Acid could do to keep her focus fixed on Engel and Spook. Sofia let out a scream of defiance as Caesar, grinning from ear to ear, barged his huge bulk into the departing helicopter. Acid kept one eye on the scene, watching as Raaz appeared behind Caesar and attempted to clamber onboard. There was more shouting. Roars of frustration and panic.

"No room," was the cry.

"Go to hell," an old man shouted.

But Raaz wasn't giving it up. She got one foot on the rim of the door and tried elbowing her way into the rear seats. Those already onboard shoved her back. No room. She screamed at Caesar to help her as the pilot lifted the landing skids off the tarmac. Another explosion shuddered through the underbelly of the complex, sending fragments of rock and dust scattering over the scene.

"Please. Caesar. Help me."

Raaz gripped on for dear life as the helicopter tried to pull away, but she was no match for Caesar's bright green, size thirteen boot when he leaned out and kicked her forcefully in the chest. With a grunt that sounded half-way between pain and bewilderment, Raaz let go of the door of the helicopter. As it began its ascent, and with Caesar watching, she stumbled backwards and banged her head on the tarmac.

Acid snapped her full attention back to Engel, keeping the Taurus aimed high, not allowing him to take advantage of the situation. "This stops right now," she said. "You can't get away. Let her go."

"Not a damn chance," Engel replied. "The fact you're so bothered about missy here tells me I still hold all the cards. So, how about this? You put your gun down, let me fly away, and I don't blow her brains out."

"What, and we take our chances on the island?" Acid said, as flames appeared up the side of the building. She lowered her aim a fraction. "What if we all win? We come with you. There are enough seats in the chopper."

"Excuse me?" Engel scoffed. "Are you for real?"

"Why not? The cop over there is dead and, you know, a cop. Screw the journalist. Take me and Spook with you. We're on the run from everyone as it is. We won't be a concern for you. And at the other end, we all say goodbye and go our separate ways." She paused, letting the words sink in. "It's the only way I can see that chopper leaving in the next few minutes. After that we're all going down with the place."

She held her nerve. Didn't move. In front of her Spook grabbed at Engel's arm, fighting for air.

"Acid, no. You can't. We can't."

"Sorry, kid. But it's the only way. Trust me." She locked her eyes on Spook. "This is the only way."

"But Sofia…"

She glanced over at the young journalist, knelt beside Welles' fallen body.

"Spook," Acid spat. "Back to me. Look at me, Spook. Look in my eyes."

She did as she was told.

"All right. Enough," Engel shouted as the entire building groaned beneath them. "Lay the gun down and walk over here. Slowly."

Acid kept her eyes on Spook as she slowly raised her hands in the air. "Cool," she told him, stepping forward. "I'm putting it down. Nice and easy."

Spook shook her head, tears streaming down her face. "Acid, no. We can't leave her."

"Look at me. It's okay. We'll be fine."

"But Acid…"

"Listen to me, Spook. It's going to be fine. You'll be okay. But don't let your focus slip. Like I always tell you. When that happens you make mistakes. Yes? People make mistakes."

"Put the gun down," Engel repeated, getting frantic now.

"Yes. I'm doing it." She gave Spook a nod. Then, slowly, methodically, she placed the gun on the hot tarmac.

The second Acid's finger left the trigger, Engel let out a hearty laugh. "You dumb bitch."

As expected, as hoped, he removed the gun from Spook's temple. Time slowed down as he manoeuvred his aim though one eighty degrees towards Acid. His finger was tight on the trigger. His eyes passionate with hate. Acid's world zoomed into micro and colour wiped from the scene. All noise and texture were gone. The bats screamed. Their chattering energy morphing into a human voice. The sound of chaos and fury. A battle cry from deep inside of Acid. As Engel straightened his arm, readying to take the shot, the kid swung her elbow, connecting with his nose and sending him off balance.

Because people make mistakes.

They let their focus slip.

And one second is all it takes.

Moving like water, fluid and constant, Acid scooped the 9mm handgun from the floor and zippered the last few rounds up Engel's torso, finishing with a fatal shot through his top lip which took out the back of his skull. His lifeless body fell to the floor in a flurry of billowing robes.

"Acid, you did it." Spook was over to her in one bound, hugging her close. As the world zoomed back into focus, she looked over to see Sofia helping Welles to his feet.

"Welles is alive," Spook cried. "It's all okay. We're going to be okay."

"We need to get out of here," Acid replied as she felt the ceiling give way in the room below, "and fast."

But Welles wasn't the only one to survive Caesar's wrath.

Over on the outlying edge of the first helipad, Raaz Terabyte was getting to her feet. Acid noticed her the same time as Spook.

"No," Spook said, resolve clipping her vowels. "Let me handle this."

Before she had a chance to reply, Spook had snatched up Engel's pistol and was marching over to her.

"I only wanted to help you," Spook shouted, waving the gun in her face. "You knew that, and you played on it."

Raaz's face was bloody and bruised, but she milked it for all it was worth. Acid held back, watching through a sneer as the pathetic cow held her hands up in pleading surrender, shaking her head forlornly at Spook.

"I'm sorry. I don't want to die. Take me with you." She spotted Acid watching and called over to her. "I can help you. I can give you Caesar. Don't think I'm going to protect him after what he did."

And yes, she'd turned on the tears. Pathetic. But Acid was surprised to see Spook was having none of it.

"The only reason we're here on this hell-hole of an island is because of you," she yelled. "You tricked me. You made me into bait."

"Please, Spook," Raaz tried again. "Caesar made me. I was only doing my job. I'm a techie, like you. We have to stick together. You said as much."

Another explosion a few floors below ripped through the complex, creating a deep fissure in the centre of the roof and sending everyone stumbling to one side.

"We need to go. Now," Acid called over.

But Spook didn't take her eyes off of Raaz. "We're nothing alike," she growled. "Screw you."

She turned around, with a look Acid had never seen from her before. It was a little unnerving, but it made Acid smile.

"Come on," Acid told her. "Leave the toxic witch where she is. Let her go down with this miserable place. We need to get going—Spook!"

Calling her name. It was a warning. Because in that moment Raaz Terabyte had leapt forward, her face twisted in taut fury, her fingers like claws. But for once it seemed Spook knew exactly what she was doing. Without missing a beat she spun on her heels and fired three rounds at Raaz. The pistol recoil drove her backwards, and she almost fell over the side of the gaping crevice that had formed in the middle of the helipad. But the shots found their mark. Two in the chest. One in the stomach. Raaz gazed down at her torso as an air of bewilderment spread across her harsh features, then she let out a strange gurgling and concertinaed to the floor.

"Wow," was all Acid could say, as Spook hurried past her and helped Sofia get Welles into the helicopter.

Acid stared at Raaz for a few moments longer, making sure the bitch was actually dead. Then, as the mezzanine level crumbled away and a tremendous explosion splintered the side of the cliff face, she hurried over to join the rest of them clambering into the chopper.

"Okay, chaps," she said, getting her head under Welles' arm and helping him into the rear of the cockpit. "It's time for us to get the hell out of here."

CHAPTER 41

Acid strapped herself into the pilot seat of the helicopter as a final explosion tore through the complex, splitting the roof terrace completely in two so the tarmac folded in on itself.

"Everyone put a helmet on," she yelled over the drone of the rotary blades. "They've got mics so we can hear each other."

A quick glance over her shoulder told her Welles was still conscious, Sofia helping him fasten his helmet in place.

"How are you doing, FBI Guy?" Acid asked, whilst flicking a set of switches into the ON position and reacquainting herself with the controls.

"I'm all right," he growled back. "Got me in the leg, above the knee. That old boss of yours is a terrible shot."

"Maybe." Acid smirked. "But he stopped you at least." She grabbed the collective control stick and tested the pitch.

"Have you flown one of these before?" Spook asked, looking out of a helmet that was far too big for her.

"Once," Acid told her. "A long time ago. But how hard can it be, right?"

As Engel's resort complex crumbled and the flames rose higher, Acid grabbed a hold of the cyclic control stick between her legs. It was all coming back to her. She gave it a bit too much welly on the pitch, but keeping a firm hold on the cyclic she was able to right them easily enough, and pulled them up and away as the final section of the roof collapsed into the floor below.

"Jesus, look at it down there," Spook cooed, pressing the front of her helmet to the side window as Acid lifted the chopper above the clouds of thick black smoke.

Engel's 'Endgame' detonators had already decimated vast areas of the lush greenery. Several smaller fires had now morphed into one giant forest fire that was spreading over the island. A few hours and the whole place would be a smouldering pile of ash. The complex too was now nothing but ruins. Another explosion had taken out the entire west wing, sending marble and steel tumbling into the ocean below. It was only a matter of time before the entirety of the building went the same way. All Engel's hard work. All the evidence of who, and what, he really was. And what happened here on this terrible Pain Island.

Acid watched the chaos unfolding, trying to make peace with the last few days, but she quickly decided that was a pointless exercise. Another scan of the controls, and a little trial and error, and she was able to plot a course north. If her instincts were correct, they were somewhere over the Indian Ocean. Meant she had associates nearby. People who could help them.

"Where are we heading?" Sofia asked, leaning over the back of Acid's seat.

"The GPS is showing a landmass about 300 miles north from here," she replied. "From there we'll be able to refuel, and then I'm thinking Vietnam."

"For real?"

"I know a couple of guys in Hanoi that can patch us up. Provide passports and safe voyage home for Spook and me."

"Oh, great for you two. What about us?"

"You don't need them. Welles can contact the Bureau or Interpol. They'll sort you out. We don't have that privilege."

"Not a problem," Welles replied. "I'll get it sorted. I reckon you've earned your anonymity with that little display down there."

Acid didn't reply straight away. Instead she settled back into her seat and steadied the controls. In front of her lay nothing but glorious blue for as far as she could see. Bottom to top. Sea and sky. Freedom. Space. It felt good. But something was niggling at her and it wasn't just the bats.

"Why did you do that, Welles?" she asked. "Go for Caesar like you did. You could be dead right now."

Welles coughed and shifted upright in his seat. "I knew taking him down meant a lot to you. Didn't want him to get away."

The words stunned her, but she didn't let it show. "You risked your life for me?"

"It's called being a team. Like I said, you should try it sometime."

Beside her, Spook stifled a smile.

"But don't worry," he added. "I ain't gone all pious and weak-minded. If he was on that island, he was a bad person. I want to rid the world of every prick on that island. But we will, we'll get 'em. Mark my words."

She nodded to herself, keeping her own jaw tight, as out the corner of her eye she noticed Spook watching her.

"You see?" she said, leaning in. "You can rely on other people now and again. You can trust them. It doesn't mean you're weak. And they won't always let you down."

Acid shook her head. "No. Sorry, kid, but I'm not having that."

"All I'm saying is asking for help isn't a bad thing. If you need it."

"Not what I'm talking about," Acid replied, allowing a smile to slacken her taut pout. "As usual, you're trying to make this about me. But this isn't about me. Not this time."

"Oh?"

"No. It's about you standing up for yourself. Not letting people get away with hurting you. Even if that means you do morally dubious things. Like killing that sour-faced harridan back there. I'm proud of you."

Spook let out a nervous giggle, her cheeks flushed. "Well, maybe we're both growing. Changing at least. Who knows, we could make a good person out of you yet."

"Maybe." Acid sniffed. "But let's not get carried away, shall we? There's still dirty work to do. You know that."

Spook sat upright, any light-heartedness draining from her demeanour. "You mean Caesar?"

"I mean Caesar."

Spook looked at her hands, nodding along to something only she could hear. "I get it." She sighed. "But not right away, yeah? Surely we can have a few weeks rest before we get back on that horse?"

Acid shrugged. "I guess we'll see what happens next. Won't we?"

"Great," Spook scoffed, sarcastically.

"Come on, Spooks," Acid said, nudging her. "Never a dull moment and all that jazz. You love it really."

"Do I?"

"What else are you going to do with your life?"

Spook didn't answer, but Acid was sure she saw another stifled smile as she turned to the window. Behind her, in the back seat, Welles and Sofia were already asleep, and with the bats calm for once and her stress levels dropping, her weariness returned. The GPS said they'd arrive at their destination in a little over two hours.

Perfect.

Despite her cavalier facade, the last few days had taken their toll, both mentally and physically. Maybe she'd suggest they rest for a few hours after refuelling rather than set off to Hanoi straight away. A little sleep would be good. Some food too. Plus a very large alcoholic drink. Something strong and smoky. She smiled to herself, almost tasting it in her parched throat. It had been a brutal experience but perhaps Spook was right – they had come out of it stronger, better people. If this better, more-rounded version of herself would last beyond the next few weeks, Acid didn't know. She suspected not. There was too much pain and resentment and chaos inside of her. But for now, calm and clarity reigned. The madness was over. And they were going home.

CHAPTER 42

"How you doing, FBI Guy?"

Welles stepped back, almost losing his place in the line for the buffet as Acid sidled up to him.

"Well, look at you. Acid Vanilla, the cynical badass, at a wedding of all places. In a dress, too. I'm shocked."

"Oh? Why's that?" Acid asked, running her hand down her figure-hugging Vivienne Westwood dress. Vintage. In black, obviously. "I scrub up okay. When I want to."

"You sure do." Welles raised his eyebrows cartoonishly. "I feel like I'm being given the stink-eye by every single guy in here."

"Hey," Acid scolded, linking arms with the retired agent as the line progressed. "There are woman checking me out, too. How's the leg?"

"Ah, you know," Welles responded, holding up his walking stick. "Still hurts, but it could be worse. Just meant I got to retire a few weeks early. But not before I filled out a pretty hefty report." He tilted his head to one side, maybe sensing her tension. "Don't worry, slick. I said I'd leave you out of it, and I did."

"And Spook?"

"Like we discussed. All taken care of. But, shit, mama, that Beowulf Caesar is certainly a character. No one at the Bureau had a clue he even existed. How the hell did he stay off the radar so long?"

She stuck out her lip. "We were good at what we did. Professionals. I take it the FBI are investigating him?"

Welles whistled, his eyes growing wide. "They sure are. He's gone dark since the island, but they'll find him. Turns out Annihilation Pest Control are the missing part of the puzzle in a whole of bunch of dead cases. So you did me a favour too, in the end."

"Well, don't you be telling anyone I helped the FBI."

"Don't worry, my lips are sealed. It is good to see you though."

"You too. My new guy came through for us. We got new passports, new aliases. Travelled here today as Sasha and Joselyn Mulberry. I'm Joselyn." Welles pulled a face. As well he might. "I know. Spook chose them."

"Well, good to meet you, Joselyn. And how you been holding up?"

"A little out of sorts, but nothing new there." Acid sighed. "I imagine the FBI's new public enemy number one will be keeping a low profile for the time being. Plus with Raaz dead, his means of locating me diminishes somewhat, so I can probably rest a little easier. But still, Caesar's a wily one. You write him off at your peril."

Acid glanced over at Spook, currently being talked at by some nerdy friend of Mike, Sofia's new husband. From this distance, she looked older than her years. But that's what happened when you lived in the shadows and existed purely on your nerves. It took it out of you. Acid made a mental note to book them into some kind of spa when they got back to London. Get some rest and rejuvenation.

Despite the fatigue and dark shadows, however, the kid had done good recently – hacking into Engel's database and wiping Acid's presence from all guest lists and information relating to the island. She caught Acid looking over and smiled. Acid allowed her a friendly (all right, slightly flirtatious, it was a wedding after all) wink before turning back to Welles.

"What about Engel's fortune?" she asked. "His legacy?"

"Ruined. In a word," Welles said, with a glint in his eye. "My colleagues seized hard drives, boxes of files, ledgers from all six of his residencies. We've got details of off-shore bank accounts, his little black book of contacts, not to mention the flight records to both of his islands for the last ten years. Let's just say there's a lot of high profile people shitting their pants right now."

Acid grinned. "Couldn't happen to a nicer bunch of chaps."

"My thoughts exactly."

She released her arm from his as they got to the front of the buffet. "I'll leave you to get some food."

"You not eating?"

"Just a liquid lunch for me. Plus, I need to go rescue Spook. But I'll see you before we go, yes? In fact, I might come to find you for a dance later."

Welles laughed, glancing down at his walking stick. "We'll see."

Acid left him scooping out a large helping of rice from a silver bowl and sashayed across the dancefloor to where Spook was sat at a table still stuck in conversation with the nerd.

"Hey there," the nerd cooed, as she sat. "I don't believe we've met. I'm—"

"Beat it, will you?" Acid cut in. "I need to speak to my friend. In private."

The man looked at Spook, then back at her.

"Go away," she mouthed, glaring at him with every fibre of her being.

Not taking his eyes off her, the young man got to his feet and, with a loud tut, slunk away into the crowd.

"Thanks for that," Spook slurred, sipping at a glass of fizz. "He was sending me to sleep."

"Not a problem. How you doing?"

Spook shrugged. "Okay. Weddings are really dull, aren't they?"

"Absolutely dreadful affairs."

"Sofia looked great, though. Beautiful. Don't you think?"

Acid narrowed her eyes. "I suppose so. By the way, I've got you a present. I meant to give it to you earlier, but I forgot."

This got the kid's attention. "A present? For me?"

Acid reached for her clutch purse under the table and removed a small purple velvet box. She handed it over. "Here."

Spook accepted the gift and turned it over in her hands. She shook it. Held it to her ear. Doing the whole bit.

"Just bloody well open it, will you?"

Acid watched as Spook carefully lifted the top off the box to reveal a single bullet. She lifted it out and held it up in the light where the name *Raaz Terabyte* could be seen etched into the casing.

"This is one of your special bullets."

"I didn't kill her. You did," Acid said. "You should be the one to lie it down with the others when we get home."

Spook put the bullet back in the box and placed it on the table. "Does this mean you'll let me help you from now on?"

"You already have helped me. You found Davros, the Sinister Sisters."

Spook screwed up her nose. "More than that. I want to help you, properly. Like I said in the helicopter, it doesn't mean you can't do it on your own, you just don't need to any longer."

Acid chewed on her bottom lip. "I'll think about it," she said softly. "Thank you."

"What? Woah." Spook arched an eyebrow. "You know, I think my hearing is playing up. I could have sworn you just said—"

"Don't push it, sweetie."

Acid reached for her drink, a double Jameson with too much ice. She took a long swig. "I spoke to Welles," she said, her attention on the glass, swirling around the contents. "Everything's cool, but like we thought, you're listed as one of the dead. From the island."

She glanced at Spook. A look of puzzlement had crumpled her slight features. "Meaning?"

"Meaning you're truly out of society now. Like me. Neither of us exist anymore." She raised her glass. "Here's to being a glorious nobody."

Acid drank, hoping the alcohol might loosen the knot in her stomach. Because this wasn't Spook's fight. It never had been. She was another casualty of the tumultuous whirlwind that surrounded Acid Vanilla.

"Screw it, so what," Spook said. "I was getting sick of being Spook Horowitz anyway. Maybe I'll change my name, like you. What do you think of Shinobi Helix?"

"You've given this some thought, I see. Would this be why you didn't erase your own name from the island's guest list at the same time you erased mine, by any chance?"

A shrug. "Maybe."

Acid laughed. "You'll do for me, Shinobi. Cheers." They chinked glasses. Drank.

"You want another?" Spook asked.

Acid crunched a piece of ice between her teeth, spotting someone across the far side of the room. "Okay, but make it a quick one. Just showing our faces, remember? You get them in. I'll be back in a few minutes."

"Where are you going?"

She got to her feet and grabbed up her purse. "Just something I need to do. Back soon."

Sofia Swann, now Mellencamp (that was going to take some getting used to), threw her arms around her new husband's neck and kissed him passionately on the lips.

"You having a good day, Mrs M?" he asked her, coming up for air.

"Sure am," she purred. "But these heels are killing me. You mind if I go get changed into my evening gear already? I really want to be able to dance."

Mike didn't take his dark eyes from hers. "You do whatever

you want. As long as you're here. As long as you're my wife. That's all I damn well care about."

Sofia smiled back. A smile she wondered would ever leave her. "Thanks. Give me fifteen minutes and I'll be back."

She rode the elevator up to the tenth floor and practically floated along the corridor that led to the Plaza's lavish Bridal Suite. Her mind was a swirl with all the possibilities she might manifest for herself over the coming years. A house in the Hamptons, two kids, and growing old with Mike. A perfect future, and one she'd almost let go of, lost forever on that terrible island.

Despite the heavy trauma she'd endured, Sofia felt optimistic. She'd already booked in a heavy chunk of sessions with Stephanie, her therapist, and day by day, with Mike's help, she was putting that awful ordeal behind her.

But not just yet.

Not entirely.

Because another reason Sofia was feeling particularly excited right now was she'd just finished the final edit on an article. Three thousand words about her experience on the island. In fact, another reason she'd slipped away from her own wedding reception just now was so she could give it one last read-through before sending it off in the morning. Sofia didn't like to tempt fate, but she could easily see the cover of *Time*. Hell, she could see a Pulitzer. Then a book. A movie, even.

She slid her key card into the lock and waited for the satisfying click-clunk as the green light let her inside. Once there, she headed for the bathroom and checked her mascara, applied a little more lipstick, before moving into the main bedroom where she let out a yelp of surprise.

"What the hell?"

Acid Vanilla was lying on the king-size bed opposite, Sofia's laptop open in front of her. "Quite the read," she mused, pursing her cherry-red lips.

"Acid? What are you…? I didn't… I…"

"You do know you can't print this, don't you? Any of it."

Sofia moved closer. "I don't mention you. Not by name, at least. Please, I—"

"I told you specifically to leave it alone."

"But the story, it needs to be told. We can't let them get away with it."

"We didn't, sweetie. They're all dead." Acid closed the laptop. "Are there any other copies?"

Sofia looked at the floor. "It's saved in my cloud account. That's all."

"Okay. Spook can delete that easily enough. We won't touch anything else."

Sofia peered through her hair as the enigmatic assassin slipped the laptop under her arm and walked up to her. "I'm sorry. I can't risk it."

She raised her head to meet Acid's intense gaze, looking deep into her eyes. "Worth a try, I guess."

Acid was a foot away from her. She leaned in close. So close Sofia could feel her breath on her cheek. "Don't ever write about what happened again," she whispered, the consonants popping in her ear canal. "Not about Engel, or the island, or me. Especially not me. Or I promise you, Sofia, I will kill you, your husband and all your family."

Sofia swallowed a gulp. "But we're... I mean, I thought you were…"

"I'm Acid Vanilla. Don't underestimate me. Ever. Do you understand?"

Sofia nodded. She sure did.

"Good," Acid said. Then, without warning, Acid's lips were on hers. They were soft, warm. Without thinking, Sofia opened her mouth and kissed her back. It was forceful, intense, passionate. And over in moments.

Acid pulled away first, her eyes sparkling in the light from the crystal chandelier above. "I'll see you around," she said. "You be good now."

She gasped a garbled response, but by the time she'd got her words out, Acid Vanilla was gone. A little in shock, she walked over to the bed and sat.

"Fia? Is everything all right?" It was Mike. He put his head around the door.

"Who the hell was that woman? Friend of yours?"

She looked up. "Did you say anything to her?"

"No. She passed me in the corridor as I was coming to check on you. Winked at me. It was kind of unnerving. What did she want? Who is she?"

Sofia lay back on the bed and let out a deep sigh of acceptance. "Don't worry, darling," she told her new husband. "She's just someone's plus one. In fact, I don't even know her name."

The End

Get Your FREE Book: Discover how Acid Vanilla transformed from a normal London teenager into the world's deadliest female assassin in *Making a Killer,* available FREE at:

www.matthewhattersley.com/mak

CAN YOU HELP?

Enjoyed this book? You can make a big difference

Honest reviews of my books help bring them to the attention of other readers. If you've enjoyed this book I would be very grateful if you could spend just five minutes leaving a review (it can be as short as you like) on the book's Amazon page.

ALSO BY MATTHEW HATTERSLEY

Have you read them all?

———

The Acid Vanilla series

Acid Vanilla

Acid Vanilla is an elite assassin, struggling with her mental health. Spook Horowitz is a mild-mannered hacker who saw something she shouldn't. Acid needs a holiday. Spook needs Acid Vanilla to NOT be coming to kill her. But life rarely works out the way we want it to.

BUY IT HERE

Seven Bullets

Acid Vanilla was the deadliest assassin at Annihilation Pest Control. That was until she was tragically betrayed by her former colleagues. Now, fuelled by an insatiable desire for vengeance, Acid travels the globe to carry out her bloody retribution. After all, a girl needs a hobby...

BUY IT HERE

Making a Killer

How it all began. Discover Acid Vanilla's past, her meeting with Caesar, and how she became the deadliest female assassin in the world.

FREE TO DOWNLOAD HERE

———

Stand-alone novels

Double Bad Things

All undertaker Mikey wants is a quiet life and to write his comics. But then he's conned into hiding murders in closed-casket burials by a gang who are also trafficking young girls. Can a gentle giant whose only friends are a cosplay-obsessed teen and an imaginary alien really take down the gang and avoid arrest himself?

Double Bad Things is a dark and quirky crime thriller - for fans of Dexter and Six Feet Under.

BUY IT HERE

Cookies

Will Miles find love again after the worst six months of his life? The fortune cookies say yes. But they also say commit arson and murder, so maybe it's time to stop believing in them? If only he could...

"If you life Fight Club, you'll love Cookies." - TL Dyer, Author

BUY IT HERE

ABOUT THE AUTHOR

Over the last twenty years Matthew Hattersley has toured Europe in rock n roll bands, trained as a professional actor and founded a theatre and media company. He's also had a lot of dead end jobs…

Now he writes Neo-Noir Thrillers and Crime Fiction. He has also had his writing featured in The New York Observer & Huffington Post.

He lives with his wife and young daughter in Manchester, UK and doesn't feel that comfortable writing about himself in the third person.

For AJH x

COPYRIGHT

A Boom Boom Press ebook

First published in Great Britain as ACID VANILLA in June 2020 by Boom Boom Press.

Ebook first published in 2020 by Boom Boom Press.

Published as THE WATCHER in July 2020 by Boom Boom Press

Copyright © Boom Boom Press 2015 - 2020

The moral right of Matthew Hattersley to be identified as the author of this work has been asserted by him in accordance with the copyright, Designs and Patents Act 1988.

All the characters in this book are fictitious, and any resemblance to actual persons living or dead is purely coincidental.

All rights reserved. No part of this publication may be reproduced, stored in a retrieval system or transmitted in any form or by any means, without the prior permission in writing of the publisher, nor to be otherwise circulated in any form of binding or cover other than that in which it is published without a similar condition, including this condition, being imposed on the subsequent purchaser.

Printed in Great Britain
by Amazon